THE SUPERINTENDENT MAKES A DEADLY GUESS

"I gather you're inclined to link three or four of the unsolved cases and attribute them to the same unknown man." Mr. Campion rose and walked over to have a closer look at the map of West London. "You haven't a scrap of evidence of any kind, have you?" he murmured absently. "You'd be more convincing with a crystal ball. I don't know Garden Green. What is it like?"

"Sad," Superintendent Luke said. "Used to be a graveyard. It's quiet. Not a slum. This chap I have in mind doesn't *live* there, you know."

"Why watch Garden Green if he doesn't live there," said Campion reproachfully.

"Because he's treating it as a hide. He's the enemy," Luke said, catching Campion's eye. "My enemy, and I'm as certain as if I were reading it on my tombstone, either I'm going to get him or he's going to get me."

TETHER'S END

Margery Allingham

BANTAM BOOKS
NEW YORK • TORONTO • LONDON • SYDNEY • AUCKLAND

TETHER'S END

*A Bantam Book / published by arrangement with
Doubleday*

PRINTING HISTORY

*Doubleday edition published October 1958
A Selection of Nelson / Doubleday Book Club, April 1958
A Selection of Reader's Digest Condensed Books, April 1958
Bantam edition / August 1983
4 printings through April 1990*

ISBN 0-553-25102-3

Published simultaneously in the United States and Canada

PRINTED IN THE UNITED STATES OF AMERICA

KRI 13 11 10 9 8 7 6 5 4

TETHER'S END

1
Business After Hours

The arrival of the bus was timed to perfection. Nobody of the slightest importance saw it at all. Traffic was slack, the theatres were only halfway through the evening performances, and no police were due on point duty until the after-the-show crush seventy minutes away.

Almost more significant still, if one were seeking a reliable eyewitness, Commissionaire George Wardle had just stepped down into the staff room of the "Porch" for his mid-evening pint and sausage and so was not on duty outside the famous old restaurant which faces the Duke of Grafton's Theatre and the dark entrance to Goff's Place which runs down beside it.

The spring rain was fortuitous but it was an enormous help. It turned out to be one of those settled downpours which, in London, seem to involve more actual water than anywhere else, and there become a penetrating and absorbing irritant guaranteed to keep the mind of the passer-by upon himself and his discomforts.

The bus came trundling along from the eastern end of the Avenue, looking archaic but not nearly so noticeable as it might well have done if there had been no fashion for vintage petrol-driven vehicles in the West End. It was a small closed single-decker of the type still used in remote country districts. Shabby but comfortable-looking, its snugness was enhanced by absurd little woollen curtains trimmed with bobbles and draped at small discreet windows like those on elderly French air liners. It was lit from within by a single low-powered bulb and only the passengers on the front seat were visible from the street. These were in tune with the vehicle, two cosy figures, plump and elderly, in decent out-of-town finery. The man wore a hard hat above his rounded beard, and his wife—for one could not imagine that he was out with any other woman—wore beads on her out-of-date bonnet and a rug wrapped round her stiff shoulders. They were not talking but dozing, as the old do, and looked warm and protected and out of the wet.

The driver swung the bus neatly into the Goff's Place entry and turned it into the tiny cobbled space behind the theatre. The Place was a minute cul-de-sac, an air shaft shared by the Duke of Grafton's and the three tall houses whose back doors and fire escapes gave on to it. These were shops and faced the other way on to Deban Street, Soho, which runs nearly but not quite parallel with the Avenue.

The original Goff had long been lost in obscurity. His Place now contained nothing but a telephone booth, a street drain transformed on this occasion into a whirlpool, and a single rather fancy light bracket sticking out over the Grafton's stage door. For the past five hundred weekdays at this time in the evening the area had been crammed with just such country coaches, up from the villages with parties to see the latest domestic musical in the series for which the theatre was noted. But tonight the building was dark. The piece had finished its run and spring cleaning was not due to begin for another twenty-four hours.

The driver parked the country bus with remarkable care. It took him some little time to get his clumsy vehicle exactly into the position he desired, and even when he had succeeded the purpose of the manoeuvre was not apparent. True, the bus faced the exit, ready to drive out again, but its rear door, by which all passengers must ascend or alight, was almost directly above the step of the back entrance of one of the Deban Street shops, while the near side of the bus was hard against the telephone booth, screening it entirely from the sight of the Avenue.

With this lighted kiosk obscured, the whole area had become appreciably darker and the driver was only just discernible in the streaming gloom as he sprang out of his seat, his black oilskins flickering below the white plastic top of his peaked cap. He was carrying a small leather attaché case and turned into the booth with it.

In the coach the old people did not move. If indeed they had arrived late for a performance which was not taking place anyway, the fact did not appear to worry them. They sat close together in the warm, dozing, while the rain poured over the tiny window beside them like a brook over a boulder. The yard itself might have been at the bottom of a fountain, so drenched and dark and remote it was from the unnatural brightness of the Avenue where the illuminated signs and the shop windows blazed at empty pavements and the tarmac glittered like coal.

In the telephone booth the driver settled himself with his back against the wall, wedged his case on a small shelf under the instrument, and felt in his pocket. He appeared to know how much money he had, a crumpled ten-shilling note and eight separate pennies, for he found them at once and put them on top of the case, but it did not prevent him from making a complete search. When he was satisfied at last he thrust the screwed-up note into the other side pocket of his coat and took up the coins. His peaked cap cast a shadow which was as dark as an eye mask over the upper part of his face, but the plane of his thin cheek and strong jaw and neck muscles caught the light. The impression was of a youngish face, probably handsome, but at the moment frankly horrible. Either through a trick of the light or because of some unexplained condition its whole nerve pattern was apparent, dancing and quivering under the stretched skin. He was also smiling as he stretched out a gaunt hand for the instrument. The telephone was one of the ordinary dial and coin-in-the-slot variety, fitted with the A and B button money-back device, but the driver ignored the printed instructions. He inserted four of his coins, dialled a number, and then slid down in the booth so that he could peer through the rainy dark at the back of the house directly in front of him. For thirty seconds he listened to the number ringing out and then, high up in the building, a pale oblong of yellow light sprang into existence. He pressed the A button immediately so that as soon as he heard his caller he was able to speak without any telltale click betraying that he was in a public box.

"Hullo, is that you, Lew? You're still there, are you? Can I come round?"

The voice, pleasant and schooled as an actor's, was unexpected, the undertone and excitement transmuted into confidence.

"Come round? Of course you can come round. You'd better. I'm waiting, aren't I?"

The new voice was harsh and possessed a curious muddy quality, but in its own way it was honest enough.

The man in the peaked cap laughed. "Cheer up," he said, "your reward is on the way. You can send John down to get the door open if he's still there. I'll be with you in five minutes."

"John's gone home. I'm here alone and I'm waiting for you here till midnight as I said I would. After that you've got to take the consequences. I told you and I meant it."

In the booth the man's bunched jaw muscles hardened but the pleasant disingenuous voice remained soothing.

"Relax. You've got a pleasant shock coming to you. Take this gently or you'll have a stroke. I've got the money, every farthing of it, and since you don't trust me it's in cash as you requested, all in this little brief case in front of me, in fives and ones." He was silent for a moment. "Did you hear me?"

"Yes."

"I wondered. Aren't you pleased?"

"I'm pleased that we should both be saved a lot of trouble." There was a grudging pause and then, as curiosity got the better of him, "The old gentleman paid up to save you, did he?"

"He did. Not willingly nor without comment exactly. However, pay he did. You didn't believe he existed, did you?"

"What I believe don't matter. You get out here with the money. Where are you?"

"St. James's, in the old man's club. I'll be seeing you. Good-bye."

He hung up and slid down in the booth again to watch the lighted window. After a moment a shadow appeared across it and the blind descended. The man in the telephone booth sighed and then, straightening himself, snapped open the catch of the leather case before him. He did not raise the lid high immediately but first thrust in his hand and drew out a small squat gun which he passed through the side slit in his oilskin into the safety of his jacket within. He then opened the case wide, revealing that it contained nothing but a dark felt hat of good quality and a pair of clean pigskin gloves. He exchanged these for his peaked cap and gauntlets and became at once a different-looking person. The long black oiled coat ceased to be part of a uniform and became an ordinary protection which any man might wear against the rain, and, with the removal of the cap, his eyes and forehead came out of their mask of shadow. He looked thirty or a very few years older and his face still possessed some of the secrecy of youth. He was good-looking in a conventional way, his features regular and his round eyes set wide apart. Only the heavy muscles at the corners of his jaw, and the unusual thickness of his neck, were not in the accepted fashionable picture. The most outstanding thing about him was an impression of urgency that was apparent in every line of his body, a strain and a determination like a climber's nearing a peak.

As he slid out of the red kiosk into the pit among the tall houses, the gun in his gloved hand inside his jacket pocket, he was, if considered dispassionately, a shocking and dreadful thing, equally horrible with any other deadly creature moving subtly in the dark places of an unsuspecting world.

He passed round behind the bus, empty save for the old people, who had not moved, and came down the narrow lane into the sign-lit brightness of the Avenue. It was still pouring, the pavements were almost empty. Wardle was still having his supper, and the Porchester's Victorian-Byzantine portico remained unattended. Nothing could have suited the man better. He had only to step round the deserted frontage of the closed theatre to gain the comparative darkness of Deban Street itself, where even now Lew was unlocking a deep-set door.

He came into the light swiftly, his head held down, and glanced briefly up the street. The next moment he halted abruptly but recovered himself and, pulling his slicker collar round his chin, he stepped under the canopy of the theatre. Directly between himself and the entrance to Deban Street there was a bus stop, and beneath it stood an elderly woman, waiting patiently in the downpour.

She stood quite still, looking square and solid in a green mackintosh cape which was dark now in patches where the rain had soaked her shoulders and a crescent above her hips. Her small velour hat glistened with drops and her stout shoes must have been waterlogged.

For the moment there was no one else on the pavement. If he passed her he must run the risk of her seeing him and recognising his back, just as he had hers. He decided against risking it, and turned the other way, back across the entrance to Goff's Place and on to Molyneux Street where he found, as he had hoped, the remains of a taxi rank. There was one cab left upon it and, keeping his face turned away from the lights of the Avenue, he spoke to the driver.

"There's an old girl standing at the bus stop just round the corner here, Guv," he said pleasantly. "She lives just off the Barrow Road. At the moment she's catching pneumonia because she thinks that it's a crime to take a taxi just for herself. Here is a ten bob. Will you go and take her home?"

The driver sat up among the leather swaddling clothes in which he was enveloped and laughed. He took the crumpled note and started his engine.

"Don't they make you tired?" he said, referring no doubt to womankind in general. "Cruel to themselves half the time, cruel to themselves. Shall I tell her your name? She's sure to want to know."

The man in the oilskin coat hesitated with what appeared to be natural modesty.

"Oh, I don't think so," he said at last. "It might embarrass her. Tell her one of her old pals. I shall keep my eye on you from this corner, driver."

"You needn't." The bundle spoke without animosity. "I'm honest. No reason why I shouldn't be. Goodnight, sir. Stinking, ain't it? I'll take 'er along."

The old cab shuddered and sprang forward and the man on foot stepped back into the shadow of a doorway. He counted two hundred slowly before walking out into the rain again. This time the Avenue was safe and the space under the bus stop deserted.

With the gun in his hand he bent his head against the rain, passed unnoticed down the lighted way, and turned into Deban Street.

2
Big Game

Just about eight months after the incident which the newspapers had christened "The Goff Place Mystery" had made a nine-days' wonder in the Press and the police had endured a great deal of unconstructive criticism with their usual gloomy stoicism, Mr. Albert Campion closed the door of Chief Superintendent Yeo's room and walked up two flights of stairs to tap on one which belonged to the newest Superintendent, Charles Luke.

Mr. Campion was a tall thin man in his early fifties, with fair hair, a pale face, and large spectacles, who had cultivated the gentle art of unobtrusiveness until even his worst enemies were apt to overlook him until it was too late. He was known to a great many people but few were absolutely certain about what it was he actually did with his life. In his youth he had often been described as 'the young man come about the trouble,' and nowadays he was liable to mention deferentially that he feared he was becoming the 'old one come *with* it,' but now, as then, he was careful never to permit his status to be too accurately defined.

It was certainly true that he had a private practice but also a fact that he and the present Assistant Commissioner, Crime, Mr. Stanislaus Oates, had been hunting companions in the days when Oates was an Inspector C.I.D. Since then Yeo, who was following Oates's footsteps, and many other eminent senior men in the service were content to consider him a friend, an expert witness and, at times, a very valuable guide into little-known territory.

At the moment he was not very happy. Old friendship

has a way of making demands on a man which would be considered unreasonable by the standards of frank enmity. When he arrived at Yeo's office in response to an urgent message it had emerged after a considerable display of bush-beating that what "the Guv'nor" really required from his old chum was a promise that he would "drop a hint" to Charlie Luke.

Mr. Campion, who was very fond of Yeo and even fonder of Charles Luke, whom they both felt to be the most interesting personality the C.I.D. had produced in a decade, found the assignment suspect in the extreme. In the first place Yeo was more than capable of dealing himself with any sort of problem however delicate, and in the second, Luke was Yeo's own protégé and white hope for the future, the son of his old colleague and an officer over whose career he had watched for twenty years. If Yeo needed help in hint-dropping to Luke, Mr. Campion felt the situation must be out of hand. Moreover, in his experience, getting a word in edgeways with Luke was a major operation on its own account at the best of times, let alone at the moment when quite a lot appeared to have been said already.

He knocked at the green door and was admitted by a clerk who withdrew as the Superintendent came across the room, hand outstretched.

Mr. Campion thought he had never seen the man in such tremendous form. Luke was a magnificent specimen who looked a little less than his six feet because of the weight of his muscles. He had a live, dark face under black hair which curled tightly to his scalp, nervous energy radiated from him and his narrow eyes under peaked brows were shrewd and amused.

"Hello! Just the man I was hoping to see!" he said with disconcerting enthusiasm. "Come in. I was wondering if I could possibly get hold of you to ask you to drop a hint to the Old Man for me. He thinks I'm round the bend."

Mr. Campion knew Yeo did, on the very best authority. However, he saw no point in mentioning it and Luke gave him little opportunity. His handshake was a minor ordeal and he got his visitor settled in the armchair before the desk with the alarming purposefulness of one who perceives a heaven-sent audience.

"I'm on to something pretty hot," he announced without preamble. "I'm certain of it but at the moment it's just a little bit on the vague side."

"That's a quality which has disadvantages," murmured Mr. Campion, who knew what they were rather better than most people. "Authority doesn't warm to the indefinite."

"It's the new rank, I know that." Luke spoke bluntly. "A Chief can have ideas and a mere D.D.I. is permitted to have a hunch. But a Super is paid to keep his feet on the carpet, his seat on his chair and his head should be a box marked 'Members Only.' I know that better than anybody and in the ordinary way I believe in it. But just now I really have stumbled on a trail. This is one of my 'sixth-sense-specials.' I've had them all my life. Look, Campion, since you're here, take a look at this, will you?"

He turned to a chart which hung on the wall behind him and Mr. Campion, who had heard about it already from Yeo, saw that it was a large-scale street map of a part of the Metropolitan Police District in west London where Charlie Luke had served as a Detective Divisional Inspector for several adventurous years. The thin man remembered most of the area as a labyrinth of Victorian middle-class stucco which had degenerated with the wars into alarming slums and was now on the upgrade once more, but the portion shown here was new to him. It was a circle, some quarter mile across, in the north of the district and sported a crop of coloured flags as on a battle map. The centre of the round was an irregular patch, coloured green to indicate an open space, which lay in the angle made by the junction of two traffic ways, Edge Street running south to the Park and the long Barrow Road going west. He leaned forward to read the large print across the space.

"Garden Green," he said aloud. "I don't know it, I'm afraid. I thought it was Goff's Place you were worrying about."

Luke cocked an eye at him.

"Oh, I see," he said. "You had a word with the Guv on the way up. Did he tell you that I'd got a delusion that Jack Havoc or the Reddingdale Butcher had come back to haunt me because I didn't bring either of them to trial?"

"No." Mr. Campion hoped sincerely that he was lying in a good cause. "I merely gathered you were inclined to

link three or four of the unsolved cases of the last three
years and to attribute them to the same unknown man."

"Huh," said Luke. "So I am." He perched himself on
the edge of the desk and looked, as Campion had so often
seen him, like some huge cat, lithe and intent. "Goff's
Place and the corpse who went by bus. Put everything
you've ever heard about that business out of your mind
and listen to me."

It was one of Charlie Luke's more engaging peculiari-
ties that he amplified·all his stories with a remarkable
pantomimic side show which he gave all the time he was
talking. He drew diagrams in the air with his long hands
and made portraits of his characters with his own face. Mr.
Campion was not at all surprised therefore when he hunched
himself, drew his lips over his teeth to suggest age, and
altered the shape of his nose by clapping his fist over it.

"Poor old Lew," he said. "A decent, straight little chap
with more patience than sense until the end of it was
reached, of course, when he was firm, as a moneylender
has to be. He had a pawnshop in Deban Street and when
he shut it in the evening he used to nip upstairs to his
office and get out his ledgers on the usury lark. His
interest was stiff but not over the odds and he'd traded
there for years without a complaint." He paused and fixed
his visitor with a baleful eye. "Someone took him for a ride
and made a mess of his office first. There was blood all
over the floor, at least half a dozen vital books were
missing, and the trail led down the stairs at the back to a
door which opened into Goff's Place and no one has seen
little Lew since. There was a lot of excitement at first but
since there was no corpse to show, it petered out."

Mr. Campion nodded. "I remember it," he said. "It
was a very wet night and nobody noticed that it was
curious that a country bus should have been waiting in the
yard at a time when there was no performance on at the
Duke of Grafton's. The police decided the body must have
been taken away in the bus."

"The police had to decide something," said Luke
bitterly. "We had to make up our minds if we were going
or coming for one thing. But it must have been done that
way, otherwise we should have been able to trace the
blessed vehicle. We advertised all over the home counties,

every police force was alerted, we inspected close on seven hundred garages. Old Lew *must* have gone in the bus, but in that case what was the explanation of the two old dears who were already sitting in it? That was the item which shook me. Who were they? What happened to them? Why did they keep silent and how sound were they sleeping?"

Mr. Campion's pale eyes grew thoughtful behind his spectacles. It was very difficult not to be moved by Luke's forceful imagination, which re-created a picture grown faint in his mind.

"Ah, yes," he said at last. "The old man with the round beard and the old lady with the beads in her bonnet who were dozing on the front seat. Some witness described them, I fancy."

"We have five," Luke said. "Five people came forward to swear that they'd glanced into Goff's Place that night at varying times between nine-forty and ten-five and had seen the bus waiting there. They all remembered the old folk and hardly seem to have noticed anything else, let alone the number or the colour of the coach. Even the waiter who passed the mouth of the yard when the bus driver was actually climbing into his seat didn't glance at him twice but could paint a picture of the passengers in oils. He was the chap who swore he'd seen them before."

"Had he, by George! That must have been useful!" The thin man was puzzled. "Extraordinary you got no further. Or wasn't it?" he added as Luke's face grew darker.

"I thought so." The new Superintendent was inclined to be offhand. "The chap wasn't specific. He thought he'd seen them in Edge Street and he was certain it was through glass. He reckoned they must have been sitting in a teashop and he'd seen them through the window as he passed by." He hesitated and after a moment's indecision remarkably unlike him turned and nodded towards the chart on the wall. "Those three yellow flags mark the only eating places in the area where he could have done that."

Mr. Campion's brows rose. He had been warned that Luke was catching at straws.

"Hardly conclusive," he ventured.

Luke sniffed. "Hardly there at all," he conceded

handsomely. "I warn you, my evidence gets thinner still as I go on. That's one reason why the Old Man is so windy. That blue flag on the corner there marks the branch of Cuppages, the cheap outfitters where this was bought in a sale." He leant over the desk, dragged open a drawer and drew out a thick brown envelope.

Mr. Campion watched him while he took out the glove it contained. It was cut for a man's left hand in imitation hogskin and was nearly new. Luke's narrow eyes met Mr. Campion's squarely.

"This is the glove left behind in the Church Row shooting case."

"*Oh dear!*" Mr. Campion's protest was so completely spontaneous and like himself that his friend had the grace to colour.

"All right." Luke threw the exhibit on the brass tray of a pair of letter scales which he kept on the desk top and it lay there, limp and unimpressive, kept in the air by the small column of weights on the other side. "I'm not trying to prove anything. I only point out that this glove left behind by the unknown gunman who shot his way out of a house in Church Row when he discovered that there were more people in the building than the woman householder, was bought in Cuppages on *that corner.*"

"My dear fellow, I wouldn't dream of arguing with you." Mr. Campion made it clear that he was not a man who argued at all. "But I would point out that the Church Row shooting happened quite three years ago."

"Just about." Luke spoke cheerfully. "It was about this time, October. The Goff's Place business was last February."

"A gap of two years and four months?" Mr. Campion's expression was very dubious.

Luke returned to his map. "Well, I wondered, don't you know," he said deliberately. "I wondered if it was all gap. See that pink marker half way down Fairy Street, just behind Cuppages? That's a small jeweller's. Belongs to an old boy called Tobias. I've known him for years. Not long ago a young woman who was on holiday from Dorset— she's a country schoolgirl there—passed by his window and went up in the air. She'd seen this in his cheap tray." He dived into the drawer again to return with a small box containing a gold ring decorated with ivy leaves, which he passed to his visitor. "She'd recognised it as belonging to her auntie and she was excited about finding it because her auntie and uncle completely vanished two years and three months ago—in the June following the September of the Church Row shooting."

Mr. Campion sat looking at the Superintendent with misleading innocence.

"I trust you don't suggest that the aunt and uncle travelled by bus, Charles?"

"No," said Luke, "No one knows *how* they travelled, or even if they travelled. That's the interesting part of the story. They were retired people, comfortably off in their own little house in Yorkshire, and they sold up and collected all their money and got on a train for London without a word of explanation to anyone except that the old lady, in writing to the schoolteacher to thank her for a white plastic handbag which she'd sent her for her birthday, had mentioned that they'd met a very nice young man who had told uncle wonderful things about Johannesburg, and how suitable the handbag would be if ever they went. That was all. Auntie never wrote again. When the niece investigated she and uncle had packed up and gone away without a word."

He paused and thrust his jaw out with sudden savagery.

"I don't want to make cases but you would think that once the police got on to it they could find some trace of these people having taken plane or ship within a reasonable time of them closing their bank account. We couldn't. We can't find a whisper of them anywhere except that auntie's ring, which never left her finger, turned up right in the middle of the area in which I'm interested."

Mr. Campion looked at the ring. It was not valuable but the design was unusual and rather beautiful.

"How sure is the niece about this?" he enquired.

"A hundred per cent." By some alchemy Luke managed to transform his thin face into a round blank one, solemn-eyed and utterly practical. "Auntie had a terrier pup who used to try to bite it off her finger. Look at it with this."

He passed him a jeweller's glass from the miscellany on the desk and the thin man made the examination carefully.

"Yes," he said at last. "What a beastly little tale. What does Tobias say?"

"So little he must be telling the truth." Luke sighed gustily. "He can't remember when the ring came in. He only put it in the window a couple of days before the niece spotted it. He was turning out the drawer in which he keeps the junk he buys over the counter and found it under the bit of newspaper he'd used as a lining last time he cleaned up. He says it must have come in with a parcel of secondhand stuff but he can't recall it. The odd thing is that the date on the piece of newspaper is just a couple of weeks after uncle and auntie left home. It proves nothing, but it's curious."

He took the ring and dropping it back in its box placed the package on top of the glove. Mr. Campion saw where the manoeuvre was leading and decided to be obliging.

"What about the last flag?" he enquired. "The one in the middle of the green."

Luke laughed as he caught his eye.

"Well, it's a good trick," he said, and, returning to the drawer once more, produced a large lizard-skin letter case of very good quality. He did not pass it over at once but sat turning it inside out and back again, showing a torn strap on one of the inner pockets. "In April this year a kid picked this up from the grass in Garden Green," he said presently. "After kicking it about for a bit he gave it to a bobby and it turned out to be just the thing the Kent police were looking for. It belonged to a car salesman whose body had been found in his coupé at the bottom of a chalk pit on the Folkestone-London road. Skid marks on the surface suggested he'd been run off, so no one was very surprised when it was discovered that he'd been carrying all of seven hundred pounds on him when he set out from the coast. When he was found he had a pocketful of loose change but no notecase of any kind although his other papers were intact. His family identified this. It's a distinctive wallet and his wife remembered the torn strap." He let his mouth widen into a ferocious grin and dropped the leather folder on to the glove and the ring. Its weight turned the scales and the brass tray clattered gently as it hit the polished wood of the desk. "There you are," he said; "it doesn't mean much but how good it looks!"

Mr. Campion rose and walked over to the wall to have a closer look at the chart.

"You haven't a scrap of evidence of any kind, have you?" he murmured absently. "You'd be more convincing with a crystal ball. I don't know Garden Green. What is it like?"

"Sad." Luke drooped, impersonating a willow perhaps. "Used to be a graveyard. The church came down in the blitz and the Council had the ground levelled and the stones set round the boundary wall. A hoarding separates it from the Barrow Road and round the back there are the usual little houses—beautiful porches, horrible plumbing. Mostly they're let out in rooms but there are some in private hands still. It's quiet. Not a slum. This chap I have in mind doesn't *live* there, you know."

There was something so convinced and familiar in his tone that Mr. Campion was startled. The Superintendent was speaking of someone as real to him as the friend before him. Luke saw the expression in the pale eyes and laughed.

"I've got him under my skin good and proper, haven't I? I worry about him, you know. He didn't make anything out of the Church Row shooting so I figure he had to catch up on auntie and uncle. He got a few hundred quid from them but not enough to square the moneylender, who must have been pressing. So he attended to that little problem but he didn't actually touch much cash if any in Deban Street and therefore, a couple of months later, he gave his mind to the car salesman. I don't know how long that drop of lolly would last him because I don't know what his debts were, you see."

"This is pure fiction," said Mr. Campion reproachfully. "It's fascinating but it doesn't touch the ground. Why watch Garden Green if he doesn't live there?"

"Because he's treating it as a hide. He's not counting it. He thinks he's safe there." Luke's deep voice had become soft. It was almost a purr, Mr. Campion thought with sudden astonishment, and he was aware of a small and secret thrill creeping down his spine.

"You can't tell what he's got out there," Luke was saying. "But it's something which gives him an entirely false sense of security. It could be a pub where they know him well but in some different character to his real one, or it might be a girl friend who doesn't ask questions—they do exist they tell me. Anyway he goes there when he wants to leave himself behind. I may sound as if I'm shooting a line but I know his state of mind about that place. He thinks he's almost *invisible* there and that things he takes from there or chucks away there couldn't ever be traced to him." He paused and his quick dark eyes met Campion's own. "It's an old idea—sanctuary they call it, don't they?"

Mr. Campion shivered. He did not know why. He hastened back to concrete matters.

"What about this new telephone?" he enquired.

The dark man chuckled and nodded towards an instrument which stood away from the others on a file in the corner.

"That's it," he said. "That's caused the trouble downstairs. You can go as batty as you like if you do it cheaply, but spend a bit of Government money on your delusions and authority starts having kittens at once! That's my private line to the Barrow Road station. If anything comes in from the Garden Green beat I shall hear of it quicker than soon. It's been waiting, costing all of thirty bob, for a couple of weeks but it'll ring in the end. You'll see!"

The thin man in the horn rims returned to his chair and sat down eyeing the little pile of exhibits on the scales.

"You make it very convincing, Charles," he said at last. "Although there's no great similarity of method you force me to admit there's a strong family likeness in the mental approach. Of course there are no bodies in the ring story but then there isn't one in the bus business either."

Luke thrust his hands in his pockets and began to play softly with the coins there.

"That idea of Yeo's about me trying to revive Havoc or the Reddingdale multi-murderer is absurd," he said. "This chap isn't a fraction like either of them. Havoc had got out of touch with the peacetime world in jug and the Reddingdale chap was a bore with a blood lust like Blue Beard or

Christie, but this man is different. He's almost refreshing. He's got a brain and he's got nerve and he's not neurotic. He's perfectly sane, he's merciless as a snake and he's very careful—doesn't like witnesses or corpses left around."

Mr. Campion studied his finger tips; he was thinking that he had heard white hunters describing game they were after with the same almost loving interest.

"You see him as simply out for money, do you?" he enquired presently.

"Oh yes, and not necessarily big money." As he spoke, the Superintendent took a handful of silver out of his pocket absently, glanced at it and put it back again. "He's a crook. He makes a living by taking all he needs from other people. The really unusual thing about him is that he kills quite coldly when it's the safest thing to do."

He slid off the desk and going round behind it sat down in his chair and swept the exhibits back into their drawer again.

"He's the enemy," he said, catching Campion's eye with a flicker in his own which was half shy. "My enemy. Professional *and* natural, and, I tell you, I'm as certain as if I was reading it on my tombstone, either I'm going to get him or he's going to get me."

Mr. Campion opened his mouth to express a polite hope that he was not beating an empty covert when behind him, on the top of the green file, the newly installed telephone began to ring.

3
Garden Green

Early in the day on which Mr. Campion went to visit Chief Inspector Luke, Garden Green achieved a beauty which was not normally its outstanding characteristic.

Sunlight, yellow and crystal in the mist, glowed through

the wet black branches of the plane trees while the fallen cream-coloured leaves made a fine carpet hiding the bald patches, the cigarette cartons and the bus tickets which in the ordinary way disfigured the discouraged grass.

A narrow concrete path ran round the green like a ribbon round a hat. At the furthest loop was a single wooden seat and upon it sat a girl.

She was not very tall but curved as a kitten, and was clad in an elegant tweed coat with matching tan shoes and gloves. At her feet was a small canvas travelling bag.

P. C. Bullard, heavyweight and elderly, who was on duty at the corner, had strolled down the path twice already to have a look at her, once in the way of duty and once for pure pleasure. Her sleekly brushed hair was honey-coloured, her grey eyes flecked with gold were widely set, and her mouth might have been drawn with a copperplate pen, so fine and yet so bold were its lines.

The man on duty was puzzled by her. He thought he had never seen anything so out of place. If she was waiting for someone who was very late she certainly did not mind, for she sat there contentedly in the cold morning, her fair skin glowing and the sunlight burnishing her uncovered head. He judged that she was something over seventeen trying to look twenty, and he was not far out except that it was twenty-four she was aiming at. Apart from her beauty, which was outstanding, the other thing which impressed him was her self-possession. The second time he passed her she caught him eyeing her and wished him a polite good morning as a matter of course.

She was up from the country, he decided. That was about it.

After forty minutes he began to feel downright anxious about her, although she showed no sign of being disturbed. If she was wearing a watch she did not consult it but remained relaxed, graceful, and apparently utterly content. Her slender feet were thrust out before her and her hands were folded in her lap.

He might have guessed that it was her destiny that other people should do the worrying about Miss Annabelle Tassie, for it was with positive relief that he, a complete stranger, saw at last a young man turn sharply in from the street and go hurrying towards her.

The newcomer, too, was an unusual type of visitor to the district. He was a small and dapper youngster with dark red hair and one of those bright little-boy faces which are so often the despair of their owners, whose tastes, more often than not, veer towards the romantic. He was twenty-two and looked no older, but there was pugnacity in the lower part of his face and his very clear blue eyes were vividly intelligent.

His dark suit was impeccable and his white collar shining, and if he had no overcoat it was because, as the newest recruit to the ancient firm of Wysdom Bros. and Company, Tea Brokers, Bread Lane, City, he did not care to wear to business his last year's garment, which was Her Majesty's khaki.

And until the end of the month he would not have quite enough money to purchase the soberly elegant affair on which he had had his eye for some time.

However, this temporary deficiency did not worry him. His most obvious characteristic, which was a natural grace and gayety of movement, made him appear a joyous figure striding over the grass as if the world belonged to him. One of the compensations of youth is its ability to accept the shifts of life as the trivia they turn out to be, and Richard Waterfield had seen nothing outrageous in the demand in Annabelle's letter that he should journey half across London at nine in the morning to meet her in some Godforsaken square of which he had never heard. It was the first letter he had received from her in eighteeen months, but he accepted the call upon him without hesitation, arranging with Messrs. Wysdom Brothers that he should take the morning off to visit his dentist.

She was an old friend and ally whom he had known as a neighbour in the Suffolk village of Dancing.

> *I will wait for you in a park called Garden Green* she had written. *On the map it looks nice and near the station and the train gets in at nine. I am sorry to bother you but I think someone living in London ought to be told where I shall be. I will explain when I see you. If it's raining we'll find a church to talk in. I mean I shan't come down on you for tea or food.*

Her directness amused him. It was one of the reasons he had always liked the child. She had a sound grasp of essentials. He had decided to buy her an ice.

He was considering this particular aspect of the problem when unexpectedly he saw her. He stopped in full stride, his ideas undergoing sudden and drastic change.

"Hullo, Richard," said Annabelle demurely.

"Hullo," he echoed cautiously, and added abruptly, "what are you dressed up like that for?"

The faintest of smiles, fleeting and content, passed over the remarkable mouth and she made room on the seat beside her.

"I thought you'd be surprised. You haven't seen me for two years and five months. It's Jenny's coat. I—er—I think I look pretty good."

Richard sat down. "I hardly recognised you," he said stiffly.

Annabelle remained content. "It's my hair," she explained calmly. "I had it done properly while I was about it. I'm trying to look as old as I possibly can."

"So I see." He spoke gloomily. He was mourning a very pleasant child who had been a good friend to him some three years before, when an agony of calf love for her elder sister Jennifer had rendered him in great need of sane companionship. This new Annabelle had blossomed like a whole flower bed, apparently, overnight, and looked to his interested eye as if she might cause a whole heap of trouble for almost anybody.

To his surprise she laid a hand on his.

"Don't be silly," she said. "It's still me."

He laughed gratefully, recovering a modicum of his superiority.

"I'm glad about that. They know at home that you're here, I hope? You're not up to anything fantastic, like trying to go on the stage or anything?"

"No." She was unoffended. "It's more complicated than that. That's why I wanted to see you, somebody reliable. Jenny knows I'm here of course, and that means that Medico Mike does too, but we couldn't trouble Mother. She's far too ill."

Her mention of Dr. Michael Robinson, his successful rival for the affections of her elder sister, reassured Richard somewhat. That mature stuffed shirt was at least hardheaded.

"I heard about your mother," he said awkwardly. "I'm awfully sorry. Isn't she any better? I didn't like to ask."

"I'm afraid she can't ever be. It was a stroke, you see." Annabelle eyed him gratefully. "It doesn't really help to talk about it. Jenny's been wonderful. She won't think of marrying Mike until...well, until it's all over. The other two are at school, still, and I've just left. I can't do what Jenny's doing because it's a tremendous feat to pay the bills out of the income, so I was going to get a job right away. Then the letter turned up and I thought I'd better be the one to answer it, and so here I am."

"So I see." He was finding it difficult to take his gaze from her face. "What letter was this?"

"Here." She produced a plump envelope from her coat pocket and handed it to him. "See what you think. It was addressed to Mother but Jenny had to deal with it. You'll have to read it all, I'm afraid, or you'll never get the drift."

Richard took the packet dubiously. There seemed to be a lot of letter, pages of it scribbled in an untidy but purposeful hand.

> *7 Garden Green,*
> *London, W. 2.*
>
> *My dear Alice,* it began, *You may not have heard of me but I should not be surprised if you have because all families talk, I know, say what we will. Well, dear, I am your brother-in-law Frederick's wife, or widow I should say, and I think you may have met Frederick before you were married.*
>
> *My dear, he was not a bad chap whatever you may have heard and was really very fond of his brother, your husband. I saw that he had passed on, poor fellow, some years ago. I am so sorry. It is difficult to talk about them, isn't it?*
>
> *My Frederick was all right really but I can understand that it must have been a shock to you all when he went off and joined me in my hotel instead of marrying where he was expected to. I*

think perhaps I ought to mention that we were married—Gold Cross Registry Office, Manchester, 27th June '31—a bit late, as you will notice, I expect, but still we did do it, and we got on very very well. When he went, poor old boy, in 1945, I was fed up, so I sold out and came to live in a bit of property my dad left me, it falling empty about that time. The address is on the top of this letter. It is not in a swanky part but I have made it quite nice.

What I am leading up to is that Freddy and I had no kids and I have no relatives left alive to need anything. I have not won the Irish Sweep but I did sell out at the best time and have always had a bit put by, being that sort of person, I expect.

To stop beating about the bush, dear, I believe there is a niece of Freddy's. I remember we saw in the paper her name was Jennifer.

Fred kept an eye on births and deaths and if he was too proud to write he always drank the health of a name he knew! Well, Alice dear, I would like to see this girl. I do not want to promise anything because I am as I am and I expect so is she, and we might not get on at all, but if you can see your way to it send her up to me, and if she is what I have in mind she will not be the loser. There is something here for her to do if she is the right sort.

Now I have read this I see it looks as if I am up to I don't know what. Do not think that. I would look after her. No silly nonsense or staying out late, or anything not quite straightforward. Anyhow, that is my idea and there is no harm in asking, is there?

To close, dear, I hope you are all right. It has been a parrotty old lifetime for us women, hasn't it, but I daresay it has made us all a bit broader-minded than we were long ago. If you decide to send the kid have a little chat with her first, because I do not want a crying set-out if I

*am not what she expects. Shall hope to see her
but will understand if not.*

Yours sincerely,
Margaret (Polly) Tassie

*P.S. She must be nearly twenty-four. I expect she's
very nice and well brought up but I have opened
this to say that if she should be really plain,
kindly, dear, forget I wrote.*

Richard read the postscript twice and looked up, his
youthful face blank.

"I suppose someone *has* heard of her before?"

"Oh yes." Annabelle appeared alarmingly complacent.
"Father and Frederick were left our estate between them,
with very little money and a lot of responsibility, but it
looked more or less all right because Frederick was engaged to one of Lord Thole's daughters over at Pharaoh's
Field. They were awfully rich. But when Grandfather died
Uncle Fred beetled off, jilted the Honourable, and left
Father to wrestle both with the estate and the scandal. I
don't think there was a row. Just an enduring coolth. No
one even seems to have considered this old darling, who
sounds rather a sweetie, don't you think?"

He did not answer immediately and she leaned over
his shoulder.

"Well, don't you?"

"I don't know," he said honestly. "You're sure Dr.
Robinson has seen this letter, and that he thinks it was a
good idea for you to come up?"

Annabelle hesitated and her grey-gold eyes wandered
from his stare.

"I think so," she said at last. "Things are rather dreary
at home just now. I imagine Mike is a bit bored with me
and the two young ones. I mean, I think that a wealthy
relative is just what he feels we need."

Richard's expression remained uncharacteristically serious and he turned back to the first page of the letter
before casting a furtive glance at the breath-taking face
beside him. Annabelle hurried on.

"We didn't write to Aunt Polly, because her letter was

to Mother anyhow, and explanations seemed too difficult and long-winded to be put on paper. I thought I'd just come up and see what she wanted, but it all sounded a bit peculiar so I thought I'd better arrange with someone reliable to know where I was."

She paused and grinned at him, reminding him vividly of herself as he remembered her best.

"You're the only person I know in London," she said. "It was the sensible thing to write you, don't you think?"

"Of course," Richard stifled an unmanly doubt. "Seven Garden Green. It's one of those houses over there, I suppose." He nodded without enthusiasm towards the grey terrace, dingy and tall in the mist, which surrounded the Green on the other side of the encircling wall.

"No, I don't think so. I came that way. That's Garden Crescent." Annabelle glanced uneasily at the maze of shabby stucco stretching in every direction. "Perhaps it's at the back here. I didn't like to go and look in case you arrived and missed me."

He smiled at her. She was terrific. That half independence, half leaning on one, was the most touching thing he had ever encountered. He got up. "I'll find out. You stay there. There's a bobby down there. He'll know. I shan't be a moment."

He sped off before she could attempt to join him and caught Bullard just as he was moving off towards the Barrow Road.

"Garden Green, sir?" In the way of elderly constables he took his time before replying. "What number do you want? Seven? That'll be the first building down that turning on the right over there. You can't miss the house. It's a museum."

"A what?" Richard was taken by surprise. His eyes looked blue and astounded.

Bullard could not forbear to smile. The boy reminded him of a startled pup, with that red-setter-coloured hair.

"Isn't that what you were looking for, sir? It's number seven, all right. It's only a small museum and there's a house attached which is occupied by a caretaker. If I recollect, she's also the owner. Name of Tassie."

"The name's right." Richard still sounded shaken. "Thank you very much, Officer. Over there? I see."

Old Bullard was loth to let him go. He was curious about the pair. Annabelle in particular had stirred his imagination.

"Number Seven's the museum all right. Only a small one, admission free. If it's any help to you, the house used to be called Tether's End."

The boy grimaced at him. "That's cheerful."

"So it is." Bullard was amused. "That's a funny thing, I've been about here thirty years and never noticed that. It's the same as 'Dunroamin' only more sarky, isn't it? Excuse me, sir, but has the young lady come up from the country?"

"Yes, as a matter of fact she has." To his annoyance Richard felt himself flushing. He looked across the leaf-strewn grass to where she sat waiting, and on impulse turned to the older man and expressed the incredulity which was overwhelming him. "She's *suddenly* got beautiful like that," he exploded. "Suddenly."

Bullard's smile was charming. "She's certainly done it, sir," he said, and moved off in his deliberate way, highly tickled. It was pleasant to see a young chap knocked all of a heap like that. Suddenly, eh? Well, that was how it always happened, and very nice too.

He dismissed the incident and started to think about himself again. It was quite remarkable, he reflected, what a memory he had got. Ask him anything you liked about the district and he could answer it pat, just like that. It was what they called a visual memory. Everything came in pictures. That little museum and the old girl who ran it, for instance. She'd only shown him round it once and . . .

At that point a picture returned to his mind with the abruptness and clarity of a price coming up on a cash register. He stopped in his tracks, his face turning first white and then red in his excitement. Standing in the middle of the pavement he felt in his pocket for his notebook, in the back of which was a worn police circular folded in four. He shook it out with a trembling hand and put on his reading glasses.

"Details urgently required of the following person: Woman, seventy to eighty years, brown complexion, wearing grey or green shepherd's plaid shawl and dark brown hat decorated with large metal beads. Man similar age, white hair round lower part of face, hard hat..."

Bullard stared at the streaming traffic in the Barrow Road. An idea had occurred to him which was credible yet so bizarre that it made him feel dizzy. It was followed by another consideration and in sudden panic he turned back to look again across Garden Green. The seat was bare. The misty sunlight spreading over the little glade showed it forlorn and empty. The young people had gone.

4

Number Seven

It was a pretty little house, built near the corner and separated from those on either side by a mass of shrubbery on the left and a high walled garden containing a studio-like building, presumably the museum, on the right. The plasterwork of the house itself had been restored and painted a delicate pink, the front door was a shiny peacock blue, and the sheer curtains at all windows were frilled and festooned.

This glory contrasted violently with some of the neighbours, but here and there down the short road which connected Garden Green with Edge Street the same sort of effort had been made. The street was on the upgrade once more.

Richard watched Annabelle's progress from the corner. She had refused to let him go with her but at the same time had appeared gratifyingly loth to part with him, and he had arranged to wait and see her safely inside.

There was a small paved garden between the house and the road and he watched her cross it and mount the steps to the porch, but after a while she emerged, made him a covert sign to indicate that there was no one at home, and walked on to the door in the garden wall, outside which there was a notice in gold on a black board.

COLLECTION OF CURIOS
Interesting Animal Furniture and other Items
acquired by the late Frederick Tassie Esq.
Hours 10 A.M. to 12:30 P.M.
Monday to Friday, Admission Free
Please enter

Annabelle paused for a moment to read the neat professional script. Her hair spilt on to her tweed collar, her shoulders were tiny and rounded under the rough cloth, and her travelling bag was held behind her in her gloved hand. For Richard she made one of those inexplicably momentous pictures, a pinpoint of wonder, gone as soon as it is born but not to be forgotten in a lifetime.

Presently she glanced back up the road towards him once more, made a little gesture of farewell, and disappeared through the door in the wall, leaving him alarmingly bereft.

Once inside, she negotiated a glass-covered passage paved with coloured tiles and mounted three red steps to a second door, which opened into a large dim room with an unpolished parquet floor. It smelled violently of naphtha and the uneasy musky scent which hangs for ever round the cured skins of wild animals, and at first glimpse appeared very crowded.

As she stood hesitating, she saw that practically the whole of the room save for the gangway, which was roughly loop-shaped, was crammed with unexpected objects whose only common denominator appeared to be the staggering human folly which had perpetrated them.

Some were protected with glass cases but others were not so fortunate, and the centre of the hall was taken up with a sort of big-game exhibit with a difference. On a carpet-covered dais two monstrous chairs faced one another. One had been constructed with dreadful cunning actually inside the carcass of a small elephant who knelt, trunk at the salute, to permit the sitter to rest within its quilted stomach, whilst the other had been made in the same unlikely way out of a giraffe whose sad head rose disconsolate just above the occupier's own. Beside them towered a moth-eaten grizzly whose ferocious snarl was offset by the fact that a Statue-of-Liberty flambeau adapted to electricity sprouted from one menacing paw, and a moulting ostrich supporting an oil lamp with a pink silk shade completed the group. All four were genuine period pieces, witnesses to a fashion as barbaric and humourless as any in history.

As Annabelle walked round the platform, the explanation of the show occurred to her at once. Here, she realised, must be the lifetime's bag of someone who had played the time-honoured undergraduate's game of Who Can Bring Home the Awfullest Thing with the abandon of youth and the cash of middle age.

She turned aside to the cases, noting the pair of clogs ornamented on the soles with the Lord's Prayer in coloured nailheads, the coat for a French poodle in black sequins and monkey fur, the six-foot replica in plaster of the bridal cake of nineteenth-century royalty, and the collection of moustache cups decorated with crowned heads and flags of all nations.

She came presently to the end of the room, where there was a very large glass case set beneath a partially opened window. The exhibit it had contained was dismantled and there was nothing now in the seven-foot cube save a painted back cloth depicting blue sea, a lighthouse, and gulls, and, in front, a small double seat which looked as if it had come off a pier.

Glimpses of sturdy iron machinery at the side of the back cloth suggested that at some time the case had housed a working model, and Annabelle, who was attracted by such things, edged round the back to discover if she could find a starting lever. She had found one and was just about to press it when a man's voice, deep and pleasant, floated in through the window above her.

"There you are, Polly," it said. "It looks very nice. But I don't see why you had to wash it yourself."

"Because I wanted my blankets clean, my boy." The second voice sounded nice but obstinate. "I appreciate that. I like a man who will help with the laundry. Are you sure you've really got to go? If I hadn't got someone coming in to lunch I'd bully you to stay."

"Darling, I wish I could, but I've got to be at Staines at one and Reading at six. This is a hopeless time to call, I know, but I couldn't pass through London without looking

you up, could I?" He hesitated and added after a pause,
"Everything's all right then, is it?"

"All right?" The query was shocked. "Of course it's all
right. Why shouldn't it be?"

"I don't know." He had a very pleasant laugh. "I was
just fishing to be sure you were glad to see me."

"Well, of course I am." The elderly voice sounded the
least bit flustered. "You're a good boy, Gerry."

"Whatever they say?"

"Oh, go along with you. When are you coming in
again? I can't promise, but next time I may have something to show you."

His reply was lost to Annabelle, whose experimental
tinkering with the lever bore sudden results. Ancient
wheels began to turn, the back cloth to revolve, and at the
same time the small siren concealed in the top of the case
began to blare loudly.

The noise was considerable and there seemed no way
of stopping it. The performance, such as it was, went on to
the end. A painted jetty appearing on the back cloth
lurched jerkily across the scene, followed by a dolphin,
and all the time a very fair imitation of a steamer's whistle
continued to fill the dusty air.

Annabelle was still struggling with the controls when
a side door to the garden clattered open and a man came
sprinting down the gangway. He laughed at her expression
and, stooping in front of the case, pulled a concealed lever
beneath it. The back cloth shuddered to a standstill and
the noise ceased.

"That's a bit better, isn't it?" It was the voice she had
heard talking in the garden. "Mrs. Tassie thought it might
be children. They get in here and play the goat with the
place." He was dusting his hands with a spotted scarf he
had drawn from his pocket and now he handed it to her
absently. "Scrub on this. It's impossible to keep all this
stuff even faintly clean."

He treated her as if he had known her for a long time
and Annabelle, to whom the approach was new, was
delighted. She considered him with interest.

Although he was almost old from her point of view,
thirty if not more, she found him exciting to look at. His
coarse fair hair was worn *en brosse* and he had deep actor's

lines down lantern cheeks. Only the heavy muscles of his neck spoiled him. His round brown eyes were bright if not otherwise expressive, and he had a long-boned loose-jointed figure which was well suited by the light khaki trench coat which he wore belted tightly round him. Annabelle grinned as she returned the scarf.

"Thank you very much. I'm awfully sorry I meddled with this thing. What was it exactly?"

He did not reply at once and she added awkwardly, "I mean, what was in it? What was on the seat?"

He remained looking at her and her impression was that she had offended him somehow, or raised an unfortunate subject. There was no actual change in his expression but she was aware of a sudden cessation of contact, like a flaw in a sound track. A moment later he was smiling again.

"Chimpanzees," he said briefly. "Two chimps dressed as yachtsmen, as far as I can remember. They got the moth in a big way and had to be written off. It's a fantastic collection. The old boy who made it was a charmer, but round the bend I fear. Have you seen the rest? My favourite is along here somewhere, just beyond the stove, a horse's hat made of fishbones knitted by some insanitary islander. Ah, here is Madame."

He nodded his excuses and went off down the room to meet the newcomer who had appeared at the garden door. Annabelle saw her with a sense of deep relief. She was just an ordinary old woman, solid and kindly, like thousands of others up and down the country. A mum if ever there was one, with a pink and white skin and smooth grey hair. The sleeves of her dark woollen dress were rolled up and she wore a neat pinafore decorated with forget-me-nots as innocently blue as her eyes.

As the man came up to her, she put a hand on his coat.

"Thank you, my dear. I can't bear that row. Must you go? Well, run along. Get all your business done and come and see me again. Is there anything you'd like to take with you?"

He laughed. "The bear, perhaps," he suggested, pointing to it. "Bless you, Polly, it's been lovely to see you." He put his arms round her and hugged her and she patted him, rubbing his shoulder with a funny little gesture which was pure affection.

The encounter surprised and slightly irritated the watching Annabelle. Without realising it, she had been counting on the idea of herself as the only relative. But these two people were fond of each other, she saw, not in love but loving.

"I'll give you bear," the woman said, laughing. "You bring me back the others first. Go on, be off with you! Come back when you can. I'm always pleased to see you, you know that. Goodbye, my dear, goodbye."

"Goodbye, old gal." He touched her cheek and went, the inspired cut of the raincoat lending his gaunt figure a swagger as he strode through the main door to the passage and the street. Just before he disappeared he raised a farewell hand to Annabelle, still standing by the empty case at the end of the room.

Mrs. Tassie stood looking after him for a moment before she came on down the aisle. She was smiling happily and for the first time Annabelle caught a glimpse of her as she must have been when Uncle Frederick had forsaken home and family and fiancée for her, not only a blazing country beauty but a character, vital as the spring.

She smiled at the girl, cleared her throat, and embarked upon what was clearly a set piece.

"Good morning," she began briskly. "Now, the little collection which you see before you is not necessarily of an educational nature. It was made by my late husband, Frederick Edwin Tassie, to entertain himself and to satisfy his own tastes, which were for the remarkable and unusual . . ." She paused abruptly and looked hard at Annabelle. "Well, dear, you see what it's like," she went on, relinquishing the formal style with unexpected completeness. "There's a lot of it, some bits much better than others. You like mechanical things best, do you?"

Annabelle blushed. "I'm sorry I started the siren. I was wondering how it worked, you see, and . . . ."

"Never mind. The things are here to be looked at. My husband loved showing his old toys to people. That's what gave me the idea. It's much better than a grave, isn't it?"

"A grave?"

"A monument." The old mouth was contemptuous. "You know, ducky, lumps of marble in a cemetery, or little glass blisters with ducks or doves or something in them. I thought the old sport would rather have his bits of nonsense kept somewhere where people who were kiddish like himself could enjoy them, so that's what I did. I spent the money on this place. It can't last, of course, but then, what does? I must go over these blessed animals for moth again soon."

"That must be quite a problem." Annabelle, who had experienced it at home, was sympathetic. "That's how you lost the monkeys, isn't it?"

"No, we never had monkeys. Frederick didn't like them. He knew he looked a little bit like one, wicked old thing." She was frowning and her still pretty eyes had become shocked. "Did Gerry Hawker tell you there were monkeys once in the steamboat? That's the thing you started."

The girl was embarrassed. "The man I was just talking to said something about chimpanzees."

"That was Gerry, the sinner." Mrs. Tassie spoke mildly. "He didn't want to be reminded. He's lost those figures, you know, that's about it." She went over to the empty case and peered in regretfully. "There were two dear old people sitting in there," she announced unexpectedly. "They were life-size and quite wonderfully done. Easily the best thing in the place. The old woman had a nice silk dress and a shawl, and a bonnet with jet bugles on it, while the old man was so real he was quite as good as anything in Tussaud's. The show was called 'The Steamboat, or Crossing the Bar,' and they used to doze there together looking as if they were on a boat, sailing off together somewhere."

Annabelle, who was too young ever to have encountered any entertainment of a similar unlikely kind, so fashionable at the end of the last century, was rendered temporarily speechless, and her guide continued. "Frederick adored it. He bought it in an auction room in Blackpool when one of the showmen sold up, and he'd be livid with Gerry for losing the figures, although he was so fond of him. I must get them back from the boy. They'd got a bit of moth and he took them to have them renovated for me, and of course that's the last I heard of them. It must be nearly a year ago."

Her laugh was half tolerant, half annoyed.

"He's left them somewhere and hasn't had time to go and pick them up. That's Gerry all over. He takes on much too much."

Annabelle was curious but still she did not speak. The sun had come out and the open door, with her overnight bag in the dark corner beside it, was suddenly very inviting. She took a step towards it but a hand closed over her arm.

"You've not come to see all this dusty old junk." The kindly voice was full of laughter. "You've come to see me, haven't you? And you thought you'd have a look around before you introduced yourself. That's Freddy's family all over. Very wise, my poppet."

She swung the girl round to face her.

"You're Jenny Tassie, sent up by your mamma to see your Aunt Polly," she announced, her smile radiant, "and you're just what I want, duckie. Absolutely bang-on, as they say. Come inside."

5

The Man Who Wanted To Know the Time

The autumn morning air was soft and smelled of rain and the London street scene was done in pastel shades under a sky of smoked pearl.

Young Mr. Waterfield lingered on the corner a little longer than the ten minutes agreed upon, in case Annabelle decided to return.

Where the roads met there was a large double pillar box and he was behind it when the man in the trench coat came hurrying out of the door in the garden wall. Richard was not only surprised to see him but, he noticed with astonishment, considerably irritated. He hung back for a minute or two to observe him.

The newcomer went over to the sports car which was parked on the opposite side of the road and was about to enter it when an idea evidently occurred to him, and he turned back not to the museum but to the house. He walked straight into the porch and emerged a moment later carrying a hat. Since he also slammed the door behind him, it was evident to the watching Richard that he carried a key. Then he climbed into the car and shot off down the short road, to be halted almost immediately by the traffic coming down Edge Street.

Richard on foot was able to cross and board a bus before the car could enter the stream, but as he settled himself on the front seat of the top deck he discovered that in the meantime the driver had edged his way into the flow and was now directly below and in front of him. Both vehicles were hemmed in by a solid procession. The traffic jam was a mid-morning special and progress was practically nil.

The driver of the sports car appeared to be taking the delay philosophically, however, and Richard had every opportunity of watching him as he leant idly on the door looking at the foot passengers as they passed by him. He had a narrow head and unusual neck muscles, and Richard noticed particularly the bravura which belonged to the generation three quarters of a step ahead of his own. His curiosity was deeply piqued. In the letter which Annabelle had shown him there had been nothing to account for this character who seemed so much at home at Number Seven.

The car fitted the man perfectly. It was a Lagonda, elderly but so tuned and titivated that only the gallantry of its basic lines remained to preserve that offhand elegance which had been its original glory. It was open and Richard, who was looking down directly into the back, could see a coil of fine rope on the worn leather seat, a starting handle with a dirty tie-on label fluttering from its shaft, and an ordinary wooden crate of the kind in which half a dozen wine bottles might well have been packed. This appeared to be nailed down, but there was no wire or cord round it.

On the top of the bus the redheaded young man in the dark suit thrust his chin out unconsciously. There is nothing actively suspicious about a sports car of interesting age, but it does present a certain menace to any self-appointed knight-errant who is compelled to travel by London General Transport.

Richard examined his resources. The contents of his pockets were just about as meagre as he had supposed and presently he unfastened the strap of his wrist watch. He turned it over with a mixture of satisfaction and regret and put it into his trouser pocket. At once his chin became more aggressive and there was a little upward curl at the corners of his mouth.

There was a branch of Messrs. Rattenborough further down Edge Street and when at last the jam disentangled itself for a minute or two, and the bus swept past the huge windows, which contained enough plate to fill a galleon, Richard descended and went round to the narrow door above which the three balls were discreetly displayed.

It was not often that he pawned his watch, which was one of his few valuable possessions, but it was his practice to do so in times of emergency. Quite apart from the sense of comfort which he derived from having the money in his pocket, the act seemed to underline the importance of the adventure or predicament in his own mind. It set a seal of authority upon it, as it were.

The transaction was accomplished without difficulty and indeed, since the watch was such a nice one, even with a certain amount of social success. He came out feeling confident and walked back to the bus stop, intending to get back to the office at once. Annabelle had agreed not to ring the office save in emergency and he had arranged to discover Mrs. Tassie's telephone number and to call her as soon as he left work. On the whole the situation appeared to be in hand.

However, at that point he saw the Lagonda again. It was in a side street, standing before the door of a barber's shop, an old-fashioned place which still carried a multi-coloured pole beside the lintel.

Richard hardly hesitated. The familiar way in which

the driver of the sports car had opened the door of Number Seven had shaken him and he found he wanted very much to know who he was. He walked past the shop, glancing in. The window was only half curtained and he caught a glimpse of a narrow, straw-coloured head above a towel in the chair nearest the glass. He pushed open the door and stepped down into the scented steam-filled room, which buzzed with conversation. The noise stopped abruptly as he appeared and five pairs of eyes regarded him with that slightly hostile astonishment which appears, in small establishments of the kind, to be the portion of the chance customer.

The man in the white coat who was attending to the driver of the sports car looked at Richard inquisitively, decided rather openly that he was nothing to worry about, and waved him to a seat against the wall, where already there was one customer waiting.

"Just a moment, sir. Percy here is just finishing. I shall be a little time on the Major, and that gentleman beside you is waiting for me. But you'll find Perce is quite all right. A very fine scissor man Perce is, aren't you Perce?"

The second barber, who was at work on the head of a fat man who was sitting like a sack with his eyes closed, took no notice at all of the remark. He was elderly, with a fine distinguished face and brooding hooded eyes.

"Perce isn't deaf," continued the first barber, who emerged as the proprietor. "He's just a foreigner. Talks sometimes." He paused to hone the cutthroat razor with which he was about to shape the two-coloured waves, and Richard eyed him with covert amusement. He was a dark pale-faced cockney, womanish without being emasculated, who possessed small hands, dull black eyes, and the caressing version of the local accent, which is to say it was thick and slightly unctuous, as if each word was some nice little gift which he felt sure the recipient would appreciate.

"You make up for 'im though, don't you, Mr. Vick?" The other man waiting, a smartish youngster of the salesman type, spoke without looking up from the sporting sheet he was studying.

Mr. Vick bridled. "I like to be friendly, I hope," he

protested, "and when I see an old customer like the Major naturally I get on to old times."

"Don't apologise," said the man with the paper. "I like it. It helps me concentrate."

"Concentrate!" Mr. Vick emitted a drawing-room scream. "You'll never win nothing that way. The only way to win on 'orses, dogs, pools, or anythink else is to take it insouciant. Fly at it, if you take my meaning."

"And then collect the lolly and come right off the 'andle. Drive round in an 'ired car with a tailor's dummy and say you're married. That was your story, wasn't it?"

The fat man opened his eyes while he spoke and shut them again the instant he had finished. Mr. Vick squealed with delight and appealed to the man whose hair he was cutting.

"That's a very old anecdote of mine," he said, grinning at his client through the mirror. "You remember it, don't you, Major? It was you who was so took with it."

"Me? Not guilty." The driver of the sports car spoke idly and his smile was casual enough. But the denial was complete and Richard, who had not heard him speak before, looked at him sharply.

"You've forgot." Mr. Vick seemed gratified. "You laughed like a two-gallon flush. I can 'ear you now."

The man who sat beside Richard folded his paper.

"Who won what?" he enquired.

"It 'appened in Islington when I was a 'prentice." Mr. Vick spoke through his teeth, his attention concentrated on some fine work he was doing with the razor. "A young fellow in a draper's picked up five pounds in the street and put it all on an 'orse called Lucky Gutter, which 'e see was running in the big race that day. It came in at two 'undred to one and the excitement pushed 'im over the edge. 'E turned 'is coat inside out, pinched one of the female dummies out of the window, put a lace curtain over its 'ead, and drove round in front of 'is young lady's 'ouse with it as if 'e was getting married. The shock upset 'er and she fell down the area, broke 'er leg, and sued 'im. It's a sad story really."

"Lucky Gutter," remarked the salesman, who had a one-track mind. "I never heard of such a name."

"There was a line of them," said the fat man, not bothering to open his eyes at all this time, "like the Cottages were later. Lucky Rooftop, Lucky Verandah, and—correct me if I'm wrong—Lucky Clocktower."

"You remember it now, don't you, Major? I see you smiling." Mr. Vick was coy.

"It's a staggering tale," said the Major, catching Richard's eye through the glass and grinning at him, "but I never heard it before."

Mr. Vick opened his mouth to protest and thought better of it. After a while he sniffed.

"You've been coming in 'ere on and off ever since the war," he began. "Tell me, Major, any more developments in the you-know-what business? You mentioned it last time."

"What was that?" The Major was friendly but cautious.

"The h-u-s-h h-u-s-h," spelled Mr. Vick rather unnecessarily, and the man in the chair burst out laughing, the colour flooding his coarse fair skin.

"Oh, that's in abeyance," he said with disarming embarrassment, "whatever it was. You haven't any old Rolls-Royces about you, I suppose? Any age, any condition, good prices paid."

"Ah." Mr. Vick seized on it. "You're in that line now, are you?"

"No, I'm not." The fair man spoke lightly. "Not at all." He closed his narrow lips and sat smiling with his eyes, while the little barber's curiosity became as noticeable as if he had shouted it.

"You've been abroad, I see," he said suddenly, cutting clean across a pronouncement made by the fat man, who was still talking of the names of race horses.

"No."

Mr. Vick was unabashed. He picked up a single wiry lock, pulled it out of curl, and let it spring back.

"I made certain this was a bit of foreign cutting," he said. "Isle of Wight perhaps."

"Or Wigan, of course," said the Major, and again his shiny eyes flickered and his glance met Richard's own in the looking glass.

"Lucky Clocktower . . ." The voice of the sporting

salesman was pathetic. "Who could get a tip out of a name like that. What does it mean?"

"Invariably fast." The eyes in the mirror laughed into Richard's and dropped as the Major glanced at his watch. "Just like this blessed thing. What *is* the time exactly?"

The question turned out to be amazingly popular with everybody. Mr. Vick turned at once to point to the fly-blown disc on the wall behind him.

"That clock is dead right by the Shakespeare Head long bar, slow by Ronnie's next door, and fast by the B.B.C.," he announced with incomprehensible pride.

"It is four minutes and twenty-three—don't stop me, twenty-four twenty-five seconds fast precisely," said the sporting salesman, looking at his wrist watch, an impressive performance which he offset somewhat by adjusting the instrument immediately.

"Wait," commanded the fat man, heaving himself up and accomplishing vasty manoeuvres under his shrouding cape. "This is the right time. This is the real time. Railway time, that's what this is." He brought out a large silver pocket watch, looked at it earnestly for some moments, shook it, and put it back. "You're not far out," he said to the barber.

Richard shot back his own cuff out of force of habit, remembered in time, and glanced up sharply to find the Major watching him through the glass again. The round eyes turned away at once but the younger man was left with the odd but very definite conviction that for some inexplicable reason he was pleased. He was certainly smiling as he turned to the salesman.

"I make it a quarter to," he remarked. "If you're right, this wretched thing of mine has lost a minute and twenty seconds in the past half hour. Exactly thirty minutes ago I was driving over Westminister Bridge and as Big Ben chimed I put it right."

Richard's pugnacious young face became blank. The lie uttered so deliberately appeared to be so unnecessary. He eyed the stranger cautiously. He looked perfectly normal and even pleasant, sitting there fiddling with his watch, but suddenly Richard became aware of something very interesting about him. He was engaged in arranging something, some definite, carefully thought-out plan. He could not rid himself of the impression. There was a wariness and a sense of suppressed force about the man which was special for the occasion, whatever it was.

Richard's speculations were interrupted by the convulsion in the room caused by the fat man getting up, and by the time he was himself in the vacated seat and had persuaded the foreign assistant not to make too much of a job of the unwanted haircut, Mr. Vick and his favoured client were in full session once more.

"If you don't know Greenwich, you don't, Major," the barber was saying brightly. "It was you mentioning Westminster Bridge put me in mind of it. But then of course there's Shooter's Hill. Kent is a lovely county. See much of Kent, Major?"

"Practically nothing." A flicker of mischief passed over the thin lips. "It's no use, my dear chap, you'll have to face it that I have no fixed abode."

Mr. Vick decided to be offended.

"Now you're trying to take the mickey out of me," he said reprovingly and stepped back from his handiwork. "Well, now, that's that, sir. That suit you? I mustn't keep that gentleman waitin' if 'e's going to get 'is bets on before the one o'clock, must I?"

It was a dismissal, and to Richard's regret, since he was now trapped in the other chair himself, the Major rose, paid his score, and took his trench coat from the peg.

He then performed the second little act which the younger man found curious. On entering he had evidently stripped off his raincoat with his jacket inside it, and now he put them on in the same way, so that the outside of the jacket did not appear. The younger man, watching the performance in his own glass now, reflected that the manoeuvre was the same as the lie about Westminster Bridge, not so much venal as peculiar, for despite the slovenly beginning he took some pains to dress himself, knotting his muffler carefully and arranging his collar with just the right degree of swagger. As he was drawing in his belt he appeared to relent towards the inquisitive Mr. Vick, who was still sulking.

"I'm going to see a hero of yours this evening," he

remarked. "I hope to do a little business with him. Moggie Moorhen."

At the name of the celebrated comedian the barber wavered and fell. A bouquet of refined noises escaped him and his sallow face warmed with pleasure.

"Are you really? My word, that'll be an experience. Just the very exact same off as 'e is on, I shouldn't wonder."

The Major turned deliberately to Richard's looking glass and winked.

"I hope not," he said dryly, "or we'll finish the evening swinging from the Savoy lighting fixtures."

He went out laughing and the door closed behind him.

Mr. Vick paused, towel in hand, to raise himself on his toes to see over the curtain.

"There he goes," he remarked with feminine bitterness. "The Savoy lighting fixtures? . . . The Bodega more likely. He's a very funny finger, the Major, and he's in a very funny mood. I noticed it the moment 'e come in."

"I t'ink," murmured the assistant who was cutting Richard's hair, "that he is of the po-lice."

"Oh dear me, no!" Mr. Vick tossed his head contemptuously. "You can relax, Perce. 'E's got no interest in your papers. 'E's a very funny fellow all the same. 'E's been coming 'ere on and off for the last eight or nine years and I've never set eyes on 'im but in this shop, and I don't know what 'e does from Adam. Not from Adam. That's quite a record for me. You could call 'im one of my failures, really."

"Mystery man," said the sporting salesman and ran a hopeful eye down the list of starters.

"You've said it." Mr. Vick dropped back on to his heels. "Charmin' man, mind you. Never shabby. Beautiful shirt 'e was wearin'. Never grouses, which is fantastic, but talk to 'im and you might be livin' in another world. After all this time there's only one thing I know about 'im for certain, and that is that every now and again 'e gets up to something—puts a big deal through." He paused. "This is one of the times."

"How do you know?" Richard spoke involuntarily. It was so much his own impression.

Mr. Vick's dull eyes acknowledged his existence.

"Because 'e's in the mood," he said confidently. "We 'airdressers get to know a lot about moods. Goin' to an 'airdresser at all is a very moody thing. Some only 'ave a trim when they're fed up. The Major usually comes in when 'e's bored, but now and again—not often, mind, but sometimes—he steps in 'ere as part of a little programme 'e's set 'imself. I can tell. I can feel 'im simmering, getting excited and above 'imself. I used to think 'e was an actor working up for a first night, but that's not it. There's no grease paint in that 'airline.'

"I picked up a packet once on Greasepoint," said the salesman. "Short back and sides, if you please, Mr. Vick, and I won't have the old curry comb."

The barber acknowledged the order but continued to talk thoughtfully about the previous customer.

"It amazes me I don't know more about 'im after all this time," he said, "but I tell you one extraordinary thing. This is the third or fourth time I've seen 'im do it, and no one would be more amazed than 'e'd be 'imself if you told 'im of it. Unconscious, it is. But when 'e's in one of these off-the-'andle now-for-it sort of moods 'e's always in a tizzy about the right time. 'E always mentions it, 'e always gets the whole shop arguin' about it, and it's a very funny thing but 'e nearly always picks up the man who 'asn't got a watch."

"Then he wasn't lucky today," said the salesman. "I wonder if I shall be. He's a crook, that's what you mean, is it?"

"No, sir, I certainly don't." Mr. Vick was shocked. "'E's a regular customer. Sometimes 'e doesn't come in for a month or two but if 'e'd been inside I should notice it at once. It takes nearly seven months to get rid of the prison 'aircut. Besides, whatever 'e is 'e's something unusual, something one doesn't meet every day."

At this point the assistant barber removed the cape from Richard's shoulders and gave his neck a cursory whisk.

"I t'ink he is of the po-lice," he repeated, sighing. "Anyhow, he has left his belongings."

He nodded towards the corner where a wooden box,

the coil of rope, and the starting handle sprawled in an untidy heap.

"There now!" Mr. Vick's scream was like a toy train. "'E brought them out of the street for safety and then forgot them. That proves 'e's no p'liceman. You'll see. 'E'll be back. I've known 'im do *that* before. Ah, what did I tell you? No sooner out of my mouth than . . . There they are, Major."

The door had shuddered open and the man in the trench coat appeared on the threshold. He was grinning and deeply apologetic, and his smile included Richard.

The wooden box seemed to be remarkably heavy and when he had hoisted it into his arms he was fully laden. Richard gathered up the rope and the handle.

"I'll bring these."

"Will you? Thanks a lot. My old bus is outside."

When he had set the box carefully on the back seat he spoke again.

"That's more than kind of you. I'm drifting down to the West End. Can I give you a lift?"

Richard was looking at the starting handle he was carrying. The worn label tied to its shaft had fluttered over and the pencilled inscription upon it was just readable. "Hawker. Rolf's Dump, S.E."

He scarcely saw it. As if it had attracted his attention for the first time the Major leaned over and pulled it off, pitching it into the gutter.

"Coming?" he enquired.

Richard looked up.

"Thank you," he said with sudden deliberation, "I should like that."

6

Luncheon Party

Matthew Phillipson, senior partner of Southern, Wood and Phillipson, family solicitors of Minton Terrace, West, was a spare elderly man with the figure of a boy and the pathetic face of a marmoset. At the moment he was very happy, an unusual condition with him, and his cold eyes had softened as he watched Polly Tassie as she bent over the stove.

He had telephoned to ask if he could drop round and see her. She had invited him to lunch as he knew she would and here he was, sitting in her kitchen waiting for his steak to be done just as he liked it, hard outside, rare inside.

The room, he reflected, looking at it with appreciation, was exactly like its owner, ordinary, comfortable, and obstinately itself. There was a red linoleum on the floor patterned like a Turkey carpet, out of date for forty years. Staffordshire china greyhounds stood on the mantelshelf, pots of gloxinia and musk, of all things, were in the window, and there was a solid kitchen table with a white cloth on it for him to sit at. He had a hassock under his feet and a waisted glass of dark ale in his hand, and under the flowered cheese-dish cover he had already discovered as nice a piece of Blue Cheshire as he had ever seen. There was, moreover, a cottage loaf, a delicacy he had thought extinct, and while she was still busy he broke the top from the bottom and was engaged in slicing off the soft sponge between the two when she turned and caught him. He laughed, his sallow cheeks flushing.

"I haven't done that for fifty years," he said.

"Then get on with it," said Polly, setting a plate before him. "Be a devil. Cut the other half. You are a fathead,

Matt. I *am* fond of you. Freddy used to say you really are the finest stuffed shirt in captivity. Now try this. It ought to be just right."

"It is," he assured her. "You're a wonderful cook. You always were. You're looking young too, if I may say so. I mean unusually so. Radiant. Has anything happened?"

"Has it!" From across the table she looked up at him, her bright blue eyes dancing. "Matt, old sport, it came off. They sent her. Not the eldest, but the second girl. Nearly eighteen, trying to look grown up. I soon stopped all that."

"Did they, by Jove?" He paused, his fork in mid-air. He was pleased but astonished. "Frederick's niece. I wondered if they would. I didn't know what to advise you to write. Well, good for them, Polly, eh? That settles a lot of problems, doesn't it? I can see you took to her. I shall look forward to meeting her. When is she coming to London again?"

"She's here now, only arrived this morning. I thought you might want to talk business so I gave her some lunch early and sent her out to look at the shops. She'll be back before you go. Matt, you're going to be startled."

"Oh dear, am I?" He was suspicious at once. "If she's a relative of Frederick's, of course, she may have *any* peculiarity. What is it?" He permitted himself a little smile. "Two heads perhaps?"

"If she had I'd still love her. But no, Matt, she's a beauty, a real true film-star knockout. Really lovely. One of those faces which turn your heart over and a body like one of the little bits of nonsense you see on the screen.

"I've been most careful not to let on I noticed anything, because I do hate conceited kids, but there's no getting away from it. You wait."

He burst out laughing. "You're clucking, Polly," he said, "but I'm thankful to hear it. As I told both you and Frederick, blood is so much thicker than water when it comes to it." He hesitated. "You'll be completing that document, then?"

"Oh, I think so. I'd only got to put the name in, hadn't I? You were right, Matt, I realised it when I saw her."

"Oh well, I'm glad," said Mr. Phillipson, sighing. "I brought it along with me, as a matter of fact. Just slipped it in my pocket in case, don't you know. I don't want to

hurry you, of course, but these things are better completed.
We'll see to it after lunch."

She exchanged his plate for a clean one and uncovered the cheese. She was smiling to herself.

"You don't really trust me, do you, Matt? You think
I'm like any other silly old woman, liable to change my
mind every ten minutes."

"No, no, I don't," he protested. "It's not that at all.
It's simply that you and I are old-fashioned people in an
old-fashioned situation, in which years of experience have
proved that any young relative, however distant, is apt to
turn out to be a better bet in the long run than the—er—
stranger without the gates."

Mrs. Tassie was making the coffee and did not answer
immediately, but as she brought the tray to the table and
reseated herself she ventured a guarded question.

"You're going to have a word with that boy for me this
afternoon, aren't you?"

"I saw him yesterday."

"Gerry Hawker?" She had started and the dark fra-
grant liquid spilled over the saucer and into the tray. "You
told me his appointment was for today."

"So it was. The rascal came a day early, assuming no
doubt that I shouldn't be able to see him. However, I
made time for him. Don't look like that, Polly. He's the
guilty party, not you."

She was busying herself mopping up the coffee tray.
"Did you tell him I knew?"

"No. I obeyed your instructions faithfully. If it's any
comfort to you, that appeared to be the aspect which
worried him most, but I think that without perjuring
myself I left him happy on that score. I conveyed that I
made the discovery quite alone. He believed me."

"He must." She was speaking almost to herself. "He
came in here this morning."

"Really?" Mr. Phillipson was shocked. "He's a cool
customer. He was trying to find out if I'd reported to you,
I suppose? What a very good thing I hadn't. That means
he still has every incentive to come back tonight with the
money as arranged. I promised him complete secrecy if he
pays up."

"Are you making him pay it back?"

"Of course I am, my dear girl." He flushed with annoyance. "That's the very least I can do. He has altered one of your cheques from eleven pounds to seventy, robbing you of fifty-nine pounds as surely as if he'd taken it from your purse. By condoning..."

"I haven't done that." She spoke sharply. "I may feel towards Gerry as if he were my own, but I won't stand for him doing anything really wrong. As soon as I noticed it, didn't I write to you at once? I feel guilty because I know I've got bad handwriting and I must have made it very easy and tempted him if he was pushed for money." She hesitated and then continued very carefully as she struggled to express herself. "Gerry has got to be pulled up good and sharp. But I want to keep out of it, not only because *I* don't want to lose his confidence but because I don't want him to lose *me*. Do you see what I mean?"

"Perfectly," he assured her dryly. "You realise that he depends on you. You're behaving like a mother thinking solely of the child. You always do. I'm not blaming you, my dear girl. In fact, I'm stretching far too many points to abet you. But I can't say I like it."

"Of course you don't. It's criminal." She made the admission with awe. "It could mean prison for him if he did it to someone else. That's why I had to do something. But he's a dear, Matt, a kind good boy when you know him. Freddy liked him very much. We first met him as a young officer in the war and he's been dropping in to see me on and off ever since. We've grown very fond of one another. He couldn't turn out to be a real bad hat after all these years, could he?"

It was a plea, and Mr. Phillipson, who was fond of her too, knew exactly what she meant.

"Oh, he's not the ordinary irresponsible type," he assured her. "There are brains there and considerable charm and he certainly seemed quite frank."

"Did he tell you he lived in Reading?" She made the enquiry cautiously and as if she feared his answer. But for once Mr. Phillipson was not noticing. He was trying very hard to be charitable.

"Outside Reading," he corrected her. "He has a part

share in a garage there, but I gather there has been some trouble with the partner's wife. I was inclined to believe his story. In my experience women in business ... well, there's no point in going into that, but the possessive wife is always cropping up in these stories. Anyway, the story he told was one I could well believe and, to a certain extent, sympathise with."

"All Gerry's stories are." Polly spoke absently. She was stirring her coffee round and round and her mild eyes were troubled.

"And what exactly do you mean by that?" he demanded. "Aren't those the facts as you know them? Has he lied to me?"

"No, dear. I'm sure he hasn't." She was flustered. "I only meant that Gerry sometimes presents things in the way that is most likely to convince the audience he happens to be talking to. I mean he might leave out the bit about the woman when talking to me, and he might make the partner his brother and the garage a factory, to sound bigger, you see?"

"Has he done that?"

"Oh no, dear, no. I'm sure I've heard about the Reading garage."

Matthew Phillipson, warm and well fed and flattered by her obvious dependence on him, sat looking at her sternly.

"Yes ... it's a very good thing the matter's in my hands," he observed at last. "I don't like clever women, Polly, never did. To me, you're worth a dozen of them, just as you are. We'll do what can be done for this wretched chap. If he honours his word and turns up with the money tonight, that'll be the end of it, but I shouldn't see much more of him."

She smiled at him gratefully but her lips were still forming the words which she did not like to utter.

"The people in your office will know all about it?" she said at last.

"No, they won't. I've prepared for that. He's coming in after five. I shall wait for him until half past, and I've kept your two letters on the subject out of the file. You marked them personal and they were kept private. I've promised him the whole thing is confidential between himself and me, and if he does his part it will remain so. He'll have had a good fright, which may prove salutary. And now, my dear, if you feel like it, we'll settle that little matter of the residue of your estate."

He put his hand in an inside pocket and she nodded absently, her mind still on the earlier subject.

"Gerry's all right," she repeated stoutly. "He only wants the right girl to love him and boss him. I've been thinking about it for a long time. What he needs is someone young and affectionate and his own class and..." She became aware of Mr. Phillipson's shrewd glance and stopped abruptly. "I'm not," she protested guiltily, although he had not spoken. "I'm neither planning nor hoping anything. Honestly, it's hardly gone through my mind."

"I'm very glad it hasn't." He was severe with her. "If this niece of Freddy's is under twenty-one, and the only thing we know for certain about Jeremy Hawker is the present very unfortunate incident, then really I can hardly advise you to let them even meet."

"Not—not if I'm there?"

"Oh, Polly!" He was exasperated with her. "Don't be absurd. You must know by this time that you can't look after everybody. If you take my advice you'll strike this young blackguard quietly off your list."

"Don't say that, Matt." She looked positively frightened. "Truly don't. I tell you I'm fond of him. I needn't worry because you'll always be about, won't you? I'll never do anything without you, dear. I do admit that when I first found out about this dreadful business I thought he needed a wife to keep him straight, and I thought of Freddy's niece, and I thought she must be twenty-four or five. But that turns out to have been the elder sister and she's engaged anyhow. This child who has come along is far too young, but she's sweet. I like her for her own sake. I'm not a fool, I shall look after her. You can trust me. Now give me the pen."

Fifteen minutes later as she was letting him out of the front door Annabelle came up the path. Mr. Phillipson looked down at her from the top of the porch steps and turned a blank face to his hostess.

"Good heavens," he said briefly.

"I know," she murmured. "I told you," and went on, glowing down at the newcomer, "Hullo, darling, how are the shops?"

"Absolutely whizz." The schoolgirl suddenly emerging from behind the sophisticated young lovely took Mr. Phillipson unaware. He found her enchanting, and although quite conscious that Polly was laughing at him for it he still displayed a fine flourish of old-fashioned gallantry as the introductions were performed.

Just before he left them he turned to his old friend. "This young lady's a very great responsibility."

Polly met his eyes. "My goodness, yes."

Annabelle laughed at them both. "I'm fairly safe out," she murmured, reddening.

"Of course you are. He doesn't mean that." Polly flew to the rescue. "He's just telling me to look after you as he looks after me, like a hen. Who gave a taxi driver ten bob to take me home when I was waiting in the rain, eh, Matt? Go along with you, you old sinner, looking so innocent."

Mr. Phillipson had not the face for innocence but he did appear astonished.

"Not I," he said earnestly.

"Oh rubbish, don't lie to me. The taximan told me an old friend. In fact what he really said was ''Op, in, Ma. The bloke is on the corner watching to see I don't scarper with the lolly. If I don't take you he'll give me in charge.' I looked back but I couldn't see you so I got in very gratefully and came home."

Mr. Phillipson continued mystified. "You've accused me of this before and I've told you I'm not guilty. It's a charming story," he said. "I'm sorry to have to disclaim it."

"Oh, Matt, you haven't forgotten the Avenue, that dreadful wet night when there were murders going on all round."

He stared at her in amazement. "You're rambling."

"I'm not. There was a murder going on in the very next street. Next day the papers were full of it. You *must* remember the moneylender who was taken away in a bus?"

"I do," Annabelle put in unexpectedly. "There were other people in the bus too, which made it idiotic. Didn't you read about it?"

"No." Mr. Phillipson wiped his hands of the whole affair. "I avoid crime except when I have to deal with it. I must go. Goodbye, Miss Tassie. Enjoy your stay in London. Goodbye, Polly, my dear. Don't worry about anything. I'll telephone you either tonight or tomorrow morning."

He went off down the path, waved from the gate, and strode away, a slender upright figure. Polly watched him go with deep affection.

"Such a sound old boy," she remarked. "So kind, and he'll never take thanks. I rely on him. He's my common sense."

The girl glanced at her curiously.

"I don't think he paid the taximan that time, though, do you? I think he rather wished it *had* been him."

"Oh, but he must have." Polly put an arm round the tweed-clad shoulders as they went into the house. "Who else could it have been? I've lived most of my life up North, I haven't many old friends in London."

"Perhaps it was the murderer." Annabelle was delighted with the mystery and her voice was full of joyous nonsense. "I know, the murderer saw you and thought you might recognise him and stop him, and so he got you out of the way. That means he's someone you know."

"Don't!" Polly's reaction was so violent it startled even herself. As the word escaped her she looked astonished. "Oh, how you frightened me," she said, laughing as she caught sight of herself in the hall glass. "I've gone white. What a horrible idea, darling. No, of course it was Matt, bless him. I knew it at the time. Otherwise I wouldn't have dared to get into the cab, would I?" She paused for a moment, her hand on the stair rail. "No," she repeated at last. "I know some damn silly boys but no murderers, thank God. Besides," she added with complete inconsequence, "I had a postcard from Gerry, sent from Yorkshire and dated that very evening. I noticed it particularly at the time. Come along, my poppet, it's nearly late enough. Let's make ourselves a cup of tea."

7

Afternoon with Music

The man who had introduced himself as Jeremy Chad-Horder, and had disclaimed his wartime rank of Major as out of date, was still chattering amiably.

"As the 1957 car said, between you and me, dearie, the trouble is I can't tell my boot from my bonnet," he remarked cheerfully as he and Richard paused outside the huge plateglass window of the Piccadilly motor salesroom. "I find that's the most important thing to remember about modern cars. If they appear to be shrinking it's all right, they're going away. I perceive it is closing time. Where shall we stagger next to top up the alcoholic content? What about the Midget Club in Minton Mews?"

"Good idea." Richard noticed with relief that he had kept all trace of doggedness out of his tone. They were both very sober, he suspected, although they had so far visited the Rivoli, the New Bar of the Café, Ley's Oyster House, and an assortment of pubs of varying elegance. At each of these establishments his companion had been recognised and sometimes with enthusiasm, but they had stayed long nowhere. The younger man had been able to hold his own financially and socially, but it had been an effort and so far he had succeeded in discovering little more about the stranger than had been apparent at the barber's.

Beyond the fact that he was obviously a charming and convincing liar, very little else that was concrete had emerged. The one thing certain was that he had no intention of letting Richard get away from him. Every tentative effort which the young man made to escape was parried neatly and some new inducement offered to keep him by his side.

Richard was interested because none of the usual explanations appeared to fit the bill. Moreover, since he was particularly anxious to discover what kind of people had got hold of Annabelle without actually spying on her, the opportunity seemed heaven-sent. The more he discovered the less he liked, and he decided to stay with the man for a bit.

The Lagonda was parked in Curzon Street and they walked through to collect it and drove to the northern side of the West End, leaving the car in a little alley which Gerry knew of just behind Minton Square. It was very full but he took an immense amount of trouble to get in, and Richard was struck by the contrast between the driving skill he was displaying and the fuddled facetiousness he was attempting to convey.

The wooden box was now safely in the boot. It had not proved practicable to carry it around with them on their quest for refreshment, and they had stowed it away on their first stop. Gerry looked in the back for it as they got out and was reassured as he remembered.

"You can't leave anything in an open car," he explained. "The whole blessed place seems to be on the twist these days. The Midget is just along here on the right. Some people call it Edna's, after the woman who runs it. If you've not met her before, you may find her amusing."

He took the other man's elbow and guided him out of the cobbled lane into the street which ran at right angles to it. There, beside a small and expensive antique shop, they found a flight of oak stairs leading up on to the first floor. A discreet sign written in copperplate so that it suggested a large visiting card assured them that Edna's Midget Club was open to members only.

At the top of the flight a small vestibule had been constructed out of the landing and in it sat a commissionaire with a visitors' book open on a table before him. He had a large friendly face and practically no top to his head, so that the peaked cap which lay by his elbow suggested the lid of a mustard pot.

He greeted Gerry with a great crow of pleasure.

"No-it-isn't-yes-it-is-'ullo-'ullo-'ullo," he said pleasantly. "Nice to see you again, sir. You've bin missed, I'll say you've been missed."

He dipped the pen in the ink, pushed the book forward and winked.

"Jeremy Blah-blah and Mr. Richard Wah-wah," he announced, blotting the entry with pride. "Straight in, sir. Go and get your welcome home."

The man in the trench coat hesitated, his face alight with the shamefaced laughing apology which Richard had begun to consider characteristic of him. Despite its admissions it was by no means unattractive and it suited the lean face and softened its deeply scored lines.

"Is she there?" he murmured.

The commissionaire raised his eyes and suddenly showed all his yellowing teeth in mock ferocity.

"All ready to eat yer," he whispered and shook with silent laughter which made him scarlet in the face.

Gerry smiled at him briefly and his forehead wrinkled like a piece of corrugated paper.

"Here's for it," he said to Richard and pushed open a door on the right.

The Midget Club was smart of its kind and what was called by its habitués 'exclusive, sort of.' It occupied the whole of the first floor of the small period house and was composed of a single L-shaped room divided by a large archway in which had once hung the panelled double doors of a more gracious age. Now most of the ornamentation had been achieved with paper, a design of white candelabra on grey on the darker walls and an explosion of gilt stars upon crimson on the lighter ones. In the first and smaller half of the room there was a long bar, its supports painted to simulate flat Regency pillars, while in the larger, darker portion of the place there was a mock window, a television set, and a number of easy chairs with coffee tables before them. The air was heavy with perfume and alcohol and blue with cigarette smoke, but the main crowd had not yet arrived.

A knot of pretty girls, doubtless young actresses, were sitting in one corner with their heads together, their voices lowered and sibilant over the latest wrong. In an alcove two dark-coated men were squaring up some private account, little black books and bank notes on the glass-topped table before them, while on a high stool by the bar, his feet drawn up under him, there sat the inevitable hunched individual whose entire body down to the smallest facial muscle appeared to be in the grip of paralysis. He sat there, patient and motionless, as if he were being slowly petrified into red sandstone, and nobody took any notice of him at all.

The one personality the room contained was behind the bar, talking to the yellow-haired lady companion who appeared to be serving there. This was a tall dark woman of thirty-two or three who wore a severely tailored suit in grey cloth and whose hair was brushed into a smooth hard shape like a shell.

From a conventional point of view she was good-looking, with regular features and eyes which were a trifle more slate colour than blue under decided brows. But her main distinction lay in her nervous force and the suggestion of quiet capability and hardness which enveloped her.

It was evident that she was the Edna of the club's title, general manageress and at least part owner.

Richard himself was a good-looking youngster, not conceited but accustomed to making an impression in his own quiet way. He was aware of her quick appraising glance and was looking at her when her eyes left him and passed to his companion. A wave of feeling, so violent that he actually saw it, swept over her, leaving her cautious and expressionless. Her educated voice, schooled to be friendly, greeted them crisply.

"Hullo, Gerry, gin?"

"And ginger. Richard here insists on bitter but doesn't mind it bottled. Can you oblige him?"

"Of course." She smiled absently, served the drinks, and took the money, moving off to the other end of the bar, only to come gliding back immediately as if she had been drawn unwillingly by a thread. "It's a long time since you've been in." The tone was bright and yet the remark sounded like a reproach.

Gerry looked at her over his glass, his eyes meeting hers and holding them.

"So what?"

Her eyes widened very slightly but apart from that she gave no sign of having heard him.

"I hope you've got a good story or two," she remarked.
"No one else has. We had the whole of the *Up the Pole*
crowd in last night and in desperation they started telling
jokes out of the show, like bears doing their tricks when
there was no bun in it."

Gerry laughed. "Which one of them said that?"

She refilled his glass and, putting her elbows on the
bar, leaned forward with a gesture which managed to
convey that she was excluding everybody else in the room.

"You haven't had any food."

"We have. Better than anything we'll get here. Smoked
salmon at Ley's. Don't keep Richard out of this. Richard,
keep your attention rivetted on this woman. I may need
you."

The boy, who was sipping the warm inferior beer he
did not want, regarded them both with polite curiosity. He
was in the picture but not of it. He could follow the words,
as it were, but not the tune.

Edna gave him a casual preoccupied glance which was
yet not unfriendly.

"That's Tilly O'Dea over there," she remarked, nodding towards a chattering lovebird of a girl in the midst of
the group of actresses. "Would you care to meet her?"

"He'd hate to. He's civilised." Gerry was pretending
that the last two drinks had been more powerful than
anyone could reasonably have supposed. "Edna, why don't
you go away?"

Richard smiled at her faintly and stepped back with
the intention of wandering off to admire the décor when a
hand closed round his wrist and drew him back.

"Keep on the bridge, Mister Christian, we may be
sinking," said the man in the trench coat.

The woman began to speak. She was flushed and her
eyes were desperate.

"Gerry, I want to talk to you. Come into the rehearsal
room for a moment. I shan't keep you long."

He stepped back and looked at her and the familiar
depreciating smile reappeared. It seemed certain that he
was about to say something unforgivable, but he let the
moment pass.

"Oh well, it would be something to do, wouldn't it?"
he observed unexpectedly. "Richard must come too. He

can dance with you while I play the piano. Then you can talk to your heart's content. Or perhaps you'd rather sing it."

"You're not so terribly amusing," she said savagely, but she came round the bar at once and led them to the end of the further room where there was a door concealed in the crimson lincrusta papering. She unlocked it with a key from her pocket, pushed them through it, and secured the door again behind the three of them.

Afterwards it seemed to Richard that at that moment he stepped not only through a physical wall between one house and another but also through some less tangible barrier.

It was as if the man he was trying to discover ceased then to promise to turn out to be some ordinary character of whom he had already met other versions and began to emerge as an individual, and more sinister.

It was not an incident which marked the change so much as an atmosphere which met him as they came into a square, comparatively light room which duplicated the one they had just left, save that here the double doors had persisted and were now closed.

It was bare save for a row of bentwood chairs set against the further wall, and a black piano standing shabby amid a thicket of music stands. Here the window was not camouflaged as in the club but was stark and ugly and looked out on a bare wall of soot-stained yellow brick not ten feet away.

Gerry sat down at the piano at once, strapping his trenchcoat belt even more tightly about him, with the buckle very high on his chest. He began to play, revealing a sound if mediocre talent but a very distinctive touch. In the harsh light his skin showed very coarse and his hair more bleached, but his hands were strong-looking and sensitive enough, with long spatulate fingers which turned back at the tips.

He was improvising on a popular number, a favourite with the crooners, "How Are You Getting on with Your Forgetting?," and as he let the familiar notes trickle through his fingers he watched with wide-open lazy eyes the irritated woman standing above him.

"Oh, for God's sake, Gerry," she began at last, "you'll be sorry if you don't hear this. This is serious."

"Nothing is serious today," he said, shaking his head and sliding into a rumba rhythm. "I can't hear a word you say. Mime it. At least that'll make it funny." The notion seemed to amuse him for he laughed and the original tune re-emerged and grew and changed under his hands.

Edna swung away and Richard, who was dancing already, caught her and swept her down the room. She was taken by surprise but she responded and her expression changed to startled approbation. Richard was one of those rare people who dance from the heart. Their movement is not only graceful but joyous and their delight in it is irresistible. She followed his lead effortlessly but her mind was still on the man at the piano, who watched her, still with the same half-smile. The standard of the performance appeared to please him because he began to play for them, and Richard, who was young enough to be able to imagine that he was dancing with Annabelle, lost himself in the pure pleasure of the exercise.

Edna spoilt it. She was still quarrelling. Richard was sorry for her but naturally was not attracted by the complex emotions of a woman ten years older than himself. As far as he could see, she was ravaged with fury against Gerry for not making love to her, and rage against herself for wanting him to. All the rest of her behaviour, he judged rightly but with an academic appreciation only, was a product of this initial situation. She was certainly suffering. He could feel the waves of irritation passing through her as he held her.

"Dance," he said suddenly and smiled at her. "Dance it off."

The colour came into her face and her slate-grey eyes softened. She might have been quite all right, he thought, if not tormented.

She made the effort but it did not last.

"I'm expecting Warren Torrenden in." She threw the name at the piano suddenly. "Does that ring a bell?"

"Who?" It was the first time she had raised any response at all from Gerry. Now he did not show any great interest but he played a little more softly so that he could hear her.

"Warren Torrenden, the racing driver."

"Never heard of him."

"Oh, Gerry, don't be such a *silly* liar. You went to Silverstone with him on the fourteenth and you were calling yourself Hawker or something. I don't know what you let him in for but he's certainly looking for you. That's what I've got to tell you."

There was no break in the music but the quality went out of it and Richard, glancing at the man, was surprised to see that his idle half-laughing expression had not changed.

"Wild lunatic nonsense," he observed affably. "Cracking insanity. Simply not true."

"But, Gerry, you were there and you were with him. I saw you. I saw you myself in the paddock. Everybody in the club saw you both. It was on television. You were standing just behind the commentator in the crowd. You were on for whole minutes."

The tune came a little faster but his smile did not change.

"Warren Torrenden. Silverstone. The fourteenth. No. Absolutely entirely not. Not guilty. Two other men."

"But I tell you I saw you. I'm trying to help you, Gerry, don't you understand that?" She was still dancing and Richard was fascinated by the phenomenon. Gerry's music and her movement formed a link between them which, although unconscious, was affecting the degree of their quarrel considerably.

"You saw someone else," he said. "It's as easy as that."

"It's not. You're caught, Gerry. This time you can't slide out of it. You see, I was watching with Peter Fellows, whom you don't know, and when I said 'There's Gerry' he said 'There's Warren.' We thought nothing of it at the time but Peter must have mentioned it to Torrenden because a few days later he came roaring in looking for you. He said your name was Gerry Hawker and I said it wasn't."

Gerry took his hands off the keyboard and leant back on the stool.

"You said it wasn't? That was helpful."

"Why? It isn't, is it?"

"The name of the man Torrenden was with probably *was* Hawker."

"But that was you. I saw you."

"No. Absolutely and entirely not."

He began to play again but she did not dance, although Richard attempted to persuade her. She remained where she was, looking down at the pianist.

"He comes in every day about half past four hoping to run into you, anyway," she said grimly. "You can answer the question very easily once and for all by meeting him."

"Very well, I will." He seemed to have settled the matter and his strumming became lighthearted again.

The other two went on dancing. Edna was not satisfied but she was happier. Richard assumed at first that it was because she had got the message off her chest, but gradually the impression was borne in on him that she was principally relieved because Gerry had indicated that he would stay at least until half past four. They danced for nearly a quarter of an hour before she brought the subject up again. It was as they were passing the piano that she suddenly stopped and faced Gerry across it.

"Torrenden is wild with you," she said hurriedly. "He tells everybody that you told him you came from Reading and had a motor business there. I don't know what you did—he doesn't say—but he's after you. He's not the type to monkey with, Gerry. He keeps trying to find out where you live. I—I didn't tell him."

The man at the piano did not seem upset by the information or irritated by her implied repudiation of his original denial. He merely nodded, as if his mind was only just on the subject. His hands still moved over the keys.

"Do you know?" he enquired pleasantly.

"Where you live? You're still at Lydaw Court Hotel, aren't you?"

"God, no! I left that dreary heap nearly four months ago."

"But I've seen you in the club here since then. You never told me you'd moved. I've been writing and telephoning you there. That's why I haven't heard, I suppose?"

"Shall we call it a contributory cause?" He laughed. "I can just see all those letters, the handwriting growing angrier and angrier, all in the residents' rack in the lounge. It must have given the old women something to chatter about. I wonder if they steamed them open."

"If they did they got an earful." She was trembling. "Where do you live now? Did you get that flat you were thinking about? Who is there with you?" She turned to Richard. "Has he got a flat?"

"I don't know, I'm afraid. We've only just met." Richard drew away. "Time I drifted off."

"Oh, don't break up the party." The protest from Gerry was astonishingly forceful. "Let's wait and meet this chap Torrenden. He's making an ass of himself, but it's a rumour one ought to scotch, I suppose. After all, one has some credit to think of."

He began to play the rumba again, very softly, talking all the time.

"It's so excruciatingly silly. I haven't even been to Silverstone this season." He threw out the disclaimer and hurried on before it could be queried. "Last week I went to an extraordinary meeting in Lichtenstein, of all places. Most dramatic. A chap barricaded himself in behind a great wall of oil drums and then suddenly emerged in a little yellow mystery wagon and cleared the board. Perfectly ridiculous. The maddest thing I've ever seen."

A slow red flush spread over Edna's face and her eyes grew several shades darker.

"Now that is typical of you," she said bitterly. "For no reason at all you suddenly come out with a statement that a child wouldn't believe. You haven't been to Lichtenstein, there was no racing there, there was no wall of oil drums and no wonder car. Who the hell is impressed? Me, who's known you far too well far too long? Or this kid who's never seen you before this afternoon?"

It was a savage outburst and Gerry's good humour appeared to increase before it, just as, when she was attempting to placate him, his ill humour had grown.

"No oil drums?" he protested lightly. "My good girl, there was a wall of them, fifteen feet high. Let me describe them. They were black, with studs all the way round top and bottom, as well as a line round the middle, and they made an absolutely impenetrable barrier with this mystery packet behind it."

He was playing joyously now so that Richard's feet began to move without his being aware.

"Edna," Gerry went on suddenly, "do you remember our cottage at Bray?"

"Why bring that up?"

"Because I like to see your face change." He was laughing, holding her glance with his own. Her sulky colour deepened and she looked cowed and as if she was going to cry, which was embarrassing because she was not at all that kind of woman.

"It wasn't *our* cottage," she protested with a return of spirit as soon as she achieved command of herself. It was clear that while she regarded Richard as too young to be anything but negligible, she resented this past incident of her sex life being trotted out before him. "If you remember, you rented that cottage furnished for a month for an elderly couple who you said were clients of yours. They'd come down from Yorkshire, had sold up their home, and were on their way to South Africa. They went off earlier than they expected and so you persuaded me down there for the odd fortnight. The poor old idiots hadn't packed properly either, so we kept coming across things they'd forgotten. The woman had even left a handbag. I bet you never sent all that stuff on to them."

Her voice died before Gerry's stare and Richard also was struck by something very odd in his face. Just for a moment it became utterly blank, not merely without expression but deserted, as if there was no one behind it.

The familiar rueful smile returned almost at once.

"Gosh, I don't remember anything about the place except that it smelled of jasmin and the river ran through the garden," he said presently. "I remember we swam at night and there were glowworms on the other bank. You were quite different down there, Edna. Not so hard..."

"Here, don't!" she exclaimed in sudden pain, flinging Richard's opinion of her to the winds. "Don't, Gerry! What the hell's the matter with you? Coming here and talking like this after staying away silent until I'm absolutely crawling up the wall. Why remember the cottage suddenly?"

He sat laughing at her gently, his charm a living thing and the intelligence, which was sorry like an ape's, showing in his flat eyes.

"Seeing you reminded me. It was terribly, terribly sweet, somehow," he said, "wasn't it?"

She made no reply but stood staring at him in a sort of helpless exasperation, her only real anger against herself.

"Well, let's see, half past four we expect Torrenden,"

Gerry went on absently. "I'd better meet the chap, since my name's been mentioned. That sort of mistake can be awkward if it isn't seen to. Then Richard and I have an appointment for five-thirty, but after that, about six, I don't see why we shouldn't come back to the Midget. Are you going to be here all the evening, or could you get away for an hour or two if we went on somewhere?"

There was colour in her face. She looked ten years younger.

"I don't trust him across the street," she said to Richard. "I've heard it so often." Her glance at Gerry was almost shy. "Joannie is behind the bar, of course. She could manage if I looked in again before midnight. I'll speak to her. You really have got to keep this appointment at half past five, have you? I'd believe you more easily if I wasn't going to let you out of my sight."

"Darling, don't be silly." He took his hands off the piano and took hers in both of his. "We're hardly going across the road. We'll be back in no time at all."

"Just long enough for one drink, I suppose?"

"No drink. Ten minutes' conversation, and then an evening on the tiles, you and me together, and we'll find a wench for Richard. It's a bet."

He lifted his face to her and grudgingly, yet very grateful, she bent and kissed him on the mouth. It was done very lightly, very naturally, but the tension went out of her like the strain out of a taut wire. Her spirits began to mount and a new and gay personality whom Richard had not suspected suddenly emerged. She was amusing, slightly ribald, and a little malicious, but very good fun, a worldly, joyful animal, ecstatically happy.

The dancing went on for half an hour or more and the fashionable semi-wisecracking was interspersed with gossip of mutual friends. Eventually Gerry glanced at his watch.

"It's a quarter to five," he said. "If Torrenden is coming he ought to be in the next room. Run along and see, darling, and if he is, bring him in here. It'll be less embarrassing for him. Come on, give us the key. Through you go."

He got up, slid an arm round her, released the key from her fingers, and led her over to the inner door, which he unlocked for her. With his hand on the latch he paused, kissed her once more, slapped her behind gently, and pushed her through the door which he closed after her and locked again. Then, moving quietly, he walked across the room to the double doors, opened them and glanced back at Richard.

"Sorry to let you in for this," he said charmingly, "but it'll save a dreary scene if we go out this way. She's a dear gal but boringly possessive."

8

Police Theory

The famous teaching hospital of St. Joan's in the West stands almost next door to the new police station in the Barrow Road. Charlie Luke and Mr. Albert Campion went down there together in a police car immediately after the call came through on the Superintendent's newly installed private line from the Garden Green area.

They were met in the vestibule by the man who had telephoned. This was Detective Sergeant Picot, who was an old friend and colleague of Luke's. He came forward as they entered, a square heavy man who, at the moment at any rate, seemed beset with the deepest misgivings. He forced a smile as they appeared and his handshakes were hearty, but he was not at all happy and as soon as he had edged them into a reasonably secluded corner he came out with an apology.

"I don't know quite how you're going to take this, sir," he said, "but I simply obeyed orders. You said quite definitely that you wanted to hear *anything* bearing on the Goff's Place enquiry, however trivial."

Luke grinned. "And someone's had a dream?" he suggested cheerfully.

"You're not too far out, that's a fact." Picot's plump face coloured. "It's a flimsy idea and it's negative, so I thought you'd better hear it from the man who brought it in. That's why I've troubled you to come out here to see him."

"The poor old boy stopped a barrel, you told me?" Luke glanced round the vast interior which looked so like a civic hall and shrugged. "Lousy luck. I hate these places. It was the usual story, I take it?"

"It was, sir. A brewer's dray was unloading outside the Bull and Mouth and a firkin of mild jumped the chute to the cellar and fell on the pavement. It rolled straight into the constable. He hadn't an earthly."

"What was the damage?"

"Left 'Tib. Fib.' fractured in two places. It might have been worse. But he's no chicken. An elderly feller called Bullard. Been here years."

"What, Harry?" Luke was genuinely grieved. "I remember him well. What sort of bee has he caught in his bonnet? He won't have imagined much, that's one thing."

"Quite." Picot's tone was flat. "I heard he was asking for me so I dropped in to see him this afternoon, and as soon as he'd told me what was on his mind I went in to the office and telephoned you. I've had him moved to a private ward so he can speak freely. He's not long out of the anaesthetic, but he's lucid. Will you come up?"

Ten minutes later a pale wraith of Constable Bullard's fatherly self was looking up at Luke from his high bed with the cradle in it. The Superintendent's sympathy was genuine and the whole force of his personality seemed to have been translated into charm. He had listened to a full account of the accident once again and had registered surprise, regret, indignation, and congratulation at appropriate moments and was now preparing to extract the information for which he had come.

As Mr. Campion watched Luke he reflected that it was easy to understand Yeo's anxiety. Both Picot and Bullard were loth to tell him any unwelcome news.

"Well, now, Harry." The Superintendent stood at the foot of the bed. "Just before the accident you came up the road from Garden Green where you had been talking to a couple of young people. They had asked you the way to a house where, you remembered, there is a little museum. Is that right?"

"Yessir." Bullard was bereft of his teeth and inclined to mumble, but his eyes showed bright against the linen. "I was walking along thinking about this 'ere museum and the oddities the youngsters were going to see there, and an idea came to me. I hope it won't upset you."

"We'll risk it."

"Well, sir, you'll recall that last spring a witness came forward to depose that the two old people whom he saw inside the bus in Goff's Place had also been seen by him in the window of a teashop in this area?"

"Yes." Luke was frowning. His hands were thrust deep in his trouser pockets and the skirts of his black overcoat fanned out behind him like the tail of a crow.

"It was that fact which made you—that is to say all of us—feel sure that this was probably the district in which to look either for the old folk or else for the murderer. Er—nothing else connects this area with the crime at all."

"Yes, that's so." Luke's frown was growing blacker.

"Well, I was one of the fellers specially briefed to keep my eyes open for the old couple, sir. I learned the descriptions by heart, like I always do, so I knew what they were like in words but not in pictures, if you see what I mean."

Luke nodded. "I follow that. Go on."

"Well . . ." Bullard indicated that he was coming to the difficult bit. ". . . This morning when I was recollecting one particular item in the museum I realised that when I recall a real thing I see it in pictures. See it all over again in my mind's eye, so to speak. So I started putting my memory of this exhibit, which was two waxworks in a glass case, into words for a sort of an exercise. They was the *same*, Mr. Luke. They was identical. You couldn't argue. What that witness saw in this area was not two people in a teashop but two wax figures in a glass case. I'll take my dying oath on it."

"Waxworks figures." Whatever Charlie Luke had expected it was not this. He put back his head and laughed aloud. "Have you seen these things?" he enquired of Picot.

"Not yet, sir. The collection is shut in the afternoons and I thought I wouldn't disturb the old lady who runs the show until I heard if you wanted to go down there yourself."

Luke glanced at Campion, who was on the far side of the room.

"How does it strike you, Guv'nor?" he enquired.

Mr. Campion hesitated. "Of course, witnesses sometimes do try too hard," he said. "There was only one man who could describe the two in detail, the waiter, and he produced rather a lot of detail, don't you think? After all, he only saw them once through the windows of a bus on a wet night and once through what he thought was the window of a shop as he passed by. The only thing definite is that he saw them through glass on each occasion. I'm afraid he's been over-anxious to help."

The Superintendent drew a long breath. His shoulders were hunched.

"That means there's nothing to connect them with the area at all," he said.

"The images are wonderfully lifelike, sir," Bullard murmured from the bed.

"I daresay they are, old boy," Luke spoke sadly. "All the same, I reckon the witness has invented the likeness. He saw the two old people in a bus and they reminded him of the two waxworks in a case. That's all there is to it. That's torn it."

It was a great blow to him. Every man in the room was aware of it.

"I'll have the waiter taken down there in the morning to confirm it," he said. "He'll realise his mistake as soon as he gets back to the place. Who owns it, did you say? Some old highbrow woman?"

"No, sir, just a widder." Bullard smiled. "The exhibits belonged to her husband and she keeps the show going in his memory. You'd like her. She's pleasant, normal if you know what I mean."

"I suppose I do, just," said Luke and his white teeth appeared briefly. "So long, Harry, get well."

All three visitors had reached the wind-swept forecourt which faces on to the Barrow Road before the Superintendent paused in his stride.

"That's the area which interests me," he remarked to Campion, nodding towards the mouth of the passage on the opposite side of the way. "If we went down there and turned right we'd be in Garden Green. This bit of news is a setback. It interferes with all my calculations. And yet you know I still feel this is the stamping ground of the man I'm after."

Picot said nothing but looked at Mr. Campion.

"He's somewhere there," Luke went on. "I know it, I feel it. I've half a mind to go down and see that museum while I'm here." He put a hand in his pocket and drew out a coin.

"Heads I do, tails I don't," he said and spun it in the air.

Meanwhile at Number Seven, Garden Green, Polly Tassie was giving her mind to Annabelle. They were in the small sitting room at the back of the house which was her own special apartment. It was set half a storey higher than the two rooms which flanked the front door and was more pleasant than either, with a lower ceiling, flower-spattered walls, and a single long window which looked over the garden and was set so low that a small wrought-iron balcony had been constructed outside it for safety's sake.

There was nothing very fashionable about the decoration, although it was apparent that it had been the subject of a great deal of thought. The effect was cluttered but comfortable and there was a note of gaiety in it which Annabelle found enchanting and slightly funny.

The loose cover of the couch on which she sat was scarlet and white calico, like the handkerchiefs of workmen long ago. The rug before the modern gas fire was a rag one, beautifully made but unexpected, and along the chimney piece there was a row of exquisite china ladies with tables by their sides and dogs in their laps, and a small china clock in the centre.

Polly, who had changed into a plain black dress for her luncheon with Matt Phillipson, had cheered it up now with a black silk apron trimmed with coloured flowers and white muslin embroidery which someone had brought her from Switzerland. She had also put on a red jersey coat against the cool of the evening, and the effect was slightly fancy-dress, a fact of which she appeared sublimely unconscious. She sat upright in her high-backed chair at the side of the hearth. She was pouring tea from a silver pot and looked as if she had been doing it for ever.

"We'll go to the pictures," she said, "and as my old Mrs. Morris doesn't come today, we'll have some food out. You can't go dancing because I've not got anyone to take you yet, and you haven't got a dress either, but we'll see to that in the morning. The first thing to do is to write to your sister and see how long you can stay."

Annabelle, who looked like a spoilt kitten curled luxuriously on the red couch, grinned disarmingly.

"I can stay until you get tired of me," she said frankly. "Forgive me, but you don't think the less fuss you make the longer it will last?"

Polly laughed. "Do you like homes?" she enquired unexpectedly.

"'Do it yourself,' and 'how to make a spare bed for yourself out of old wine boxes'?" Annabelle sounded dubious.

Polly was amused but her enquiry had been genuine. "No. I wondered, are you terribly interested in where you live? I'm too much that way. Whenever I go into any sort of building, church, cinema, anywhere, after a bit I always find I'm worrying how I could fix it up if something happened and Freddy and I had to live there."

"Where the furniture would go?" Annabelle was delighted by the fantasy.

"Where the sink would *have* to go," said Polly solemnly. "How the drains run, and so on. I remember having to meet your uncle on Euston Station once. They had open fires in those days, but even so the main waiting room was very bleak. It was enormous and such an uncosy shape. By the time he arrived I was in quite a state and like a mug I told him about it. He laughed all the way home. He said I was a monstrous fool, but he saw why I made him comfortable."

Annabelle rocked on the couch in joyful superiority.

"No, I'm not like that," she said. "I like this room, darling, and I have got a nesting instinct, but I should never feel I must make something of Euston. I love these cups, by the way. They're old, aren't they?"

"Early Victorian. My great-grandad bought seven services all alike." Polly was very happy. "He had seven ugly daughters, which was a calamity at that time of day."

"A bit of a facer at any time," murmured her visitor.

"Ah no, but this was awful." Polly spoke with feeling. "It wasn't considered the thing to send them out to work, so he had either got to get them all married or sit and listen to them lamenting. If he'd only had the one, he could have given her a nice fat dowry, but since there were seven he did the right thing and divided the fortune equally. He let it be known locally that each girl would have a tea set too, and then he sat back and took what came. My grandmother got the proprietor of the inn, who was a fine-looking man, and this is the tea set."

"Did your mother worry where the furniture was to go?"

"I shouldn't be surprised." Polly was content. Her blue eyes were lazy and the room was warm with security. "Mother was a great housekeeper. When I was a girl we still made beds from our own goose down. You'll sleep on one tonight. There's nothing like it. Beds haven't improved in my time. Draughts have."

"Draughts?"

"Currents of air, usually freezing." Polly was laughing deep in her throat. "I've stopped them here all right and overdone things as usual. There's a patent outfit on that window and another on the door, and now I have to leave one or the other open or the gas fire goes out. What are you laughing at, you wretched child? You think I'm an old fool, don't you?"

"I don't." Annabelle was pink with amusement. "I think you're wonderful. I only wish you'd come and stop the draughts in our house. . . . Oh, am I what you had in mind, Aunt Polly?"

The spontaneous question, premature, naïve and overeager, touched the old woman to the heart.

"Better," she said swiftly. "Much better. I think you've got the character, I think you've got the brains, and I think you've got your feet on the ground." Then she added for prudence's sake, "You'll never be more clever than you are now, you know that, I hope? That's the mistake most young people make. They think they're *clever for their age,* my God!"

Annabelle looked scared. "The mind ceases to develop before one is twenty, is that what you mean?" she said.

"Twenty?" Polly was greatly entertained. "You'll be lucky if you get to twenty undisturbed. My father didn't hold with educating girls, so I'm not very up in these things, but I always understood that the idea of education was to get one's mind as sharp as it will come before the party starts. Once the heart gets going you need all the wits you've got, my goodness."

She was not looking at her visitor but she was aware of her stiffening. The deer was emerging, she thought, timid and curious at the forest's edge. She ventured to be more explicit.

"I was never out of love myself after I was twelve," she announced cheerfully. "At fifteen I nearly died of it. He came to the local theatre for a week and he looked so neglected, with his green tights runkled round his ankles, that I cried whenever I thought of it. On the Friday he came into our bar and I saw that he had a great blue nose and was sixty if he was a day. Even that didn't quite put me off."

She was still looking at the fireplace and not wholly laughing.

"I thought that if he would only notice me I could cure him, you know," she added devastatingly.

Her audience exploded. "There were girls like that at school," she said. "What happens to them? Do they ever get over it?"

"I don't know." Polly looked so lugubrious that they both laughed and Annabelle gave in.

"I've been in love myself," she said primly, "but not as bad as that."

"Ah." Polly pounced on the admission. "Who? The parson, perhaps?"

"Good heavens, no. He's got grandchildren and makes sheep's noises in church."

"Not mistresses at school?"

"No. They don't count." It became evident that Annabelle was thinking round for a suitable candidate. "There's Richard, of course."

Not nearly good enough! Mrs. Tassie succeeded in

checking the words in time. She made a sincere effort to be reasonable.

"And who is Richard?"

Her visitor was ready to chatter. After a careful biographical sketch, a minute physical description, and a somewhat arbitrary delineation of character, she came to the heart of the matter.

"When he was in love with Jenny I was breathlessly keen on him," she admitted, looking so like a Greuze that Polly was startled. "But I was young then, and nobody suspected. I did feel it terribly, though. I thought he was the only person in the world and that I'd lost him. Then he went into the army and I forgot him and I didn't see him again until this morning."

"Really?"

"I asked him to meet me, you see, because I'd never been alone in London before. Naturally I was rather interested, but when he arrived he was only an ordinary boy. Quite a nice one. I'll have to look him up, by the way. Will that be all right?"

"We'll invite him on Sunday." Polly tried not to sound as if she was preparing for an enemy. "What do you like about him? Do you know?"

Annabelle considered earnestly, seeking for the exact truth no doubt.

"The back of his neck, I think," she admitted at last.

"Oh dear," said Mrs. Tassie. She paused and added, "Twenty-two, you say? And in tea?"

"You said that as if it meant three feet high and half-witted. He's not terribly tall, as a matter of fact, but he moves awfully well."

"Well, we'll see." Polly was irritated with herself for feeling irritated. "You've never thought you'd like to marry someone older and more exciting... more difficult?"

To her horror the innocent eyes turned towards her with the awful seriousness of an intelligent baby.

"Oh." The tone told her nothing. "Someone like that fair man who stopped the siren for me this morning?"

There was a brief and startled silence during which the older woman's cheeks grew slowly red. She opened her mouth to speak but was saved, literally, by the bell. A distinctive buzz from the front door surprised them both.

"Who on earth is that?"

Annabelle rose at once. "I'll go and see." Her pink mouth widened uncontrollably and her eyes narrowed with mischief. "Suitors perhaps, Aunt Polly."

9
The Visitors

Polly stood in the studio in the garden, a bright neat figure surrounded by all her formidable junk. She was smiling at Charlie Luke engagingly.

"What do you *want*?" she demanded unexpectedly. "I've shown you all Freddy's old rubbish and I've told you there's nothing else like it in the house, and yet here you are growing more and more depressed while I watch you. What's the matter?"

Luke's dark face with its strong nose and narrow dancing eyes split into a smile.

"I'm ungrateful," he agreed. "That's right. It's a staggering show. Your husband must have been . . ." He hesitated.

"Very fond of it," she said firmly. "You don't want to shut it, do you? It's not doing any harm."

"None in the world." He looked round once more, a spark of laughter in his eyes. "It's old-fashioned, out of the ordinary, and highly educational. No, I don't want to shut it."

She sighed with relief and her glance travelled down the room to where Mr. Campion and Annabelle were enjoying the usual first conversation among people of their kind, an exploratory expedition, part genealogical, part geographical, concerning mutual friends in the country. Polly was glad the child was there to take the pale affable stranger out of her way. Luke belonged to a type that was more to her taste.

"Well, then, what is it?" As she spoke she touched his

sleeve and was aware of the steel muscle beneath it. He was treating her, too, with the direct knowing intelligence which she had always liked in a man.

"I was looking for some waxworks," he said, turning to her.

"Looking for them?" He did not quite understand the nuance in her tone, but her face was placid enough. "What a pity," she added sincerely. "I had two, but they've gone. They were in that case there."

"How long ago?"

"Oh, they were here last winter. They were thrown out at spring cleaning. Why?"

Luke did not reply immediately. He had known in his bones that Picot and Bullard were going to be right, the moment he had put his nose in the hall. His secret hope had been that the waxworks were going to turn out to be nothing at all like the waiter's description, so that the teashop theory could be raised again, but as soon as he saw the empty seat in the glass case his heart misgave him. He knew that three of the flags on his map would have to come down.

He took a packet of frayed papers out of his pocket and consulted the original description which he already knew by heart.

"Can you remember these things, Mrs. Tassie?"

"Of course I can. We had them for years. An old man and an old woman in Victorian costume."

"Fancy dress?" His eagerness puzzled her yet set her mind at rest. At any rate he did not seem to be worrying about what happened to them. She did not want to have to tell a lie.

"I couldn't call it fancy dress, exactly. The clothes were old-fashioned, but you could have gone out in the street in them. The old lady had a red dress and a shepherd's plaid stole and a round bonnet in black silk which had gone a bit brown, but it had lovely beads on it, just like the newest idea."

"What colour were they?"

"Oh, black." She spoke with complete authority and the Superintendent did not look up.

"What about the man?"

"Well, he was the real trouble." She appeared

embarrassed. "He was dropping to bits. His head was respectable because long ago, when his long beard got awful, Freddy had him out and cut it into a tidy round, and he had his hard hat cleaned and reblocked at the same time. But last year I noticed that the suit really had gone. It was black turned green and the moth had got it. I half wondered if I ought to put him in a pair of Freddy's trousers but I couldn't bring myself to. It seemed so shocking. Do you see what I mean?"

"I do." Luke put away his packet of notes and sighed. He was bitterly disappointed. The description tallied. The witness had made a silly but commonplace mistake. "I do. Once the moth appears, far better to chuck the lot out. Well, ma'am, thank you for your information."

Polly wavered. Her eyes were anxious and she moistened her lips with the tip of her tongue.

"Ought you to have seen them? Was it important? Does it matter that they've gone?"

Luke smiled at her. The police have a technique with the useful but not unnaturally inquisitive householder.

"No," he said cheerfully. "It was a question of satisfying my own mind. People who give evidence sometimes make mistakes. A chap who sees some people we're interested in—through the window of a bus, for instance—can be reminded subconsciously of somebody else, say an actress on the screen. So when he comes to make his deposition to us he gives us all sorts of details, clothes, expression, everything. But the person he's describing may be the woman on the screen, not the one whom he only saw for a moment in the bus. It's a thing we have to look out for all the time."

"I see," she said gravely. "And you thought something like that had happened with my waxworks? Were you right?"

"I'm afraid we were," he admitted, grimacing at her. "Our witness must have come in here one day when they were here. He made the mistake quite innocently. They always do."

Polly shook her head. "It means all your work is wasted, I suppose?" She sounded as worried all of a sudden as he felt, he reflected wryly.

"It happens."

"Oh, I know." She was deeply sympathetic. "When we had our hotel Freddy and I had a very good friend, County Superintendent Gooch. He'd be quite twenty years older than you and it was up North so I don't suppose you've heard of him, but he told me that police work was like growing seed. For every quarter ounce you got you had to sift a bushel of chaff."

"Ah, he was a member all right!" Luke's heart went out to the northern practitioner and the old woman smiled at his warmth.

"Dick Gooch was a kind man," she remarked. "He taught me one or two very useful little hints, I remember."

Luke's quick eyes met her own inquisitively. He liked her; she was his sort, he reflected.

"Such as what?" he murmured. "The tidy dose of chloral in a rowdy's half pint?"

Polly's brows rose into croquet hoops.

"Shush. That's not a thing to mention even in fun." She spoilt the effect immediately by adding in a lower tone, "It's a very useful thing to know, though, if a woman does happen to be left alone in charge of licensed premises at any time. They sleep very peacefully and nobody is any the wiser."

Luke controlled a shout of laughter. She was restoring his temper.

"Did you ever have to use it, ma'am?"

"Certainly not, Superintendent," said she and they both laughed, and, turning away from the empty showcase, made a move to join the other two.

Annabelle was talking, her country colour glowing, her face animated. Charlie Luke leaned towards his new friend.

"You've got a knockout there, ma'am, if I may say so. Your own niece, or your husband's?"

He expected her to be delighted and she was.

"Oh, Freddy's," she whispered back. "Such a nice child, too. Not in the least conceited. I've only known her for a day, but I love her already."

"A day?" He paused to stare at her. She was not looking at him but continued placidly.

"I invited the elder sister but she couldn't be spared, so they sent this one. Only this morning. But she's very like Freddy. The same temperament and the same common sense. He and I got on like a house on fire from the moment we met. Some people make friends like that. They do or they don't in the first ten minutes."

Luke grinned. He found her soothing. She restored his self-confidence.

"And you're one of the ones," he suggested.

She beamed at him. "And so are you," she declared, startling him, "and it's a very funny thing to find in a policeman. It must be very awkward at times. Still, you're tough and I suppose you can take it. Now is it too early for a drink, or can I offer you some tea?"

They had just reached the others and Luke shook his head. Annabelle was full of news.

"Mr. Campion's wife is Amanda Fitton, Aunt Polly," she announced. "We know her sister at home. She lives in almost the next village. And you," she added joyfully, turning to Luke, "you must be the man who married Prunella last year. Will you give her my regards, please? She'll remember me, Annabelle Tassie."

"Only last year?" Polly pounced on the information and regarded the Superintendent with a new and to him terrifying enlightenment. She closed her lips at once but as she let her visitors out of the garden door she shook his hand and wished him good luck very earnestly, so that he had no doubt at all to what she referred. She made him laugh even while she embarrassed him, a human old party if ever he saw one.

Mr. Campion did not follow Luke immediately but lingered for a moment or two chatting to Annabelle. He was dithering slightly in the way which those who had cause to know him best might have found a little sinister. His pale face was as vacuous as in his youth and his pale eyes were lazy behind their spectacles.

"It's such a jolly neighbourhood, don't you think?" he was saying earnestly as he waved an idle hand which took in the hideous studio behind them and the so-far unrestored tenement house opposite.

"Jolly?" Annabelle, who was literal-minded, sounded dubious, and Polly, her smile still happy from her encounter with Luke, sailed in to the rescue.

"It's been good in its time," she agreed, "and people

are rediscovering it and painting it up, which is always exciting."

"Of course it is. And so convenient. So near the shops."

It was Polly's turn to be astonished. To her mind, the hardwear shops at the Barrow Road corner of Edge Street were hardly the kind to attract him.

"Well, I find them useful," she said, "naturally. But they're not very posh. One would hardly buy clothes here, or . . ."

"Oh, I say, wouldn't you? Not some things? I mean to say . . ." The stranger appeared to be wrestling with the conversational subject as if it was a wet sheet which had fallen on him. "I understand there's a magnificent store somewhere down here called Cuppages, famous for its sales and for men's gloves. Is that true? Have you ever bought men's gloves in a sale at Cuppages, Mrs. Tassie? As a present, I mean, not—not to wear of course. S-silly of me."

The involved stuttering speech was sufficiently long to permit the words to register and Polly stood stiffly, her head slightly on one side and her indulgent smile fading. From behind his spectacles Mr. Campion observed her with interest and saw first astonishment and then incredulity, followed by a flicker of instantly suppressed alarm, appear and vanish on her kindly face. When she bade him goodbye she was on guard.

Luke had waited a yard or two down the street for him and now they walked towards the corner together to pick up the police car which had been parked discreetly just around it. Luke seemed disposed to apologise, if strictly in his own way.

"I'm Charlie Muggins in person," he remarked. "I know it and I don't want to hear any more about it. Wherever the Goff's Place beauty is, he's not in that chamber of horrors. That's one item we can enter in the book and sign for."

"You think so?"

"Don't you?" Something in the light voice had made Luke turn to stare, his arched brows rising high. "That old girl was on the up and up, and the dummies she described were clearly wearing the clothes which our witness had in mind."

"Oh yes, I agree." Mr. Campion conveyed that those were not quite the lines on which he was thinking. "A pleasant woman," he continued cautiously, "but with one peculiarity which might be significant in the circumstances, or so I thought, didn't you?"

"No," said Charlie Luke, who was irritated with himself. "Since you ask me, chum, no. I'm satisfied that I've been led up Garden Green as far as Goff's Place is concerned. I admit it and when I get back I may possibly go in and tell old Yeo so, just to see his happy smile. You can take it from me that there isn't anything that isn't dead ordinary about that woman. The world is packed with old ducks just like her. There's millions of 'em, all born on a Friday, loving and giving. What's peculiar about Aunt Polly, for God's sake?"

Mr. Campion hesitated. "I was thinking of her museum," he said. "To keep up a nuisance of a place like that, which she doesn't think is funny, as a memorial to a man who was delighted with it, argues that she loved him in a particular way. She identified herself with him."

"Okay." Luke was splendidly unimpressed. "There's no need to get a trick-cyclist approach to that one. That's how uncomplicated people do love. They gang up. I'm you, you're me, that's the big idea, so what?"

"*So where is the rest of the family?*" said Mr. Campion simply.

It was a convincing point. Luke pushed his hat on to the back of his head and walked along considering.

"She's bound to have someone to be fond of, I grant you that," he said at last, "or she wouldn't be standing up. The girl has only been there a day so it can't be her. The old lady must have friends, obviously. You think she's mothering something, do you?"

"I don't know at all." The thin man shrugged his shoulders. "No one's living in the house. She may have many interests. I got the impression that there were several people in and out, didn't you?"

Luke frowned. "A coke hod in the kitchen was standing on an old copy of *Sports Motor* and there was an old cigar butt among the London Pride edging the little path to the front door. There was an overall too big for her hanging in the scullery, and someone had left a bunch of water cress on the kitchen window ledge," he recited casually. "Yes, of course there are people about her or she wouldn't be as she is, but no, Campion, our chap can't be amongst them. The witness who saw the old folk in the bus happened to confuse them with the waxworks in her museum. That is sufficient. If the murderer was known to her as well, the coincidence would be amazing."

Mr. Campion drew a long breath. "There is one possible explanation of that point," he was beginning when they turned the corner and Luke's wireless operator sprang out of the car and came towards them, a written message in his outstretched hand. The Superintendent glanced at it and turned to his friend with sudden energy.

"This is more like it," he exclaimed joyfully. "This is what we've been waiting for. They're fairly certain they've got the bus. It's been hidden for eight months behind a bargeload of empty oil drums. Hop in, old boy. We'll drop in to the office for the full gen and then we'll slip down and inspect it. It's in a square mile of scrap called Rolf's Dump. Ever heard of it?"

10

The Object of the Exercise

"So tea is served to residents only? My dear man, we *are* residents. Our baggage is coming up from the airport. That is why we are sitting here waiting. Run along, do. We're tired. We've come a very very long way. We want crumpets, and for God's sake see the butter is fresh. Cake, Richard? No? Very well then, tea and crumpets."

The man in the trench coat stretched himself in the

deep brocade-covered chair and waved an impatient hand at the ancient waiter, who plodded away mumbling.

"This old place has got the kiss of death written all over it, but it's useful," he continued, looking round the dim lounge of the Tenniel Hotel and keeping his voice down as people do in a huge public room in which they find themselves virtually alone. "The lease is just running out and it's going to be pulled down to make way for Government offices. But meanwhile it's quiet and reasonably civilised."

Richard, who was sitting on a couch beside him, followed his gaze with open disapproval. To his mind the place was a tomb and, worse, an anachronism. He fancied he could smell the dust in the pile carpet patterned with fleurs-de-lys, and one corner of the high ceiling, the cornice of which was as elaborate as a wedding cake, was badly discoloured where some mishap to the plumbing had done its worst.

Gerry's elaborate lie to get the unwanted tea had annoyed him and he was also puzzled. His guide had insisted that they should sit just here in the centre of the longest wall, although there was apparently no other visitor in the place. Richard could see no purpose in the decision unless it was part of the manoeuvre, in which case, as seemed more and more probable at every moment, he felt he was liable to find himself involved in something very dubious very soon. The only real advantage in the position appeared to be that they had a direct view across some forty feet of lounge, through an archway, down a white-painted corridor, and into the side vestibule of the hotel through which they had entered. From where he sat Richard could make out the row of telephone booths there, at this distance no larger than so many dolls' houses.

"Are we waiting for somebody?" he enquired suddenly.

The flat expressionless eyes of the man beside him opened very wide.

"Good heavens, no. Why?"

"I wondered. I thought you told Edna you had a date at half past."

Gerry ducked his chin. "That? Oh, I had to be

definite or we'd never have got away. You fell for her, did you? She's got something, God knows quite what, but a certain something."

Richard coloured and his jaw became more aggressive even than usual, but he stuck to his shy, slightly offhand manner.

"She seemed to know you pretty well."

"But not well enough, dear boy." Gerry produced the archaic form of address with a flourish. "I saw quite a bit of her at one time and she played hard enough for me, but it never took, as they say of inoculation. I was damned careful it shouldn't. That's the secret of my success."

"What is?"

"I never let anything tear the skin. I've never been faintly fond of anything or of anybody in my life." He spoke lightly but with satisfaction. "I'm deadly serious about this. I spotted the plain mechanical truth of it as a child. You could almost call it the Chad-Horder discovery. Any kind of affection is a solvent. It melts and adulterates the subject and by indulging it he loses his identity and hence his efficiency. By keeping myself to myself in the face of every conceivable attack I have remained successful, bright and indestructible. It's a simple recipe for a hundred per cent success. I hand it to you gratis, Richard. Consider it a token of my esteem. Ah, here are the crumpets."

They arrived cold and slightly burnt and soggy, in an Edwardian white-metal contraption which should have contained hot water and did not. Gerry did not appear to notice any fault worth commenting upon. He poured tea from a plated pot, sent the mutinous waiter, a black-browed toad in the seventies, labouring back for lemon, and appeared to enjoy himself hugely.

He was revealing a personality with a faint but positive streak of conventionality, which was unexpected, but now more than ever, Richard was aware of the strong element of deliberation in him which he had first noticed in the barber's shop. He was going about some business, conducting some carefully considered undertaking which, Richard felt uncomfortably, was going according to plan. How he himself was supposed to figure in the performance Richard had no idea, and it occurred to him that it might be as well to find out, but before he could make any move in that direction he was forestalled by Gerry, who might have been thought-reading.

"I tell you what I have in mind for this evening and I don't want any refusal," he began suddenly, with an engaging air of frankness. "I've been hanging on to you like a leech all this afternoon and you're not going to escape me now. This is the position. I live in a rather decent little residential hotel, Lydaw Court, Kensington, and they've got a party on tonight. There is, as usual, a preponderance of women and I've promised I'll bring a young man to partner some of the girls. Don't worry, my dear chap, we shan't be expected to change, but I can offer you a decent meal and very nice company, and you'd be doing a most charitable act. How about it?"

Richard blinked. The offer possessed a curious quality of conviction. Suddenly he was quite certain that the man did live in just such a place as he described and that he himself had been picked out as a likely candidate for the invitation, even as far back as their encounter in the barber's shop.

Meanwhile Gerry had produced a visiting card.

"We may as well be formal," he remarked depreciatingly. "Never mind if you haven't one on you. Where do you live, by the way?"

Richard gave the number of his Chelsea lodgings and watched the other man write it down in a small notebook neat as a stage prop, which he replaced very carefully in his inside breast pocket. Something slightly extraordinary about the movement caught Richard's attention. Gerry had held the side of his trench coat and the edge of his jacket together when he reached for the pocket, so that no glimpse of the inner garment appeared. There was nothing wrong about the performance; it was merely odd, and Richard was reminded of how he had removed the two coats together and put them on again in the same way in Mr. Vick's shop. The card was engraved and read:

Mr. Jeremy Chad-Horder

Lydaw Court Hotel
Kensington, W. S.

He looked at it for a moment and glanced up.

"I thought you said you'd left this place," he observed bluntly.

"That's right. I told Edna so." Once again the shame-faced laughing apology flickered over the lantern face. "Something had to be done. Frankly that was why I drifted in there today. Our receptionist at Lydaw Court is an extremely decent woman and very useful to me. She's been getting fed to the teeth. Edna has been pestering her, ringing up at all hours of the day. The poor woman told her I was out sixty-three times in a week. She made a note of it. It was getting absurd."

Richard sat looking at him, his young face inscrutable.

"So Edna's letters weren't hanging about in the vestibule?"

"Good God, of course they weren't. That *would* have been dangerous. I said that to discourage her." He began to laugh. "How romantic you are," he said. "I rather like it. It's Old World. Let me see, Edna is about eleven years older than you. That's as it should be. You're the age to have chivalrous instincts and she's the age to work hard to evoke them. Oh well, if you insist, we'll wander back to the Midget after I've made a phone call."

The offer constituted such an extraordinary volte-face that the young man gaped at him and at once a hint of caution appeared in the flat eyes and the suggestion was withdrawn at once.

"On second thoughts, please not," he said. "I couldn't bear it. Besides, the food at the old Lydaw is really exceptional when they make the effort, and, oh boy, will they be trying tonight! That's settled then, is it? Waiter!"

The old waiter, who was resting his weight surreptitiously on a gilt and marble console on the further wall, detached himself reluctantly, ploughed forward, and stood lowering. Gerry smiled at him.

"Some more of your excellent crumpets. Hot, this time, and not quite so black round the edges."

The ancient face remained expressionless.

"For two, sir?"

"Certainly for two. I see no more of us, do you? For two only."

"None for me," said Richard hastily.

"Oh, but you've got to. I'm going to telephone a girl I know and I may be hours. You must have something to amuse you while I'm down there in the box."

"I'll go on drinking tea."

"Will you? Oh, very well. Bring some more tea, waiter, and no crumpets. No crumpets to sound for us on the other side. Off you go."

He leant back in his chair and glanced at his watch.

"I must go and call up my poppet in the wilds." He took a handful of change and a ten-shilling note from his trouser pocket and looked at it. "The only thing against this lovely gal is that she lives deep in the shires, and the charge for a three-minute call down there is three shillings and sevenpence," he remarked as he began to sort the coins in his hand. "She will certainly expect six minutes' chitchat from me, and because she really is quite something I may feel like continuing even after that. The phone boxes here are normal and work on the principle of the coin in the slot, therefore I shall require nine separate shillings, three sixpences, and three pence. From you, Richard, I require two separate shillings and a tanner for half a crown. Can you do it?"

It took them a minute or two to make the little adjustment and by the time the fresh tea arrived the three small columns of coins were arranged on the table. Gerry took up the teapot and chattered briskly as the waiter's gloomy presence moved away once more.

"What an evil-eyed old drear," he observed. "He'll remember me, won't he? He loves me not. Don't get me wrong about this girl, by the way. I've not been captured. It's just that she's delectable, lusciously young, and she's fallen for me and so . . ." He peered at his watch again. "And so I humour her. Well, now, it is a quarter to six."

"Is it?" Richard was astonished. He felt his own naked wrist and glanced round for a clock. Gerry displayed his forearm with a good Swiss watch upon it.

"There you are," he said. "On the dot. She'll have just come in. My God, Richard, you should see her. She's extraordinary. Lovely. Very smooth golden-brown hair, cut so that it just brushes her tweed collar. Enormous grey eyes and a perfect skin. She can't be out of her teens and she looks edible. Wait here for me, old boy. As you know, I just haven't got the money to be more than ten minutes. There are the phone boxes, see? Down there in the hall at the end of the corridor. You can keep me under your eye all the time."

He sprang up, gathered the change from the table, and strode across the vast room, getting smaller and smaller as he passed down the long passage to the vestibule. Just before he reached it he turned and waved his hand and saw Richard raise his own and settle back in his seat.

After that point in distance it was not really possible for any normally sighted person to pick out much detail from either direction, although the two figures were still visible to each other, or would have been had either been watching. As it was, Richard saw the man he knew as Jeremy Chad-Horder bearing down upon the telephone booths, glanced away for a moment and lost sight of him. Not unnaturally he assumed he had entered one of them.

In fact the man in the trench coat had approached the line of booths and had walked along swiftly beside it as if he were seeking one which was unoccupied. When he came to the last of the line, which was out of sight of the mouth of the corridor, he turned smartly round behind it and stepped out of the small doorway normally used by hotel servants bringing in luggage, and which flanked the canopied side entrance.

Outside it was neither dark nor light, but at that brief twilit stage when London's sky, streets, and buildings appear all to be draped in different shades of blue, and the newly lit lamps and the side lights of the traffic are yellow and inadequate against the fast-vanishing daylight. It was also the rush hour and the man in the trench coat melted into the wave of home-going workers like a drop into the sea.

Gerry moved quickly and with that complete lack of hesitation which he had displayed as he had prepared Richard's mind for his telephone call. Never once did he falter or make an unnecessary step, but carried out the entire operation with the smooth efficiency of a dance routine on the stage.

All central London is covered by a network of small rights of way which can make moving about in it remarkably simple to anyone who has taken the trouble to work out his route. By making use of a mews, a furniture shop with a back entrance, and a passage kept open by ancient custom to give access to a no longer useful pump, Gerry reached the Lagonda parked where he and Richard had left it in something under two minutes.

As he had expected, the long car was now almost alone in the cobbled lane and lay deep in the shadow cast by the steep sides of the dark houses which lined it. He walked over to it and unlocked the boot, to take out the box, the rope, and a worn ex-army beret which was lying under them. This last he put on at once, and, taking off his trench coat, locked it away. Finally, after tightening his muffler, he turned up the collar of his jacket and buttoned that double-breasted garment up to his chin.

His next move was extraordinary but it was made so casually that even had there been a watcher it must have passed unnoticed in the uncertain light. Leaning over the back of the car where he had rested the box, he ran first one hand and then the other along the running board, and as he straightened himself he rubbed his face with his dirty hands. At last he took up the rope and shook it out, revealing it as a loop carefully knotted. This he placed round his neck where it hung halfway to his knees, lifted the box into the sling it made, and set off down the lane in the direction opposite to the Midget Club.

He came out into Minton Terrace in a matter of seconds and the overhead lights of the traffic way showed the remarkable change in his appearance.

The heavy-duty van delivery man is a familiar figure in modern London and is one of the very few workers whose trade still dictates a distinctive dress. While his shoes and trousers are as respectable as his pay packet, his jacket, which receives most of the wear, is liable to be torn out in a matter of days. He is apt, therefore, to wear old secondhand garments which can easily degenerate into picturesque rags by the end of the week.

No one who glanced at Gerry as he shouldered his way across the pavement could have thought there was anything strange about him, yet his navy chalk-striped jacket had been made for a bigger man and was oil-stained and ragged, the elbows out and padding protruding from the shoulder where the sleeve was coming away.

The beret, which completely covered his distinctive hair, was dusty, and his face was dirty enough to be virtually unrecognisable. The rope sling gave him a professional air and the rough wooden box was typical of millions. Above all, his manner was convincing. Every movement he made, every line in his taut body, and the impatient half whistle from between his teeth, were calculated to convey to one and all that he was late, that shops and offices were closing, and that somewhere in the gloom his van was waiting, its driver swearing in its cab.

His performance was particularly convincing as he came bounding up the stone steps of Number 24, Minton Terrace. This was a very fine block of offices built in the florid style of the early years of this century. The carved walnut door stood open and the moderate-sized entrance hall, with its white marble floor, Turkey carpet, and elderly commissionaire dozing in his hooded hall-porter's chair, was bright and busy as the little gilt lift travelled up and down serving the home-going staffs from the upper floors.

The offices of Messrs. Southern, Wood and Phillipson occupied the whole of the basement floor, but they closed at five and the staircase which ran down behind the lift was deserted.

As Gerry strode across the hall towards this well, no one appeared in his path. At the top of the stairs he paused to drag a small ragged receipt book from his left side pocket and dropped the wooden box on to the marble for a moment while he looked for it. The box hit the stone with the vicious double crash of a pistol shot, a savage noise which seemed to epitomise the roughness of the role he was playing. At any rate, the old commissionaire, although he frowned helplessly at the clatter, made no attempt to admonish him.

Having found, apparently, the necessary receipt form, Gerry lifted the box again and rattled down the stone staircase with it, still whistling between his teeth.

The small passage below was not very well lit and contained only two mahogany doors, both of which bore the name of Mr. Matthew Phillipson's firm. The newcomer lowered his box very gently on to the ground beside the first of them, replaced the receipt book in his left pocket, and thrust a hand deep into the right one. When it came out again it was holding a gun.

There was a bell on the door and he pressed it with his elbow and flipped the knocker with the nose of the weapon, so that it fell noisily. The breathy whistle through his teeth did not cease.

The right time, but not by the watch he had shown Richard, was half past five exactly. From somewhere behind the heavy door there was a thin tinkle of chimes and the man with the gun at the ready waited. Apparently he was without any emotion.

As the door opened and old Matt Phillipson's face appeared, still wearing the contented expression from his encounter with Polly, Gerry fired carefully and once again the distinctive noise, as of a heavy wooden box falling upon a polished stone floor, a sound as sharp and violent as a pistol shot, echoed up the well of the staircase.

Gerry did not close the door, but, bending swiftly over the old man, he thrust his hand into the inside breast pocket and drew out the plump black wallet hidden there. Then he swung the box up into his arms again and stamped up the staircase with it.

All the time he was listening for a hue and cry behind him, but there was none. As he had hoped, Mr. Phillipson had kept his bargain and had waited alone.

As Gerry reached the hall the lift came down and he was swept out of the building amid a flurry of young girls, typists from the pool on the top floor.

There was no need for him to explain the fact that he still carried the box, for the old commissionaire was surrounded and not looking at him, but his original plan had contained cover for this point and he did not alter it. From first to last he behaved as what he so nearly was, a well-trained animal without imagination or moral sense, and it was probably because of that that he aroused no instinctive alarm in the crowds through which he pressed. There was no danger signal from him, no smell of fear.

As he reached the doorway he peered out into the misty shadows and bellowed to his nonexistent van driver.

"Wrong 'ouse, mate! Try the Square."

He plunged out into the throng. Despite the crowds

he reached the mouth of the alley in nine seconds and was beside the car, now in considerably deeper shadow than before, in a further ten. It took him four minutes to lock the box away, rearrange his jacket and scarf, put on his trench coat, and scrub his face with a couple of clean handkerchiefs. There was no outcry from Minton Terrace, no sound of police whistles. Presently he was not even out of breath.

He had reckoned on it taking him an extra two minutes to get back to the Tenniel, because the furniture shop would now be closed and that short cut denied him, but in the narrow street which was his alternative route he passed behind an open truck held up by the lights and he threw the looped rope in the back of it. He was still holding his beret rolled up in his hand. There was nothing upon it to distinguish it in any way but he had planned to get rid of it, and because the exact method of doing this had not been worked out, he was worried out of all proportion by the little problem now that it arose. He had been alone in the pump passage but had not dared to drop the cap there, and came out into the street again still holding it. Finally the matter was solved for him.

Half a dozen yards before the turning leading to the long slope up to the Tenniel a dog appeared in his path. It was a big yellow animal with a large benign face and a long waving tail, who had been let out for brief personal reasons from one of the blocks of luxury flats further down the hill. It came up to him and he stooped to pat it, thought better of the impulse, and offered it the beret instead. To his surprise and secret relief it took it promptly and galloped away with it into the gloom.

Gerry strode on. He was making excellent time and already the lights of the hotel were visible from the top of the street. He hurried and was almost level with the door which would lead him back to the row of telephone booths when a second unrehearsed encounter occurred. There was a patter of light feet behind him followed by a familiar but not instantly placeable laugh. They brought him swinging round to confront Mr. Vick, of all people, looking unexpectedly small and prosperous in a blue melton coat and a velvety black homburg. The barber was delighted.

"Why, Major!" he cried exuberantly. "It *is* you! What
a coin-*ci*-dence!"

Since Gerry remained silent, his face wooden, Mr.
Vick hurried on.

"It's quite a liberty, I know that," he said, "and I hope
you'll forgive it, but as I was only saying this very morning
that I've known you donkeys' years and never seen you
outside my shop, when I actually caught sight of you just
in front of me turning out of Petty Street—well, I had to
follow you all the way up the hill just to make up my
mind."

He took a breath and stood smiling, his inquisitive
eyes bright in the lamplight.

"You're just off to catch Mr. Moor'en, I suppose?" he
added wistfully. "My word, Major, you don't 'alf walk fast,
you know."

11

Richard to Play

"In t'ree weeks this 'otel will be an 'ole in the road. I
shan't be 'ere no more. I shall be livin' wit' my daughter in
Saffron 'Ill. It don't matter to me what I tell you, see?"

The old waiter was only just intelligible and had
Richard known more about London he would have guessed
that he was listening to a local dialect rather than a foreign
accent, inasmuch as the man had no other tongue and had
never had any other home.

To look at, he was remarkably like a toad and moved
with some of that pleasant creature's spry difficulty. At the
moment he was bending sideways at the tea table, leaning
heavily on his hand. His dark-skinned face flecked with
little black patches was tired with the wear of a lifetime
and he spoke to the boy like some comically allegorical

figure of Age talking to Youth—hurriedly, timidly, and out of the corner of his mouth.

"If 'e should come back I'll give 'im your message if you say so," he went on furtively, "but I shouldn't leave no message. I shouldn't say you waited no hour for 'im. You've just met 'im today, 'ave you?"

"Well, yes, I have as a matter of fact." Richard was exasperated with himself, principally for not being much older and more informed. His vivid blue eyes were fierce under his dark red hair and the old man looked away nervously and flicked at a crumb on the table with his napkin.

"'E told you I would know 'im again," he muttered presently. "Did you 'ear that? I don' think you did. When I was a young man I wouldn't 'ave 'eard it, but now being old I did and I thought." He coughed. "You un'erstand now, don' you?"

"Not entirely," said Richard frankly. "Have you seen him before?"

The waiter looked round with elaborate casualness but there was not a soul in sight in the vast domed hall. All the same he lowered his voice still further.

"'E come in yesterday, just walked round." There seemed to be some deep significance in this statement, for he stood watching for a moment before he tried again. "'E cased the place," he said. "Cased it. Don' you know that word, sir?" Receiving no response, he became very foreign indeed. "How you say, sur-vey for da crook."

Crook! The familiar and likely word registered on Richard with something like relief. But his new friend raised a protesting hand and became so Latin as to be almost incomprehensible.

"No," he said, "no, no, I don't know nothing about that. But don' you send 'im no message and when the police come and ask you if you know where 'e was today you say no, jus' like that. You don't know 'im and you don' know 'is name, you never saw nor 'eard of 'im before. You don' want to get mixed up with 'is troubles."

"An alibi?" The explanation, so obvious as soon as it was pointed out to him, startled Richard rather than astonished him. He had begun to expect his new acquaintance to turn out to be some sort of confidence trickster, but not to discover that he personally was being used by him as a shield.

The old waiter, who was watching his face with interest, ventured another observation.

" 'E left 'ere twenty-five minutes after five," he remarked.

"How do you know?" Richard recalled the wrist watch held out for his inspection and the repeated insistence that the time was a quarter to six.

The waiter's grey face split into a gap-toothed smile and he jerked his thumb towards the tall archway in the wall behind them.

"I 'ear the glasses," he explained. "Bar opens 'alf past five."

"I see." Richard ran an absent-minded finger round his collar. It was patently obvious that for some reason of his own Gerry had thought it important to have some completely disinterested person to vouch for him during the twenty minutes between five twenty-five and a quarter to six. The more Richard thought about it the more uncomfortable he felt, for he realised that had the man returned from the telephone booth after any reasonable interval the chances were that he would have been tricked into answering for him. "He hasn't been out of my sight since this morning." He could hear himself saying it.

"Why didn't he come back?" He spoke aloud and the old man shrugged his shoulders.

"Who knows?" he enquired with magnificent sophistication. "You go off and enjoy yourself. Forget 'im. You don' know 'im no more."

Richard laughed. Had it not been for the one uncomfortable fact that Gerry had appeared so remarkably at home in the house which had swallowed Annabelle, the advice would have suited him perfectly. As it was, he paid the bill, assured the old man of his gratitude, tipping him sufficiently to convey sincerity, and went along to the telephones himself.

To his relief he found Mrs. Tassie's number without any difficulty and was surprised to hear such a warm comfortable voice answering him. The moment he heard her he began to feel that his terrors were silly. It was such an ordinary voice, a little fluttered because a young man was asking to speak to a girl, but sounding not even sophisticated, much less sinister. It belonged to a different world, he felt, to the one in which he had spent the day.

Annabelle was fetched immediately and as he heard her burbling over the wire his heart jumped, a surprising and interesting phenomenon. A little to his chagrin, she appeared to be enjoying herself enormously.

"The aunt's all right," she assured him in reply to his question. "Wait a minute. No, it's perfectly okay. She's being tactful. She's gone upstairs. She's an old poppet, Richard, just rather lonely, I expect. She's a bit formal though. You know, a bit as if she'd been Uncle's girl friend rather than his wife. Old-fashioned careful. Understand?"

"I think so. Can I come round and see you?"

"Not tonight."

"Why?"

"I'm being taken to the movies. It's the char's day off and we're eating out." Her eager child's voice hesitated before rushing on again, anxious to soothe. "I'm dying to see you and you're going to be invited to a meal on Sunday. You see what I mean by formal. I shall get her out of it, of course, but it's ingrained so it'll take a week or two. Be ready to accept for Sunday. Best clothes, I think, for the first time. I do so want her to like you. I can't ask her now because she's a bit upset. Some visitors came and seem to have worried her."

"Very well." He was trying to sound neither amused nor disappointed. Annabelle was a sweetie. He could see that amazing new beauty of hers as vividly as if her face were before him. For some reason it made him feel old and careworn. "Listen," he commanded briskly. "Before you go, tell me, who is the man, thirtyish, fair, tall, slightly boiled eyes, face haggard-handsome..."

"In a sort of trench coat?"

"That's the chap. He came out of your museum gate about fifteen minutes after you went in. Know who he is?"

"Yes. Gerry Hawker."

"Horder?"

"No, Hawker. H-a-w-k-e-r. Think of the bird. He's a pet of Aunt Polly's."

"Is he? Does he live there?"

"*Here?* No, of course not. He's just someone she's

known and treated as a sort of son for years. He lives in Reading and was passing through London today, so he called in to see her. Why, you don't know him, do you?"

"No. But I saw him coming out of the house...."

Annabelle laughed contentedly. "You couldn't possibly by straining it have been jealous, could you? I should like that." She made it sound a request and he scowled at the telephone.

"I certainly couldn't. What are you talking about? You behave yourself."

She sighed with mock regret. She was enjoying herself hugely, he suspected.

"Shame. I feared you might not have fallen for me at first sight. This is Aunt's influence. You'll enjoy her. She's as romantic as a valentine. As far as I can gather she adored her husband and wants every girl to have the same glorious experience. I fancy she was hoping to get me off with the Gerry person."

"Oh God, don't do that."

"Of course I won't. Don't be silly. He must be close on thirty-five. But I think that was the idea originally and why she was asking for the twenty-four-year-old daughter."

"I see," he said slowly. "Do you expect him back this week? Before Sunday?"

"I don't know. Aunt Polly didn't say. Why, what is all this? What's the matter with you?"

"Nothing much." Richard's face was hot with anxiety. "However, if you do see him do *not* mention my name, that is vital. Do you understand?"

"Then you do know something about him? Or does he know something about you?"

He could feel her interest quickening.

"This is all very mysterious and sounds exciting."

"Well, it isn't," he said flatly, "but I beg you to shut up about me and to do all you can to get me asked over to see you just as soon as you can. I'll tell you all I know then."

"All right. But don't be so bossy. You needn't worry. I'll keep your beastly name out of it, whatever it is."

The unfairness was too much for his stoicism.

"It's not me, it's you I'm thinking about."

"Oh, Richard, how charming." She sounded just about

as sophisticated as a six-year-old in lipstick. "I'd call you 'darling' if it wasn't so old hat. What's wrong with the poor man? I thought he was rather a honey, if he hadn't been so old. Aunt Polly says she could cure age when she was sixteen, by the way."

"She says what?"

"Forget it. Actually that wasn't quite fair. She didn't mean it. I was just making a good story. What do you know about this man Gerry? I'm fascinated."

"I'm not," he said bitterly. "Shut up about him now. I'll ring you tomorrow."

He hung up and stood looking at the silent instrument. As far as he could see, the position was more than awkward and he was not at all sure what he ought to do about it. Finally he decided to verify what facts he had, and once more took up the directory.

The receptionist at the Lydaw Court Hotel had one of those refined yet fruity middle-aged voices which suggested to Richard tessellated pavements in palm courts and very well looked-after cane furniture with spry old ladies and depressed young ones sitting about in it, waiting either for a meal or bedtime.

"Mr. Chad-Horder?" She said with very much more warmth than had appeared in her original greeting. "No, he's not in yet, I'm afraid. We're expecting him at any moment now. He's later than he said already. Can I give him any message?"

"No, please don't bother." Richard was bearing in mind the old waiter's advice, but he was curious. Lydaw Court sounded such an odd place for a man like Gerry to live in. "Have you a—a dance there tonight?" he added on impulse.

"Yes, indeed we have." The voice was archly enthusiastic. "One of our regular Thursday evenings. Excuse me, but are you one of the gentlemen whom Mr. Chad-Horder thought he might be able to bring?"

"No, I'm afraid I'm not. Thank you very much. Goodbye."

"Wait." The command was imperative. "I really must ask you to leave a name. Mr. Chad-Horder is very particular. He will insist on knowing who called." At this point even she appeared to notice that the approach was a trifle highhanded, for an embarrassed laugh escaped her. "He always asks if there have been any calls or messages, and I do like to be able to tell him," she added and sounded suddenly pathetic.

Richard, who was not a natural prevaricator, looked round for inspiration which he found in the largest type in the place, the cover of the Directory.

"Tell him Mr. London," he said hastily. "Only a general message. Just that I made a call."

He rang off and the woman in the desk at the Lydaw Court Hotel jotted down four somewhat ominous words on her memorandum pad. "Chad-Horder. London. General call."

Richard came out of the booth undecided on his next move. He had found out a little about Gerry as Chad-Horder, but almost nothing about him when he called himself Hawker. It seemed unlikely that Edna would be of much help, even if she were not actively unco-operative, and Torrenden, the racing driver, sounded difficult to approach.

As he stood hesitating he suddenly remembered the starting handle and the label upon it. Gerry had removed it but not quite quickly enough, and Richard could see it clearly in his mind's eye and could read the words on it. Hawker. Rolf's Dump.

He asked the way from a young constable on the corner outside the hotel, who went to considerable trouble to look it up in the pocket street directory which each man on duty carries with him.

"It's some distance, sir," he announced after study. "East, right round by the Regent's Canal. If I were you I should take a Number Seven bus to Liverpool Street and ask again."

He was a big gangling youth with squat widely spaced teeth and a permanently anxious expression and he eyed Richard's conventionally clad figure dubiously before he returned again to the shaded area on the section of the street map in the book in his hand.

"Are you sure you want to go there?" he enquired, bending a little to show the page. "That's it, Rolf's Dump. There's miles of it, see? All along the canal. It won't be what you might call very salubrious this time of night."

Richard grinned at the man. He was his own age. He wished they could have gone together.

"I'm afraid I must get there," he said. "Thank you very much. Do you happen to know what sort of place it is?"

"Sorry, I can't say. It's in a built-up area, see, so it won't be noxious materials. It's too big to be private so I think you'll find it's parcels of scrap all owned by different dealers which are waiting there for re-sale. The stuff would come and go by barge, I should say, on the canal. No trouble at all, sir. Good-night."

Richard walked on towards the bus stop, hoping he was not making a fool of himself. He realised he was taking a very long chance but he decided to press on.

Two and a half hours later, however, his mood had changed. By that time he was convinced that he was behaving like a lunatic. The journey had proved formidable. He had travelled by a series of buses far into the East End of the city and had finished up at last in bright moonlight in a strange flat no man's land which appeared to consist of wide acres of condemned slum houses, relieved here and there by the huge towers of the blocks of new council dwellings, all very modern and impressive against a limpid sky.

With considerable difficulty, and against the earnest advice of everybody who had directed him, he had discovered the Dump at last. It lay dark and uninviting on the other side of the fifteen-foot barrier made partly of board and partly of wire, which lined one side of the road on which he walked quite alone. For ten minutes now he had seen no living soul and nothing which looked faintly like a door into the enclosure.

Fortunately it was one of those clear nights which seldom occur over London because of the haze, but are dazzling when they do. The moon was as big as a tea tray and its light was so strong that colours were discernible by it, while all the shadows were ink black, their highlights silver. Yet even under this enchantment there was nothing even faintly attractive about Rolf's Dump. As far as Richard could discover through occasional unobscured patches in the wire fence, it consisted of a sort of moon landscape composed of mountains and craters of unlikely objects such as truck bodies, street-lamp standards, rotted baskets, derelict machinery, cases of out-of-date tins of food, wheels, water tanks, and a thousand other examples of waste material all arranged in orderly masses. And beyond these he caught the gleam of a narrow waterway. It was very quiet. The city's roar was here reduced to a murmur and there were very few nearer sounds.

From the middle distance he could hear the hollow crashing of a railway and once or twice he thought he detected voices and movement from the far end of the Dump itself. But he was not sure. He could see no lights in that direction.

The road he walked on was extraordinary. There was not a house on it. The buildings on the side opposite to the fence were roofless and ruined, the filthy glass in the windows broken and ghostly in the moonlight. They had been stables at one time, Richard thought, and now looked like relics of an age as dead as the pharaohs.

He stumbled on, cursing himself for an idiot, the worn stones greasy under his feet, until unexpectedly he came upon a much broader road running at right angles to his own and leading apparently directly into the Dump itself. The way was barred by a pair of stout doors which were very tall and completely black against the sky.

For a moment he thought he was defeated and was on the point of turning away when it occurred to him that he might as well try them. He was looking for the lock when he discovered a small postern built into the left-hand door.

It opened to his touch and he was about to step forward when a terrier, who was tethered just inside, sprang up barking hysterically and a voice, also uncannily near, let out a stream of comment equally violent.

"What d'yer want?" it demanded finally.

"Mr. Hawker." Richard was too startled to invent. The name had been in his mind and he uttered it.

"Orl right." The voice was lowered and had become conversational. "Shut up, Jack! Down boy. 'E ain't 'ere, I don't think," it continued. "I didn't 'ear 'im come in yet."

12

At the Rose and Crown

At just about the same time as Richard was asking for Jeremy Hawker at Rolf's Dump, the man who called himself by that name when it suited him was standing against the round bar in the Rose and Crown. This public house stands directly behind the old Royal Albert Music Hall, a famous vaudeville theatre before the war and later the home of lavish musical shows. On this particular evening Morris Moorhen was appearing there in *Bowl Me Over*. The performance had been on for forty minutes and the long interval was due in five.

Mr. Vick, who was standing next to Gerry, bright spots of colour on his cheekbones and his elegant black hat well on the back of his head, was having a much better time than anyone who merely saw the scene could possibly have supposed. The Rose and Crown was never a place of gaiety. Its main trade was done at lunch time and in the evening it was apt to present an ill-lit and deserted appearance.

At the moment the only other two people in the place at all were behind the bar. There was the tender, a solid youngster who looked as if he had troubles of his own, and the manager, who was a white-faced, gloomy-eyed man, who sat aloof in an alcove built into the mahogany and looking-glass contraption, part sideboard, part office, which stood in the centre of the bar like a hub in the centre of a wheel. He was taking no notice of anybody but was reading an evening paper which he had folded into a narrow strip like a harlequin's wand.

Mr. Vick was drinking large dark glasses of unidentified sherry with a recklessness either of ignorance or insanity, and by now he was garrulous, affectionate, and noisy as a macaw, which he was beginning to resemble. His drawing-room scream became more and more frequent and the arch hero worship which he lavished on the man in the raincoat was mounting.

Yet the principal change which had occurred during the evening had taken place in Gerry. In the three hours since his carefully prepared alibi had been destroyed at the very moment of its success by the chance meeting with the inquisitive little barber, he had altered in appearance. His flesh seemed to be clinging more tightly to his bones. There was a slight stiffness in his body and the muscles of his face, while the blank expression in his flat eyes, normally infrequent, had become almost habitual. Moreover, his normal casualness of manner had become exaggerated, so that the barman, who was not bothering to give serious consideration to the matter, would have sworn offhand that he was the more drunk of the two.

This was an assumption which could not have been more wrong. By pleading that he was driving, Gerry had avoided alcohol all the evening and had achieved an icy sobriety in which his mind was working with unusual clarity. He had arranged many alibis in his life. It was part of his nature to be careful. So far he had never needed one. But always they had been there, like safety nets, ready to save him if by chance the unexpected occurred.

Yet this time, by sheer fortuitous bad luck ascribable to no mistake on his part, the alibi had broken down and he was surprised to find that it was important to his faith in himself that he should replace it somehow.

Mr. Vick had not been as easy to dominate as he had hoped when, in the first moment of panic outside the hotel, he had decided to abandon Richard and concentrate on the barber. The little man had a quicksilver intelligence, bright and unstable. No thought appeared to be, as it were, safe in his head for a couple of minutes together.

"In ten minutes you'll be in old Moggie's dressing room, Major," Mr. Vick was saying with a bobbysox shiver. "Oh my word, I do wish I could see you two together! It would be worth putting down in a diary, that would. I believe you're selling him a song. Don't deny it, I can see it in your eyes, I'm psychic. You could, you know. There isn't much you couldn't do, is there, Major? Be a sport and tell me, go on, do." He turned to the bartender. "He won't tell me anything," he went on, his voice breaking. "We've been together all the evening..."

"Ever since opening time." Gerry spoke with mock weariness.

"Ever since *after* opening time," corrected Mr. Vick with dignity.

"Hell to that, I've been suffering from you ever since *before* opening time. When we met it was so early we had to go and get the car before we could have one. You've been drinking that liver-paralyser steadily ever since, but I should have thought you could have remembered that."

"I do." Mr. Vick seemed surprised by the fact. "You said we'd got to go and fetch the car because it wasn't opening time." He paused and added flatly, "Six o'clock."

"Half past five, old boy." The correction came a fraction too sharply and the bartender raised a harassed face from his meditations.

"London area, half past five," he echoed obligingly.

The man in the trench coat met his eyes and laughed. "I've had him on my hands since a quarter past five and I'm still sane," he said with just the right air of affable indulgence. "I shall have to leave him here for ten minutes while I nip into the theatre. Don't give him any more of that stuff than you can help."

"It's a nice sherry." The bartender pushed over the bottle for inspection. "It's good South African."

"Is it?" Gerry stood reading the gay label, a new superiority in the curl of his lips, and the manager, who had been watching him, suddenly slapped his paper wand across his plump knees.

"Now you look exactly like your granddad, Gerald," he remarked. He had a fat man's voice, friendly and broad, with a South London accent. His sad eyes had brightened in his white face. "I wasn't sure at first," he went on. "You're more like the old man than yourself, as I remember you. I'm completely unrecognisable, I suppose? What is it? Thirty years? Twenty-two or three, must be." He thrust a hand over the bar. "I'm Dan Tilley. Our garden backed on to your grandfather's in Urquhart Road, remember?"

There was a moment of utter silence. The man in the

trench coat blinked, as if a bullet had struck him, and for a second his face wore the expression of innocent surprise which goes with it. Then he pulled himself together. He was controlled, but still unnaturally grand. He took the proffered hand with exaggerated deference.

"Why, yes," he began, conveying that he was utterly at sea but determined to be polite. "Yes, of course, Dan—er—Tilley. My dear fellow, twenty-odd years, what a very long time. Too long."

The manager flushed. He was embarrassed and had no skill to hide it. He took refuge in a sort of truculent pleasantry.

"'Lord Almighty,' that's what we called your old man," he said. "It was your name for him, not mine. You seem to have forgotten it was me helped you to get away. You did get to Australia, did you? I never heard of you again, you know, not from that day to this."

Gerry remained wooden, the faint half-smile still on his lips, but at this point Mr. Vick decided to intervene. He had climbed on to a stool and now sat there, his hat hanging half off his head, his gaze fixed upon the manager, whom he appeared to see for the first time.

"*I've* known the Major for ten years," he announced with startling distinctness. "We are two dear old friends out on the loose. I don't know who you are *and I don't care*."

"Hush." Gerry spoke reprovingly. This definite line so crudely taken had made up his mind for him. No doubt it had occurred to him that a drunken witness is of little use without a sober one to vouch for him. "This is the original Danny Boy, the first chum I ever had," he went on with an abrupt return of friendliness. "I didn't know you, Dan," he said, turning to the manager. "You made me grow cold for a moment. You brought back my childhood. Good God, you old sinner, now I look at you you haven't altered in the least. Put on a Fair-Isle sweater and navy knickerbockers and I'd know you anywhere. You say the same damned things, too. I resent the suggestion that I resemble the old man."

"You do though, Gerald, in feature." The manager was mollified. He was revealed as a slow-thinking person, loth to leave any subject until it is utterly exhausted. "I'm not saying you're like him in any other way, of course. He was a one, and his second wife. They thought themselves somebody." He sucked his teeth by way of emphasis. "A clean paper collar every day and a set of the Encyclopaedia Britannica to read up at night. He went through the world on those two, old Lord Almighty did." He laughed reminiscently. "Oh dear, he used to make my father so wild. They used to go up in the train together to their pore little offices and be rude to each other on a big-headed level all the way. Just a bit more educated and more refined than anyone else in the street, that's how your granddad saw himself. It shook him when you ran off, you know. Did you go to sea as you planned?"

"Briefly." Gerry's wry smile suggested youthful false steps safely retraced. "I never saw the house or the old people again, though. My God, what an atmosphere to drag up an orphan child in. I can see that place now," he added, with a flash of pure sincerity which completely transformed him. "Suppressed dirt, suppressed starvation, and a soul-chilling atmosphere of superiority to the rest of the ignorant herd."

"Huh," said the manager. "Everybody knew that they could sell him at one end of the street and buy him at the other. Silly old clod," he added with a flicker of resentment still alive after twenty years. "He had a lower intelligence than most."

"Oh, no, he was a very brilliant man. I think you really must grant him that." The man in the trench coat made the statement with a conviction not only out of character but clearly misplaced. The effect was conventionally shocking, as if he had put a straw in his hair suddenly. "Quite, quite brilliant," he repeated with a fleeting smile of contented superiority which made everybody in the room, including the drunken barber, vaguely uncomfortable. The revelation was no more than a glimpse. Immediately afterwards he was his usual sophisticated and charming self. "It was no home for a kid, anyway," he said.

"I should say." The manager wagged his head again. "No one blamed you for going. The old girl told a lot of lies, I believe," he added slyly.

"What about? What sort of lies?" The questions came very sharply and the manager coloured.

"Just what you'd expect," he muttered. "I wouldn't have blamed you, mind you, if you had helped yourself to something to go on with. They'd made your home impossible, I mean to say."

"Lies, of course." Gerry's dignity was pitying. He seemed to be a different person altogether when on the subject of his childhood. "Poor woman, I think her life may have been difficult. She wasn't clever, you know."

"Look at the time, Major, look at the time!" Mr. Vick went off like an alarm clock himself. He was pointing at the bold-faced clock over the door and was in imminent danger of falling off his stool.

Gerry burst out laughing and exchanged amused glances with his newly found oldest friend.

"Take care of him until I come back," he said. "I just want a word with someone in the theatre. I shan't be ten minutes."

"I'd like to see old Moggie and old Moggie'd like to see me," said Mr. Vick, emerging into the open after the bait which had been dangled before him all evening.

"I doubt it." Again the childhood friends exchanged glances and as Gerry went out of the back door nearest to the theatre the manager's soothing voice reached him as it addressed Mr. Vick.

"If you've been on sherry since opening time, sir, I wonder if you'd like a change? What about a nice Fernet Branca cocktail?"

The man in the trench coat walked swiftly down the pavement, avoiding the stage door in the blank wall of the theatre. There was a contented smile on his lips. "Since opening time." The words were so satisfactory that he repeated them aloud. It was the point he had been trying to establish all the evening and now that it had been done, and he had a new alibi in place of the other which had gone astray, he felt infinitely happier even though he was quite confident he would not need to use it.

Perhaps if his attitude to the precaution had been less superstitious and more practical it might have occurred to him that two alibis for the same vital quarter of an hour, one in Richard's mind and one in Mr. Vick's, might be more dangerous than none at all. That realisation came some minutes later.

Crossing the main street he turned into one of those small eating houses which seem always to be built on the same rectangular plan. They possess two short counters set one on either side of a narrow entrance, and a passage between leading into a square steam-filled room where plastic-topped tables are surrounded by quantities of spiky bentwood chairs. This was a poor place with shabby painted walls and dusty light bulbs, and the single waitress, a pallid flat-chested youngster, was only too obviously the daughter of the grim old lady at the urns. A group of seedy-looking youths who might have been planning anything from a burglary to a skiffle group sat round the largest table in the far corner, talking together, and did not look up as he came in. The rest of the room was empty.

He chose a small table under the ledge of the right-hand counter. It placed him in a corner diagonally opposite the whispering group, and as he edged round to get the angle behind him, the bunched skirts of his trench coat scattered the light-weight chairs. Beneath the coat the pockets of his ragged jacket were heavy and he frowned as he sat down. The chance meeting with Mr. Vick had upset the whole exercise. He was carrying far too much incriminating stuff for complete safety and the wooden box was still in the car.

Yet he was by no means panic-stricken. His attitude was far more dangerous than that. He felt impersonal, almost as if his whole interest in the matter was academic.

There was a wireless set turned low on the counter and as he sat down he heard the chimes of Big Ben heralding the news. He ordered coffee and sat there sipping it while the prim voice of the B.B.C. announcer went through the happenings of the day.

There was no police message, no mention of a West End crime.

Presently he pushed his cup away and drew out the black wallet which he had taken from Matt Phillipson's body. It lay plump and neat in his hands, where it looked unremarkable. By far its greatest bulk consisted of a cheque book, he noticed with mild regret, of no use to anybody now. But in the opposite pocket there was a reasonable wad of pound notes and a couple of fivers tucked among all the usual miscellany. It was when he was looking to see if there were any more that he discovered the two letters, clipped together and kept there for safety away from secretaries, as Mr. Phillipson had promised Polly. Gerry recognised her familiar sprawling handwriting and a flood of tingling blood rose up from his stomach to suffuse his face.

Apprehension, breath-taking and terrible as anything in his childhood, took possession of him and he spread the sheets out with hands that trembled.

There it was, clear and irrevocable, in words which could have come from no one else.

> "... *The money doesn't matter but you must tell him, dear. Make it clear how wrong and how dangerous it is, but leave me out. Once he knows I know, the mischief will be done as he'll be afraid and keep away and there'll be no one to keep an eye on him....*"

The coarse skin on the lined forehead was damp. Gerry hardly dared to read the second letter. As he turned to it the nerves in his face contracted into a net of pain, and the blood in his heart felt icy.

> "....*Thank you, Matt, what a dear old sport you are. Thursday night, then. I'll be thinking of you both. If you can just give him a good fright it may pull him right up and make him see sense. He's all right when you know him, one of the best. Give me a ring afterwards or better still come in and see me. Love, Polly.*"

The man in the trench coat sat looking at the trembling sheet. She knew. She knew of the appointment and would know therefore of everything else.

With the realisation, the odd hypothetical quality in his appreciation of events left him suddenly and gave place to stark vision, a difference as great as between sleeping and waking. For the first time he saw his two alibis for what they were, two over-elaborate sums cancelling each other out.

Gradually he became aware of a shadow, and looking up saw the little waitress standing close before him.

She was spreading out her elbows in an attempt to shield him with her thin body from any chance glance from the other table. She was very young, her black dress very poor, and the little gold cross on the thin chain round her neck very small. Her circular eyes were black, too, and shyly reproachful as she looked from his face to the table before him.

Glancing down, he saw that he had forgotten the wallet. It lay wide open before him, the money exposed.

"Put it away," she said softly, "you're drunk, aren't you?"

He pulled himself together at once and his charm lit up his face like a lamp.

"Bless you," he said, quickly, gathering up the notes and thrusting them into his breast. "I'm sorry. I was reading a letter. It's a bit of a knockout... from a woman."

The little face, pale-skinned and muddy, flushed with sly amusement as she attempted badinage.

"She's found you out, has she?"

He shivered and the sudden glimpse of helplessness appearing in his face thrilled her.

"It seems so."

"I see. Well, you'll have to do something about her, won't you?"

For a time he stared at her in open horror, silent as the full implication of the words sank in. Then:

"Yes," he said slowly. "Yes, I shall."

13

Someone at Home

"If you don't know where the shed is I can't show you. 'E's got no business coming in at night at all, let alone sending down strangers. There's a lot of valuable property standing about 'ere, though you might not think so."

The night watchman at Rolf's Dump was still a voice in the dark so far as Richard was concerned, although by now he was standing only a few feet away from him. Here in the Dump the moonlight had created a world of ink and silver with no half tones. The watchman was lost in a black wall rising up into the sky, but the dog, a white terrier, smooth-skinned and shivering, sat visible in the path, presumably at his master's feet.

Richard took two coins silently from his pocket and let the light fall upon their broad silver faces. There was no response. The voice continued to grumble.

"I've 'ad plenty of trouble down 'ere already tonight," it said. "The police 'ave been 'ere all day over on the other side of the estate. They've still got the key of the foot gate in Toley Street. Did you notice them as you came past?"

"I'm afraid I didn't. Where would they be?"

"Over 'ere be'ind me, about three quarters of a mile back, against the 'oarding."

"No. I didn't see anybody."

"They've gorn then. Good job. There's nothing more nosey than the police. As for the public, they're interfering, gabby, can't keep their traps shut. You would think a gang of labourers could load a ton or two of empty oil drums on to a barge without interfering with what they found be'ind them, wouldn't you?"

"What did they find?" Richard felt in his pocket for a third coin. Again there was no movement as he displayed it, but as he placed it with the others the chink sounded and response was immediate.

"I don't know if you can see me setting 'ere, sir." The voice was many shades warmer. "Wait a minute." There was a scuffle and a bright light appeared, revealing a little old man sitting on a kitchen chair in a sentry box of a shelter built into the hillock, which was entirely composed of old wooden wheels. He was wrapped in an assortment of coats topped by a sleeveless leather jerkin belted with a piece of cord, and from under the peak of his cap, which he wore pulled down far on his head, a pair of spectacles with the thickest of lenses peered at Richard hopefully.

The young man offered him the money and almost

dropped it. The hand which came out so eagerly missed his own and there was a moment of confusion before the coins were safely transferred. The man was virtually blind and not admitting it, a discovery which explained a great deal.

"It was because the engine was all right, you see, sir." Having stowed away his seven-and-six, the old man became a friend and his tone was confidential.

"The engine," said Richard, completely at sea.

"The engine of the bus, sir. It went, that's what surprised everybody. It started up at once, although it had been there for three years, they say, and couldn't nohow have been moved since last spring because of the oil drums being right in the way, you see. They were put there in the spring."

Richard did not understand in the least. The entire statement struck him as a *non sequitur*. He did not say so but his silence was expressive and, aware of his lack of success, the night watchman tried again.

"It was the loaders what found it out," he said hoarsely. "They was nosin' about yesterday after they shifted the drums and they saw that seven old buses had been hemmed in behind this load they was movin'. They over'auled them, seein' what they could pinch, I'll bet, and one was perfectly all right. When they went to lunch they 'ad to talk about it in the boozer, someone 'eard them and re-ported them, and before anybody knows what's 'appenin' the rozzers comes sniffin' in. That's what democracy 'as come to. One word in a pub and down come the flippin' police anxious not to miss anything useful. We're a nation o' scroungers."

The information contained in this piece of involved thinking was of little interest to Richard, who was no reader of murder cases and was unaware of any police search for a bus. His interest was solely in Gerry.

"Does Mr. Hawker work here?" he enquired at last.

"Only in 'is shed, private like. 'E don't own anythin' stored 'ere."

"I see. He rents a workshop here?"

"That's about it. A little workshop. 'E tunes up racin' cars down 'ere, or limousines." The watchman sounded admiring but vague and it occurred to Richard, who had become something of an authority on the subject, that Gerry must have been talking again. Since the night watchman had not the evidence of his own eyes, his information could only come from one source.

"Is he often here?" he enquired.

"On and off. Sometimes 'e works 'ere at night for a week. O' course I'm only 'ere at night meself. I couldn't say what 'e does in the daytime. I thought you was a friend of 'is?"

"Well, I've just spent the day with him."

"Oh." The reassurance seemed sufficient. "Well, 'e always 'as a word with me when 'e comes in late. Two years now I've 'ad this job and 'e's always been very nice when he troubles me to open up for 'im. Reely very nice." The coins clinked softly in his pocket, an accompaniment to praise. "Very nice indeed. 'E's a feller you can take to, ain't 'e? Always the same, I say, always the same."

It became clear that this was about as far as they were going to get. Richard turned away to look down the moonlit track which wandered away through the nightmare landscape.

"Perhaps I'd better go on down to the shed. Where is it? Do you know?"

"Course I do. I seen it scores o' times." The nearly sightless eyes stared angrily at a point some three feet beyond the one where Richard was standing. "But I ain't got time to take yer down there now. You'll 'ave to go by yerself. People 'ave work to do, don't forget."

With a reproachful wriggle he settled himself an inch or so further back in the shelter and switched off the light.

"It ain't far down there." His voice, hoarse and satisfied, came out of the darkness. "It's in a holler, he tells me. There ain't no other building in the place that I've ever 'eard of. When 'e comes in I'll tell 'im you're there."

Richard thanked him without deep enthusiasm and went off grateful for the moonlight. Without it the Dump, which was eerie enough in any case, must have been a place of terror. Although it was by no means a rubbish heap, it was yet not odourless and he was constantly aware of dark sliding shapes, inexpressibly evil, flickering out of his path.

He strode on doggedly, refusing to ask himself what on earth he thought he was doing and what good could possibly come of the excursion. His chin was tucked in angrily. At least he was doing something. At any rate he would find out all he possibly could about Mr. Jeremy Hawker before he next saw Annabelle.

He came on the shed unexpectedly. A gap in the row of hillocks which lined the road revealed an artificial depression which had perhaps once contained the foundations of a considerable house. A steep drive led down into this basin and at the bottom, surrounded by a scattered collection of old motor bodies, discarded tyres, a broken carboy or two, and other similar debris, there was a ruin. It was built mostly of brick and might once have been a kiln or a bakehouse or part of the cellars of the original building. There was no way of telling. Now there was nothing left but a nest of roughly roofed brick boxes, a broken chimney, and a single tall shed with a tin roof on it and wide coach-house doors.

Richard turned down into the hollow without hesitation. It did not occur to him to query the shed. It suggested Gerry to his mind and he did not doubt for a moment that it belonged to him. There was no one around. The whole place was as silent as a churchyard. The building proved to be bigger than he had thought on first seeing it, however, and the tall doors were padlocked.

He circled it, stamping through the tall twitch grass which grew sparsely on the uneven ground. There was a great deal of rubbish about, he noticed, bricks and old cans and pipes lying in the weeds and all picked out bright and misshapen in the icy light.

It was as he approached the smaller door at the back of the shed that he experienced the first twinges of the extraordinary series of sensations which descended on him later. He knew what fear was, naturally, but he was not of a highly nervous or hypersensitive disposition. He had done his share of service overseas and was not inexperienced, yet as he approached that second door he was aware of some intangible menace which made the short hairs at the back of his neck rise and prickle. It was not a sound which had alarmed him, for the silence was oppressive. He sniffed dubiously. The whole dump reeked but here there

was something else, something new to him yet so old that
his disgust was instinctive. He shrugged his shoulders
irritably and pressed on.

The old-fashioned thumb latch on the small door
lifted readily enough but the wood was fastened lower
down and from the inside. Either a bolt or another padlock
secured it. On impulse he put his shoulder to the peeling
painted surface and, a little to his dismay, for he had
hardly meant to break into the place, it gave at once. He
felt the iron staples pulling out of the rotten wood.

The building he entered was in complete darkness
save for a shaft of moonlight, strong and clear as a searchlight,
which poured in through the single skylight high in the
roof on his right. A square of light, bright and barred,
rested partly on a workbench which lined the left-hand
wall and partly on the pile of rubbish which had accumulat-
ed beneath it, an area never so visible in the normal way
when the doors were open.

It was practically the first thing Richard saw, a collection of dusty rubbish of a kind found in most motor
workshops. There were paint and oil tins there and bottles,
a pail on its side, part of a pump, a ball of crumpled paper,
a set of rods which might have been part of a broken deck
chair, and among them, lying open, with its lining pulled
out, a white plastic handbag.

Why he should have found the sight of it so sinister
Richard never knew, but as he stared at it his heart moved
uncomfortably. It looked so fresh, so very unused, and yet
so completely ravaged, lying there in the bright moonlight.

He came forward and stumbled over something lying
in the fairway. He had no torch with him but, with the
help of his lighter, he was able to discover that it was a flat
slab of polished marble which is still found sometimes on
old washstands. There were two wooden wine boxes of the
type which Gerry had been carrying round with him in
the Lagonda, one larger and one smaller lying beside it.
They each contained a quantity of ordinary bricks, a
meaningless collection from Richard's point of view.

What he found more interesting was a glimpse of an
inspection lamp lying on the bench just out of the moonlight.
He picked it up and followed the lead along to a plug with
a switch beside it. He pressed it over without much hope

but was startled by his success. Not only did the wire-caged lamp light up but a hanging bulb in the roof sprang into life. He was in a curious barn of a place, much older than he had supposed from its appearance outside. There were beams across the tops of the walls and the floor was made of stamped earth with here and there a patch of brickwork or the ringed flag marking a well head. The walls seemed to be cluttered and were in darkness and the corners were crowded with junk of all kinds. A petrol engine, stripped and glistening with oil, stood blocked up on one side of the centre area, and inside the main doors there was a clear space just about large enough to take the Lagonda.

The handbag was hidden now, lost in the general mess under the bench. Richard squatted down to find it and drew it out at last. It had been white once but was now thick with dust, yet his first glimpse had been truthful. It was not worn and might have been new when its lining had been torn out. He put it back where he had found it and, rising to his feet, stood breathless in the oppressive atmosphere.

He was frightened. The realisation shook him still more. There was something indescribably awful about the smell of the place, something worse than dirt or vermin or the prickling stink of acid. His own weakness made him angry, but his anger induced an obstinacy which kept him ferreting round the shed, hunting for something, he did not know what. There was sweat on his forehead and damp in his clothes, but he stayed there, looking about for anything which would give him a clearer picture of its owner and a lead on what he was about.

The fact that the shed was lit up and its skylight visible across the dump did not occur to him. If it had, it was improbable that he would have worried. He was not afraid of Gerry. He thought he was a crook and wanted proof of it, but it had not crossed his mind that his crimes might extend beyond theft in some small form.

Gripping the lamp, he went all round the place slowly, picking his way. He found a flight of steps suddenly, all but falling down them as he thrust his way round a pile of old coats hanging against the further wall. They were wide steps, very shallow and bricked in the old way, and they led apparently into a further room which, he decided, must be one of the little nest of brick boxes which he had noticed from the roadway. There was a curtain of tarpaulin over the entrance and the draught whistling round it suggested that the building was almost if not quite roofless. The flex attached to the inspection lamp was only just long enough to reach the entrance and, as Richard pulled aside the waterproof curtain and shone the beam in, he caught a glimpse of red walls streaked with green and the glister of white fungus. He turned the lamp towards the far corner and stood transfixed, his skin crawling.

Two old people sitting close together, mouldering fancy dress hanging from them and their faces strangely wooden and brown, were perched on a plank between two barrels. They did not move. Only the old woman's eyes, which were glassy and bright under a bonnet trimmed with beads, seemed to meet his own.

Richard panicked. The lamp dropped out of his hand and he ran blindly across the shed, stumbled recklessly among the pitfalls, the marble slab, and the wooden boxes, and pitched himself out of the door through which he had first entered into the moonlight.

As the cleaner air enveloped him he pulled up, struggling with himself, very much aware that he must force himself to go back. He was so torn by the conflict that he did not see the two shadows bearing down upon him and the grip on his arms took him by surprise.

"Now then, now then," the time-honoured police warning was warmly human in the nightmare.

"In there..." Richard did not recognise his own voice. "In there. In the cellar by the lamp. Two old people just sitting there."

"Are they, by God?" The voice of Superintendent Charles Luke spoke out of the blackness of a buttressed corner and his top-heavy form, kite-shaped and powerful, went crashing into the shed.

14

Hide My Eyes

"I like this cinema." Annabelle surveyed the dark red and gilt oppressiveness of the Como with frank satisfaction as she waited for the lights to fade for the big picture. "It's like settling down to dream in a great State bed. Flicks are rather like dreams, aren't they?"

Polly did not answer at once. She was getting herself thoroughly comfortable in the seat she liked best, with the plush-covered ledge for her bag and nothing save a misty expanse of air between her and the giant shadows. She was hatless because it was evening, and had achieved a considerable presence without looking particularly smart. Her clothes were of good material, very plainly made, and her kindly face wore the solemn preoccupation of a child's.

"Dreams," she echoed suddenly. "I suppose they are. That's why I like them best without colour. Now listen, my dear, you say you really have heard of that man Mr. Campion before, and that the tale about him is that he is not just a silly ass?" She made no pause between the two subjects and Annabelle was amused.

"That is what they say. Do you know how many times you've asked me that since I first told you—before we started out? Four."

"No. Have I?" Polly dropped her carefully gloved hand over the younger one. "How dreadful! I'm sorry. He worried me, poor chap. He seemed so very unsure of himself."

Annabelle turned to her accusingly. "Darling, you're not as silly as that. You're pretending. You knew that was his act. It's an affectation of his time. Young men invented it in the twenties. But *obviously* he went out of his way to say all that stuff when he was leaving."

116

Polly's frown deepened. "What did he mean? Do you know?"

"No, I don't. I've been wondering." Annabelle had the grace to colour. "It wasn't directed at me, quite, was it? It was about a sale of gloves at a men's shop called Cuppages, and had you bought a pair for anybody as a present? Had you?"

The old woman stiffened. Her nose lengthened and her eyes were frosty.

"I may have done," she said coldly. "I'm often in and out of Cuppages and I enjoy sales. But I don't see what that has to do with anybody else. That's my business, surely."

She was rather alarming in this mood. It was the abrupt cessation of the good will flowing boundlessly from her rather than any manifestation of anger, Annabelle decided.

"He thought you'd say that," she explained defensively. "That was why he wrapped it up like that. I thought he was trying to tell you something without committing himself."

Polly did not speak. Her mouth formed words but she rejected them and the last glimpse the girl had as the lights of the theatre went down was of her strong calm face grown introspective and her blue eyes wide and dark.

Annabelle lost herself in the film. It was a frolic of the new romantic school about unsuspected passion and was delightfully decorated with fancy dress and smooth acting. It held her complete attention and she was several worlds away by the time she returned to the silent figure by her side and saw to her astonishment that Polly's expression had hardly changed. She was still staring straight at the screen as if she was looking through it and her face seemed to have grown older.

The lights distracted her at last and she turned with a start and smiled.

"Did you enjoy it?"

"Yes, I did. It was so pretty, wasn't it? Awfully silly, though. I mean, fancy not facing it."

"Facing it?" The woman seemed appalled. "What made you say that?"

"Because it was all about it." Annabelle began to laugh. "You wicked old thing, you've been to sleep."

"Not really. I was thinking." Polly picked up her bag briskly. "But I think we'd better go now, if you don't mind. We'll go along and see Mrs. Dominique for dinner. While I'm there I want to make a telephone call. You're not tired yet, are you?"

"Gosh no. This is terrific fun, Aunt Polly. You don't know how I love it. I've never done much of it, you see. Who is Mrs. Dominique?"

"Sybylle? Oh, a very old friend of mine. I knew her when we were girls." Polly's voice had warmed again. "She and her husband started this restaurant of theirs, the Grotto, in Adelaide Street, just after the First World War. It's been one of the very best of the Soho places ever since. Freddy and I always went in when we came to London, and long ago she used to come up North and stay with me and bring the children. You'll like her. She's hard because she's had to be, but she's a very clever woman."

"What about Mr. Dominique?" enquired Annabelle, who was taken by the name.

"Adrian? He died, poor fellow, the same year as Freddy. Now she runs the place with her son and his wife, and their son is coming along. They still have most of the old staff, which is amazing, and the cooking is wonderful. You'll like it."

"It sounds terrific." They were in a taxi now and Annabelle's murmur contained a vein of timidity. "Aunt Polly, I don't want to be a beastly expense."

"Well, you're not, girl." Polly was rough in her attempt at reassurance. "I want to see Sybylle. I should have come alone if you hadn't been with me. I often do on a Thursday."

"I wasn't thinking of the restaurant. I meant the taxi." Annabelle was hot-faced in the darkness. "You see, I happen to know you usually take a bus because you mentioned it only this afternoon."

"*I* did?"

"Yes. You told your solicitor you were waiting for a bus in the rain while murders were going on all round you."

"Not murders, dear. Don't say such things."

"But you said it. Your Mr. Phillipson got frightfully prim and said he never read about crime, which was a bit much, I thought, coming from a lawyer. It was silly of him anyhow, because he'd deprived himself of the super-mystery of the two old people who were seen asleep in the bus which must have taken the body away. I wonder what happened in that case," she added brightly. "We ought to have asked Superintendent Luke while we had him in the house. He's on the murder squad."

There was dead silence in the cab.

"How do you know?" The question came huskily at last and Polly coughed to explain it. "He didn't tell me anything like that."

"He wouldn't." Annabelle was blithely confident. "The police never do tell one anything. Even our old bobby at home pretends to be as close as a rock. I happen to know because Jenny knows the man's mother-in-law, and she told her that Prue had married someone big on the murder squad. It's one of those exciting things one does remember."

She paused as the full implication of her revelation sank in.

"I shouldn't worry about him coming to see *you*, though," she added awkwardly. "He may have got moved or anything."

"Oh, good heavens, I'm not worrying." Polly spoke too heartily to deceive anybody. "Here we are. It's just round this corner. I liked the Superintendent, I thought him a very nice man. . . . Don't go talking about him in front of Mrs. Dominique."

The Grotto, which had been a favourite restaurant of two generations of discriminating London eaters, was not very large and not, to look at at any rate, particularly elegant. It possessed that mellow, slightly worn appearance which has nothing to do with shabbiness, and its atmosphere was as warm and private as the dining room in an old-fashioned family house.

Its one long narrow room was dim save for the table lamps and had a very low ceiling and a thickly carpeted floor. The diners sat on upholstered benches arranged round the walls. The narrow tables were shrouded with quantities of coarse white linen, and the service quarters were all at the very far end of the apartment.

In the midst of this further wall there was an open

office doorway and before it, high and grilled, stood a little cash desk where Sybylle Dominique sat as she always had sat, keeping an eye on everything, keeping order, and above all keeping her professional status as a shopkeeper plain to everybody.

She was a very small woman, slight and dark-skinned, with a faint moustache, intelligent eyes, and unnaturally black hair cut close to her head and worn with a fringe. There were several good diamonds on the small hands, which betrayed her age as somewhere nearing seventy, but her black dress was as severe and matronly as Polly's own.

She looked up as they appeared and bowed as formally as if Mrs. Tassie was a recent acquaintance, and went back to her books as the maître scurried forward to greet the newcomers.

It was a much colder welcome than Annabelle had expected, but gradually, as she began to recognise the formality for what it was, the ensuing performance fascinated her and she saw that just as one could take one's hair to a master hairdresser, so presumably did one take one's stomach to a master chef. There was the same earnest solemnity about the preliminary consultation, the same suggestion of ritual and obedience to iron convention.

The fact that everybody concerned knew each other remarkably well made no difference at all. The meal, which was not elaborate, was ordered as though it was a trousseau at least, and it was only after the apéritifs had been served that Polly paused to introduce her niece to the tall sad-eyed maître, who turned out to be Peter Dominique, the son of the owner, who had visited Polly when he was a little boy.

He shook hands, dropping his high priest's or professional manner, and emerged as a charming if slightly browbeaten person who was very anxious to speak of "Uncle Freddy," of whom he had clearly the kindest of memories.

"You will go and talk to Mamma, won't you, Polly?" he said earnestly. "She is a little lonely, you know. She sees everyone and no one. It is a very dull life for her now. All the customers appear to her as children eating. The

parents with whom she was of an age and who were flesh
and blood to her cannot come any more. Will you have
your coffee in the office with her, perhaps?"

"Yes, I will, Peter, please. I'd like that. But first I
must make a telephone call."

"Not before the meal?" He was hurt and shocked and
Annabelle understood that since he was a friend, it mattered.
"See, the soup is here. You can telephone from the office
when you join Mamma."

Polly glanced at the small enamel pocket watch in her
bag.

"It's old Matt. I mustn't ring too late or he'll be in
bed. What about the child? Can I leave her here?"

"Why not?" Mr. Dominique smiled with his sad eyes.
"You feel she may be shy? Shall I find Florian? Would she
care to see him?"

"Oh, is he at home?" Polly's natural enthusiasm escaped her before she remembered how worried she was.
"I thought you were starting him in the kitchens at Aix."

"In a few weeks. At the moment he is downstairs,
very unhappy. I should like you to see him."

"I should love it," she assured him and nodded and
smiled as he drifted away to allow her to enjoy her
consommé.

She drank it as quickly as its heat would permit and
obviously did not taste it at all.

"You won't mind staying here, will you?" she said to
Annabelle, her eyes very blue and anxious as she peered
into the young face. "I want to talk to Sybylle. She's my
oldest woman friend and she's got a very good head.
There's nothing like business to clear the mind. If you live
alone as I do, you can start imagining all sorts of silly
rubbish until you're terrified of your own shadow."

Annabelle's eyes widened appreciatively. "I know you
can. It's always happening in the country. People have
great quarrels and make it up again, all without seeing or
communicating with each other in any way, but I shouldn't
think you had to bother about that, Aunt Polly. You're not
frightened of much, are you?"

Polly shivered. "You be quiet, and eat your *scampi*.
Now that I'm sitting here in this dear old room I do

wonder what I'm fidgeting about. Your uncle and I always had this table and they try to give it to me still whenever I come in. They're a very good family, the Dominiques."

"Is Florian the grandson?"

"Yes. Be nice to him. They're very proud of him. He's just left Chichester, where he did very well."

"The school?"

"Of course. He may be a little grand. They're tremendously wealthy. It spoils a child sometimes."

"What for? The kitchens at Aix?"

"Oh no. He expects that. It's a tradition. Anyhow, don't worry. Just be yourself and you'll be all right."

Annabelle was silent. Since seeing the film, she had felt a little like a puppy which after being a considerable success has suddenly ceased to amuse. Polly was thinking about her no longer. Meanwhile the food was extraordinarily good and the service an art, under Mr. Dominique's personal supervision. The whole thing was a revelation to the girl, a glimpse into a *mystique*.

Polly decided against a sweet for herself and when Annabelle's ice arrived she rose to her feet.

"I think I'll run along now," she said. "I've caught her eye. I'll send for you before we go. Sybylle is certain to want to meet you. She was very fond of Freddy."

She went quickly down the room towards the desk and Annabelle, a trifle forlorn, sat looking after her. She had just time to see Mrs. Dominique climbing carefully down from her perch when a discreet cough at her elbow brought her round to find herself looking up at one of the most typical senior prefects of a British public school that she had ever set eyes on.

Annabelle had some experience and her eyes took in the large solemn youngster and noted his superb self-possession and slightly anxious enquiry about herself with complete understanding. The two regarded each other blankly for a minute as if they had met on a desert island, and then shook hands with open relief.

"You're the niece."

"You're the grandson."

"Oh well, then," he smiled at her, the sun coming out on his face as he passed her with honours, "I mean to say, that's all right, isn't it? Do you mind if I sit down?"

Meanwhile, in the tiny green-walled office behind the cash desk, amid a lifetime's collection of trophies, photographs, and caricatures, Sybylle Dominique stretched up like a kitten on her toes to take her old friend's face between her hands.

"Ah, my Polly, how are you my pet? How good it is to see you. You look like hell, dearest, complete hell. What is the matter, eh? What is it? Come and sit down and tell me all about it."

She had one of those voices which, after tinkling in youth, are apt to crackle in age, but the graces and little affectations of her heyday still hung about her by no means unpleasantly. She had always been a genuine person and her intelligence had survived.

The two elderly women in their good black clothes sat down together on the small settee which fitted neatly into the wall behind the door, and there was a pause while a waiter brought them coffee and little glasses.

"I've been watching you," Mrs. Dominique said. "The girl is quite remarkably beautiful, but are you sure she's twenty-four?"

"Eighteen. It's the sister."

"Oh, but that is no good at all. Polly, what are you thinking of? Eighteen? The child's a liability. They haven't met, I hope?"

"Hardly. She's very sweet, Sybylle, very sensible."

"But much too young." Mrs. Dominique spoke flatly and dismissed the subject. "Have you seen Gerry?"

"Only for a minute or two this morning. He was on his way through London."

"And was he all right?"

"I thought so, dear. How do you mean?"

Mrs. Dominique poured the black coffee into the half cups and dropped a hand on her old friend's knee.

"Why do you want him to marry?" she demanded. "I don't believe in interfering. I thought it over after what you said last time. You like him, Freddy liked him, he's charming and fond of you both in a nice way. You don't know these girls of the brother's family. I should make my will in favour of the person I liked best and forget it. That's my advice."

"Yes." Polly was not listening. She drank her coffee very quickly and put down the cup with a rattle.

The other woman eyed her inquisitively. "You haven't any reason? There isn't anything you haven't told me?"

"No." The lie was suddenly quite apparent and Mrs. Dominique settled back and folded her hands.

"Ah well," she said, "who can judge, eh? Who can advise? Never mind. Now, who have I seen? Practically no one. Old Matt Phillipson came in the other day with a client."

"Yes." Polly interrupted her. "I must telephone him. I want to get hold of him before he goes to bed."

"Plenty of time. He stays at his club until half past eleven these days. He can't sleep like the rest of us. I trust him though, don't you? One of the best. We've both got a lot to be grateful to Matt for. He's looked after us for a few years, my goodness! Kind, too, and always discreet. If you want something awkward done, shout for Matt."

"Sybylle." Polly turned towards her. "Sybylle, do you remember, quite a long time ago, Gerry and me and some gloves?"

Mrs. Dominique sat looking at her, her dark eyes very bright and knowing and her lips smiling.

"Ah," she said, "so that's it, my Polly. He's flown in a temper again, has he? They do, of course. You were lucky in Freddy, dearest. He was a sweet-tempered man, and you had no sons so you don't know. Most of them aren't like that."

"That's right." Polly sounded relieved. Her calm face, which could still look beautiful on occasion, had cleared. "That's right, Gerry was only angry, wasn't he? He'd lost the gloves I'd given him and he was irritated by it. That was all, wasn't it? That really was all?"

Sybylle Dominique allowed a little, grunting, old woman's laugh to escape her.

"Whatever the cause, it was quite a performance," she said. "It nearly put me off the boy for good. Temper! He teetered like a monkey and all about nothing. We were only teasing him, weren't we? Both of us, at the table just outside here, very late. He'd taken you to a show and you had the last two covers to be served. I had mine with you." She broke off, her eyes widening. "It must be years ago. I know he sent me some flowers the next day with a little note and I decided I'd have to forgive him. It shook me, though, because it was so unexpected. He's always been so charming. It was your clipping out of the *News of the World* which upset him."

"I don't remember that." Polly had become obstinately stupid. "I don't remember any more about it than what you've just said."

"Then although you're younger, my memory is better."

The little woman threw herself back on the couch with a crow of amusement.

"I remember you suddenly brought out a terrible police picture of a single glove with an awful stained wrist, which you'd cut out of the paper. You pushed it over to him and said, 'Aren't those like the gloves I gave you?' and he turned on you as if you'd bitten him." She slid a tiny arm through the other woman's own and squeezed her. "It wasn't very tactful, dear," she said, laughing. "It was something a murderer had left behind."

"Oh no, Sybylle, no!" Polly's cry was from the heart. It escaped her involuntarily and the woman beside her set down her glass and wriggled round in her corner so she could look in her face.

"Polly."

"Yes?"

"What's happened, my dear? What is it? Come on, out with it."

"Nothing. Honestly, Sybylle." She was making a great effort, forcing herself to meet the enquiring eyes. "Truly. Well, almost nothing. Just some silly man who appears to be a private detective called and asked me in a roundabout way if I'd ever bought a pair of men's gloves to give away as a present. . . ."

"What did you tell him?"

"Nothing."

"Good." Mrs. Dominique had become the business-woman again, shock-proof and packed with resource. "A *private* detective. That's nearly always divorce. You won't want to get involved in that. Oh, how irritating of Gerry, silly man! He's attractive, you see, and women are quite relentless. Well, never mind, better find out now than later."

She was sitting very upright at the edge of the settee, managing to suggest somehow a miniature black poodle begging.

"Don't worry, dear. Perhaps it's as well. This girl is out of the question because of her age, and it'll give you time to find another, or her to grow a year or so older. Women age faster than men."

"I don't think it was divorce." Polly made the statement and closed her lips. Mrs. Dominique watched her mouth and said, "Oh," flatly, and there was silence for a moment.

"Polly," she began at last, taking a long breath, "this is only an idea. Only something I'd do myself just to be on the right side. I mean, dear, no one would ever dream . . ."

"What are you thinking of?"

Mrs. Dominique hesitated and presently busied herself pouring out cold coffee.

"When one is fond of a son, real, adopted, or step, one has no rules," she began oracularly. "I know that. One forgives. That is all there is to it, and the whole nature of the attachment. That's life. But, dearest, one still ought to *know*. One should take common precautions, both for his sake and for one's own."

"How do you mean?" Polly's blue eyes were suspicious and the other woman put a little arm round her shoulders.

"Dearest, we have both been friendly with this charming boy for ten or twelve years now, and yet what do we really know about him? Nothing that he has not told us himself. Now wait, wait . . ." She held up her free hand imperatively, although Polly had not spoken. "I only want to take that appalling look off your old face, bless you. Why don't you let me find out the facts about him really discreetly, so that no one ever knows an enquiry has been made?"

"Through the trade?"

"No, easier than that. Superintendent Cullingford often comes in here to see Pete. A most charming man. He's Security himself, but these fellows all know one another. If . . ."

"No." Polly was very pale and her eyes were dark again. "No, Sybylle, promise. No. Not a word."

Mrs. Dominique sat looking at her anxiously, true apprehension appearing for the first time on her small face.

"All right, dear," she said, "all right. Now you want to ring up Matt. He's a real true friend, that man. You can trust him. There's the telephone. I shall just be in at the desk."

She went out in her precise dignified way and the portly sommelier, who happened to be passing, hurried himself for the honour of helping her up into her high chair.

Alone in the office, Polly took up the telephone and gave a Hampstead number. After a minute or so a voice answered her and her face cleared.

"Hullo, Mrs. Harper. Is Mr. Phillipson in yet?...Hullo? Hullo, my dear, what is it?...Mrs. Harper, what's the matter? This is Mrs. Tassie...He...*what?*...Oh, where? Where?...In his office tonight?...Shot?...Oh no, *no, no, no!*"

"Polly, hush. My dear, the diners." Peter Dominique, pale and startled, closed the office door hastily and came over to her in time to take the receiver from her hand.

15

Police Machine

The young plain-clothes man, stepping carefully to avoid the gap where floor boards had been removed to be examined for bloodstains by the police laboratory, edged down the little bus toward the two model figures arranged on the front seat and adjusted them slightly.

Mr. Campion, who was standing next to Charlie Luke in the darkness, watching the proceedings, thought he had never seen anything so macabre in his life, yet all the horror was implied and not actual.

The moonlight was still very strong, although it was clouding over in the east, and at this end of the Dump, which was a graveyard of vehicles of all descriptions, with an open space before it where the wall of oil drums had been, the scene was like a deserted battlefield. The black shadows were suggestive and the highlights incongruous.

In the midst of it the shabby, homely little bus stood panting. Its engine was noisy but sound enough and its single interior light made a faint pool of yellow in the black and silver world.

The two figures had been tidied as much as possible and the glimpse of them, which was visible through the looped and fringed curtains of the front window, was unexpectedly convincing. They had been designed and made in the heyday of such models, when time was no object, so that even now when they were practically in pieces they remained extraordinarily lifelike.

The plain-clothes man climbed out again and Luke, who was playing with the coins in his pockets, took a sighing breath. Campion could see his sharp face and crop of shorn curls silhouetted against the floodlit sky. He was taking a considerable chance in backing his hunch and no one knew better than he how dangerous it might be for him.

If the shed should prove to be the innocuous workshop of a reputable man who decided to stand on his rights, and the figures proved to be his innocent property and nothing to do with the bus, then questions very difficult to answer might easily be put not only to the Superintendent but to his superior officers, whose attitude to the Goff's Place mystery had been expressed already.

"Right," Luke said as the plain-clothes man's slim body dissolved into the pool of dark behind the bus. "Now I think we'll have the principal witness, Sergeant."

"Okay, sir. Shan't be a jiffy. He's outside in the car."

The voice in the shadows to their left betrayed a tremor beneath its heartiness. The sergeant was a local man from the Canal Road Station nearby. It had been one of his men who had followed up the chance word from the oil-drum loaders overheard in a public house, and who had made the discovery of the bus itself. The incident had entailed a great deal of work for his office and for a time there had been frustration, when it had appeared as if the Tailor Street Station in the West End, Headquarters of the C.I.D. Division to which the Goff's Place case properly belonged, could not supply the witnesses required. At last two of them had been located—one, mercifully, the all-important waiter whose recollection had been so particularly vivid. Now the test which was to decide if the whole exercise had been a waste of time was about to take place.

"I should have waited for Donne." Luke's confidential murmur buzzed like a whole hive of bees in Mr. Campion's ear. "Have you met him? He is the D.D.C.I. of Tailor Street. You'll like him. Funny vague sort of bloke until you know him, then you see where you made your big mistake— not unlike you, really." He paused. "No offence, of course."

Mr. Campion smiled in the darkness.

"This is his pidgin, I suppose."

"Very much so. Goff's Place is in his manor and he did the original homework, such as it was. Worry, mostly." He laughed softly but still managed to make the sound ferocious. "He'll be along soon but they've just copped in for another showy homicide up there. Some old legal eagle got himself written off in Minton Terrace this afternoon. Donne was in the thick of it when I caught him on the telephone." He cleared his throat and spoke more softly than ever. "But I thought I'd better find out about this particular exercise before old Yeo takes it into his head to blow down here himself."

He turned his head quickly as a murmur of voices reached them from the winding path behind them.

"Now for the witness," he muttered. "Hold your breath." There was a brief moment of quiet, during which the far-off noises of the city became noticeable, and then, from a yard or so behind them, a strong cockney voice, villainously refined, said distinctly:

"Oh yase." Nobody spoke and he repeated it. "Yase. That's them all right and that's the bus. I'd know it anywhere, anywhere I'd know it." The speaker then moved closer, paused, and presently made a remark which in the circumstances was absolutely terrifying. "The old lady's awake now, I see. Of course she was all out, sleeping like a rock, when I see her before, when the bus was in Goff's Place."

"Half a moment, sir." The sergeant's voice, brisk and resourceful, was welcome. Someone had giggled hysterically and Mr. Campion felt for him. He hoped it was not himself. There was a muttered consultation near the bus and presently the young plain-clothes man appeared again, edging his way along it. He moved the head of the figure nearest the window very slightly, so that the eyes were in shadow.

The effect of the manoeuvre was oddly reassuring to most of the audience but the impact on the witness was completely different and much more violent. He swore abruptly and unprintably and in an entirely different accent now that the refinement was absent.

"Now that I did not know," he said at last and his tone would have carried conviction even in the Old Bailey. "That's got me, that 'as, right in the wind. Images! 'Strewth, you wouldn't believe it, would yer?" There was a long pause and he suddenly said "'Ere, what about . . . ?"

The new idea which had presented itself to his mind was apparent to Luke before he expressed it.

"Wait a moment, son," he chipped in hastily. "Don't say anything now about any other occasion on which you may or may not have seen any part of the exhibit. One thing at a time. All we want to know at the moment is if, in your opinion, this is the vehicle you saw in Goff's Place on the date as recorded in your statement. Sergeant, you'll see to this, will you?"

He led Mr. Campion away quickly, picking his way towards the moonlit path which led down through the Dump to the shed.

"He'll remember on his own where else he saw them," he confided in the same sepulchral rumble. "Once we start helping him, we're suspect. Must be. The old girl in Garden Green says she put those figures out. We'll find out what she meant by that tomorrow. She probably paid the dustman to take them away."

"Do you think these are hers?"

"Oh yes, I do." Luke's peaked eyebrows were briefly visible as a shaft of light passed over his face. "I do. I mean to say, they're remarkable. They take people in. There can't be two sets of jokers like that wild in the pack." He hesitated. "She was on the level though, I thought, didn't you? She knew nothing."

Mr. Campion did not commit himself. He was saved from the necessity by the appearance of the local Inspector from the Canal Road Station, a compact bustling man called Kinder, only just above regulation height. He came hurrying through the chequered darkness, his torch beam bobbing on the path before him.

"The first shot is a bull, Inspector," Luke said, and Campion heard the man's grunt of relief.

"An unqualified identification, sir?"

"He seems quietly confident." The Superintendent appeared to echo the mood. "It's in the bag, barring act of God. While we wait for the other witnesses I shall authorise a search of the shed. I'm going down there now."

"Yes, sir." Kinder was far too experienced to criticise. Instead he opened the subject he had come to discuss. "Young Waterfield, Superintendent," he began, "he's made a very full statement and there is only one point in it which isn't entirely satisfactory. His address has been checked and his proofs of identity are all right. He has spent the day with the man who owns the shed, and he's not the type to break in and enter save in the way of friendship, as it were. Do you still feel that we should hold him until this fellow Hawker, or Chad-Horder, turns up?"

"You don't?" Luke's laugh was not lighthearted. "What's the unsatisfactory item in his statement?"

"Nothing very much. I simply felt he wasn't giving us quite the lot. He says he first saw Hawker in a barber's in Edge Street about eleven this morning, but he isn't particularly clear why he went there. It's not the place where he usually gets a haircut. He simply says he found Hawker interesting, but he doesn't say why or why he spent the day with him instead of going to work." He paused. "None of the possible explanations which leap to my mind apply," he added primly. "He's a decent kid from a good and influential sort of home, and my instinct is to let him go. It may be that he's right when he says that he began to think Hawker was a crook who was trying to use him to alibi some job between half past five and six which went wrong. Waterfield may just fancy himself as a detective."

Luke's teeth flashed in the half-light.

"Same like me," he said cheerfully. "All right. Do what you think best, chum. He's all yours. All I want is an eye kept on him so that when I need him I can have him brought in on a dog lead. Have you got the staff for that?"

"I think so, sir."

"Fine." Luke's shrug was not visible in the shadows but both men would have sworn to it. "I'm expecting Chief Inspector Donne from Tailor Street, by the way. I shall be obliged if he could be told to look for me down here in the shed."

"Righto, sir. I'm just going along to the exhibit now but I'll send someone back with the message." Kinder continued towards the bus and Luke and Campion pressed on towards the shed.

"He's quite right, blast him," Luke said presently. "I can't go holding nice little lads from literate families who can write to Members of Parliament just because I've got a hunch I may need 'em. Of course I can't. Who do I think I am, I wonder?" An obstinate grunt escaped him. "I tell you what, though. On the strength of an identification from one bird-headed grillroom hand from a temperance hotel I am going to take this shed apart if it costs me my ticket. There's some discreet homework going on there now."

They walked on to the hollow together and Mr. Campion was struck again by the extraordinarily sinister appearance of the small group of ruined buildings amid the debris, the single skylight window in the tin roof yellow in the moonlight. The door at the back of the shed was still open and as they came in, one of Luke's own men, a sharp-eyed youngster called Sam May, emerged from the shadow round the entrance to the further chamber.

"There's one or two objects of interest about, sir," he began. "Nothing actually actual yet, but a lot of curious stuff. Will you step down here for a minute? Mind the bit of marble as you come."

Luke waited to look down at the slab and the two wooden boxes of bricks beside it.

"What's that all about?" he said to Mr. Campion.

"How to make 'a chic marble-topped coffee table as a surprise for her birthday'?"

"I doubt it." The thin man in the horn-rims touched the edge of the stone with the toe of his narrow shoe. "It's been bedded in, see, with a spot of sand. It suggests to me an experiment of some kind. I don't quite see what."

"There is something experimental down here or I should have my conk seen to," murmured Detective Constable May, who appeared to be enjoying himself. "This way, sir."

He led them through the tarpaulin curtain to the partially roofless cell where the figures had been found. A second Detective Constable, an older man from the Canal Road Station, was waiting for them. He carried a powerful torch of the kind that is mounted on a wire stand and was directing its beam at the solid door of a well head set in the worn bricks of the floor. He looked thoroughly shocked and the area round his eye sockets was pale.

"Evening, sir," he said as Luke appeared. "I've closed this again. It's not very nice."

Luke made no movement towards it. His angular shadow, made giant size by the low-based lamp, towered menacingly above the scene.

"Can you see anything down there at all?"

"Not a lot, sir. It might be crude oil to look at, and Gawd knows how deep it is. It's sludge of some sort, that's certain."

"Huh. Anything else?"

"Nothing conclusive. There are four empty carboys which at one time have contained sulphuric acid, just outside over the wall here. We found two galvanised tanks in the shed itself, and there's a stirrup pump, or the remains of one, among the junk under the workbench."

"You're thinking of the Haigh case."

The detective eyed him woodenly. "Well, it's not unnatural of me, sir, is it? I mean to say, if we've got the bus and the passengers, but we haven't got the money-lender . . . ?"

"Exactly." Luke's grin was savage. "However, don't forget first how long he's been missing, and then that if the forensic boys had waited until the end of the week to do their homework in the Haigh case, even they admit there wouldn't have been any evidence to convict on. I should feel happier if you'd found nothing to indicate that the owner of this shed had ever heard of sulphuric."

"I see, sir."

"Of course, we're not chemists," murmured the optimistic May in the background. "Give those chaps half an hour in here with their bits and bobs and there's no telling what they might be able to find."

Luke turned to Mr. Campion as they stepped back into the shed proper.

"Have you ever heard Yeo on the subject of chemists?" he observed wryly. "He says they're like war weapons. There never was a prosecution chemist born who hadn't got close at hand a defence chemist to cancel him out, and in his opinion the same thing goes for pathologists and trick cyclists. What else have you rooted up, Samuel?"

"Not a lot yet." Constable May, who had followed him out, was regretful. "We've only just scraped the surface. But there's one or two hopeful things about. Take a look at this little fitment on the bench, sir."

He pointed to a block of small drawers in rough oil-stained wood.

"It's a repairing watchmaker's cabinet, I should say. But look what's in it."

He pulled the drawers out one after another and Mr. Campion, who was watching, felt a trickle of cold creep down his spine. Yet there was nothing so very extraordinary to be seen in the dusty six-inch-square containers. It was only that in one particular drawer, instead of the usual gritty miscellany of nuts, staples, rings, washers, screw hooks, and eyelets which filled the rest, there was a collection of other less typical items: a new cheap lipstick in a pale colour, a complete set of studs of ordinary quality, a quantity of steel hairgrips for use on grey hair, a nail file and pair of tweezers combined, a cheap butterfly brooch with the enamel chipped on one wing, a plastic cigarette holder, a key ring with a medallion attached, a penknife with a Masonic emblem etched on it and a dozen or so other worthless trifles, none of which possessed any individuality but which taken together struck a chord in the memory of every man present. As detectives they were all familiar with that most usual of exhibits, the contents of the deceased's pockets or handbag. The pathetic collections are always strangely similar. They consist of little personal items of no interest to anyone but their owners, and, by the time they reach police notice, to no one at all.

Luke stood looking at the drawer, his shoulders drooping. He was moved and angry and also, they saw, when at last he looked up, frustrated.

"Horribly suggestive, but what does any of it prove?" he said savagely. "Damn all."

"There's this, sir." With some of the placid pride of a retriever Sam May produced the remnants of the plastic handbag which Richard had first discovered, and, holding it with a pair of metal tongs, laid it before his boss. Luke shook his dark head regretfully.

"Good multiple-store stuff, son," he said. "Made and sold by the million. Beside, all this is old. It's been sorted and scattered. The chap has had time. What we need now..." He broke off abruptly.

Chief Inspector Henry Donne of Tailor Street, the division which includes the West End of London and is one of the most important, came quietly into the room. Mr. Campion, regarding him with interest through his spectacles, saw with a start what Luke had meant. Donne was one of those loose-boned fair men who in youth look older than their years and in middle age look younger. His face was concave, with a strong chin and a lumpy forehead, but his eyes were smiling and slightly shy between very thick light lashes. He had a record of remarkable successes achieved through sheer application and was reputed to be without nerves of any kind.

He looked at the Superintendent, who as far as this particular investigation was concerned was his immediate superior, and smiled faintly.

"Nice little place you've got here, but unaired," he murmured, but slyly, as if the habit of joke-making was an affectation with him which he hoped would be forgiven. "I hear two witnesses have already identified the bus."

"Two?" Luke was pleased. "I can uncross my fingers. I'll get you to take a look at what we've got, Henry, and then, if you agree, we'll get Pong Wallis down from the labs with a full turnout and let them take the place to pieces. Meanwhile we can concentrate on the man who rents it. I've got a chap waiting for him at his home address now and I see no reason why he shouldn't bring him quietly in. The bloke has no idea that we're on to him."

Donne glanced round the shed again. "What connects the man who owns this outfit with the bus?" he enquired.

"The two figures. They were found here. Oh, I was forgetting, Henry. You don't know Mr. Campion, do you?"

He performed the introduction and the two men shook hands. Campion was faintly dismayed to notice that he was being appraised in the light of a legend and an example encountered in the flesh for the first time.

"What happens if the chemists find nothing conclusive here, Charles?" he demanded in a somewhat hasty attempt to give his new acquaintance something else to think about.

"Then we'll have to do some more homework." Luke was returning to form in a splendid way. The old energy and fierce good humour was pouring back into him. "We've got a very interesting statement from the youngster who spent most of today with the man we're interested in. This boy is under the impression that he was being used as an alibi for a period somewhere between five twenty-five and six this evening. If he's right, the man was up to something about that time in your manor, Henry."

"Mine?"

"Probably. He was based on the Tenniel Hotel and appeared to expect to get there and back in something over fifteen minutes. Can you let us have a full list of likely incidents before the night's out?"

Chief Inspector Donne opened his mouth and closed it again.

"About that time there was a fine drop of homicide going on some four minutes' walk from the Tenniel," he said at last. "On the face of it it doesn't seem very likely that it can connect, but you never know. A van delivery-man walked into a basement office in Minton Terrace, shot dead the old solicitor who opened the door to him, lifted his wallet, and walked back up a flight of stairs to the entrance again. The commissionaire heard the shot but assumed it was the noise made by the box the van man carried falling on to the marble floor. The bloke dropped this box in the front hall as he came in and it went through the old boy's mind then that the noise was unusual and like a shot. My chaps are down there experimenting now. What could one put in a wooden wine case so that the row when it hits a marble floor sounds like a gun?"

The idle question died away in the silent outhouse and his audience, who were looking at him as if he were something out of science fiction, turned as one man and their glances bent towards the washstand top embedded in the sand and the wooden boxes and the bricks beside it.

16
Farewell, My Pretty One

Inspector Kinder of the Canal Road Station was almost as energetic as he was obstinate. He made up his mind that it would be safer not to hold Richard and, having extracted from Luke the permission to release him, he rushed the matter through with the result that the young man was set down at his Chelsea lodgings by an auxiliary police car not equipped with wireless a good fifteen minutes before word came up from the shed that he was needed again. Unfortunately for Kinder, by the time a detective from the Chelsea Division got round to the address young Mr. Waterfield had left the house once more.

It happened very simply. When Richard stepped out of the car it waited at the kerb until he had let himself in with his latchkey and shut the door. He waited on the mat inside until he heard the vehicle move on, and then went down the hall to the alcove where the telephone was kept. The lights were dim down the narrow way and there was no sign of life in the landlady's quarters in the basement, which prepared him for the fact that the instrument proved to be dead. There was a notice on the wall above it, written in a firm feminine hand, explaining the position.

This telephone, which is for the use of Residents Only, will be disconnected at 10:30 every evening. The service will be resumed at 7:30 A.M. Residents are requested to note that incoming messages can NOT be accepted by the caretaker.

Experience had taught Richard that there was no relaxation from this rule and so, after waiting a discreet five minutes to let the police get well on their way, he went quietly out into the street again and walked across the road to the telephone kiosk on the corner. There was no answer from the number he called, but he was not particularly surprised. Annabelle had said specifically that she and her hostess were to eat out after the movie. His aim was to catch her immediately she came in and before she went to bed.

So he strolled on towards the city centre, calling the number from each group of telephone boxes as he met with them.

A coffee-stall keeper obliged him with a pocketful of coppers in anticipation of success, and he spent the whole of the next hour, while the police of two divisions were looking for him, telephoning from kiosk after kiosk and getting his money back every time on the no-reply signal.

It was a long stroll through the deserted late-night streets but he was deeply preoccupied and did not notice it. He was aware he had no hope of persuading Annabelle to do anything she didn't want to do over the telephone, but he fancied that if he could get her to meet him out on the Green again early in the morning, he could put up a very convincing argument and get to his office in reasonable time as well.

It had not been easy to keep all mention of Garden Green out of his statement to the police. They had asked him more than once how he had come to choose Mr. Vick's barber's shop when it was so far from either his lodgings or his work, and he had known at the time that his replies were unconvincing. All the same he had stuck grimly by

his story and was rewarded by the knowledge that so far, at
any rate, Annabelle had not been dragged into anything
"unpleasant."

Richard used the word to himself with a nuance
worthy of his own great-grandfather. Masculine chivalry,
protecting and romantic, out of fashion for forty violent
years, was returning in his generation. He was still not
connecting Gerry with any crime more serious than theft,
for the police had been very reticent, but this to his mind
was quite unattractive enough and he felt very strongly
that Annabelle should be taken right away from it all and
be safely down in the country before this friend of her
relative reaped the trouble which was coming to him.

As the moon sank, the clouds thickened and there
was a promise of rain in the air by the time he reached the
corner of the park. By now he was used to hearing the
telephone bell ringing out in the gay little house which he
recollected so vividly from his glimpse of it in the morning.
The sound of it was a distinctive hollow trill and he could
see in imagination dim quiet rooms and silent furniture
waiting for the newly radiant Annabelle as she came up
the path. He saw her standing aside for a blurred but
vaguely unattractive old lady to fit her key in the lock, and
then hurrying forward as the telephone summons greeted
her.

The only fault with this picture was that it did not
materialise. When he reached Park Lane and turned into
the first telephone kiosk the signal he received after
dialling the familiar number was not the unanswered
ringing tone but the continuous whine which indicates
that the line is out of order. This was so unexpected that
he dialled it again and finally got hold of the operator.

The impersonal voice was courteous but firm. It did
not care how often he had rung or how recently, it
explained with patient coldness: the number was now
unobtainable, not because the line was engaged nor yet
because someone had wedged the receiver to prevent the
bell ringing, but because some definite fault had developed
since he last called and the address could no longer be
reached by telephone.

The news was irrevocable and worrying. Richard came
out of the box, frowning. Before him the wide road ran on

beside the Park towards Marble Arch, Edgware Road, Edge Street and finally the Barrow Road. He scarcely hesitated but set off grimly down the pavement.

About the same time, on the other side of central London, Madame Dominique and her son Peter were saying goodnight to Polly on the steps of their private entrance to the Grotto, a few yards down the small alley which bounded the back of the building. Annabelle had already reached the main street and was waiting on the corner with Florian, who was still in attendance. They were both delighted with themselves and their laughter was softly audible to the little group in the doorway.

Sybylle Dominique was holding Polly's sleeve. She looked minute standing between her tall son and the other more motherly figure.

"Don't worry more than you can help. Take something rather than lie awake," she was murmuring urgently, her feather-weight strength concentrated in an effort to comfort her old friend. "That housekeeper of Matt's didn't know a thing. The police hadn't told her, they don't."

Polly looked down at her. Her face was only just visible in the grey light and the skin showed taut over the fine bold bones.

"They'd have let her know if it had been suicide or accident," she said bluntly.

Sybylle Dominique drew a long uneven breath.

"Oh, Polly," she said softly, "oh, Polly."

"Goodnight."

The two elderly faces met and the soft cheeks touched.

"I don't *know* anything, Sybylle." Polly's words came painfully. "You understand, dear, don't you? I'm upset, but it's really only because I'm thinking about poor old Matt. Don't let me put . . . anything else into your head, will you?"

"Of course not, my girl, of course not." The tiny crackling voice was full of pity. "Gerry . . ."

"What about Gerry?" Terror flared in Polly's tone, but the whisper was very low.

Sybylle's grip on her sleeve tightened.

"There's *some* good in that boy or you couldn't love him, dearest," she said. "That's a law of God and Nature and none of us here will forget it. I'll give you a ring in the morning, my dear. Now off you go with that staggeringly beautiful child of yours, before my poor little Flo drops on his knees in the gutter. Poor little beasts, isn't it frightful what they've got to find out before they come to the end of *that* story?"

She was talking to ease the tension and Polly put her arms round her, big handbag and all.

"You're a dear, Sybbie, you always were. Goodnight, love. God bless."

Annabelle and Polly caught the last number fifteen bus of the evening from the bottom of Regent Street. Florian escorted them to the stopping place and stood looking after the vanishing red monster bearing them away. The old woman led the girl up the stairs to the deserted top deck and along to the front seat, but Annabelle paused to wave to him, sending him home ecstatically happy.

The girl was shiny-eyed and delighted with herself. It had been a honey of an evening. Alone, grown up at last, and with someone new and city-bred to impress. She turned to Polly as soon as she sat down, concentrating on her for the first time since the meal, eager to thank her and to confide.

"Aunt Polly," she said seriously, "do you know this has been probably the most wonderful evening of my whole life."

Polly, who had been staring down the curving street picked out in lights, heard the words as if they were far off and utterly meaningless. Her bleak eyes took in the glow on the young face and closed before its unbearable fatuousness.

"Oh, darling, aren't you well?" There was disappointment in the girl's cry as well as compassion, and Polly was stung to life by it.

"I'm tired, that's all. You had a good evening, did you?" She settled herself on the jolting seat, tucking her heavy black skirts about her, folding her hands over her bag, and raising her elbows so that the girl could slip her hand through the crook in her arm to steady herself. "Flo seems to have turned out well," she ploughed on. "He was pompous as a small boy."

"Was he? That's all gone now. I liked him. He's awfully sensible but terribly young in years." Annabelle was inclined to sigh over it. "Richard really is more the right age, against mine I mean."

"Richard." Polly remembered the name with a sigh of relief. "That's the pocket-sized tough with the red hair?"

"Did I say tough?" Annabelle was dubious. "He is, of course, but there's nothing rough about him. He's formal, if anything. You'll approve, I think. But look, Auntie, what's interesting me at the moment is this. Florian says he can get Fellows tickets to the Zoo on Sundays and he knows all the keepers. I could go with him one day, couldn't I? Apparently there's a ginger pig there who's exactly like Robinson Tariat, the playwright. Florian says it's rather the thing at the moment to go and see it and give it . . ."

"Annabelle, I want to talk to you." Polly was aware of being brutal. "That is why we've come back by bus. I'm sorry, my dear, but you've got to go home."

There was complete silence for a while and then the girl said, "Oh. Oh, I see."

It was only too obvious that she did no such thing. Her lovely face wore a mask of blank dismay and her round eyes were full of tears already. Polly regarded her helplessly.

"I'm sorry," she repeated.

"Oh, it's all right. . . . Is it because I'm too young, or have I done something?"

"Neither. Circumstances have altered, that's all."

"Oh." There was another long pause and the girl sat up, drawing her hand away and stiffening. "I only enjoyed the good time because it was given to me," she remarked presently. "I didn't *need* it. I mean I hope you'll let me come and see you anyhow—sometimes."

"No." Polly winced at the stare of bewilderment and took hold of herself irritably. "No, dear, I don't want you to. That's what I'm trying to tell you. I want you to go home first thing tomorrow morning and to put your whole trip up here right out of your mind. I want you to forget that I ever wrote to your mother or that you ever came to see me. I shall give you a note to take to your sister. I don't want her or you to answer it, or ever to try to see me again. I don't suppose you'll want to, but anyway I'd rather you didn't. Is that absolutely clear?"

"Not *ever*?"

"Not ever. Don't make it sound like that, child. Don't be absurd. It's best. In fact you'll find it's vital."

"But what have I done?"

"Nothing at all. Nothing at all. It's entirely my affair. Nothing to do with you at all. You're out of it. Now forget it until we get home. Did you have a nice dinner?"

"You know I did, you had it with me. Oh, don't treat me like a child. What is it? What's happened? Can't I help you?"

"No. Be quiet."

"But you thought I could and said so in the letter. That was why you wanted me. Has it changed?"

"Yes."

"Could it change again?"

"No."

"Are you sure?"

Polly was silent. She seemed to be considering the question, or facing it perhaps.

Annabelle was watching every variation in her expression.

"Oh, I thought it was going to be wonderful," she burst out in a sudden abandonment of childhood's grief. "Can't I come back ever? Are you sure, Aunt Polly? Are you sure?"

The old woman turned her head. Her mind was shuttering.

"Quite sure, dear," she said and was suddenly calm. "Quite sure. Now let's forget it and enjoy the ride home. London's very lovely at night."

"I shall hate it always after this."

"No, don't say that." Polly was speaking absently and she patted the hand on the tweed-covered knee.

Annabelle turned on her like an infant. Angry tears flooded her eyes.

"Won't you miss me?" she burst out. "Won't you miss the fun we would have had? Don't I remind you of Uncle Frederick? Don't you want a good daughter to keep you young?"

"Hush," said Polly. "Hush. Look, that's Selfridge's..."

They left the bus on the corner of the Barrow Road and went slowly up to the house. The old woman walked heavily and her shoulders were a little bent, but she was occupied and kept sane by the necessity of managing and comforting the child.

"Now when we get in," she said, "I want you to go up to my sitting room, light the gas fire, and pull the curtains, and wait for me."

"What are you going to do?"

"I'm going to my desk for a minute to drop a note to Jennifer. Then I shall heat some milk and bring it up with me, and as we drink it I'll tell you what I want you to do. I want you to be off very early tomorrow. Could you get up at six?"

"Of course I could and I expect there's a train, but..."

"No buts. Just do what I say. I'll give you the note for Jenny tonight. Get up as early as you can and come down to the kitchen and I'll give you a cup of tea and you can be off before the char arrives. Oh, and Annabelle, I don't want you to buy a paper until you get home."

The girl looked at her sharply but she did not ask questions.

"Very well," she said.

The house looked pretty and bright even by the light of the old-fashioned street lamp outside the gate. Polly unlocked the front door and turned on the light.

"Now you run up."

"Let me get the milk."

"You can if you like. You'll find everything in the kitchen. Or are you frightened to go down there alone in the dark?"

"No. It's not that sort of house, is it? It's so gay and feels so full of people, even when no one's here. I do love it so." Annabelle's young voice was uncertain but she controlled it with a valiance none the worse for being conscious. "I'll take the milk straight up."

She went off down the two or three steps to the kitchen and Polly turned into the tiny room on the right of the hall door, which was practically filled by an old-fashioned roll-top desk with a telephone on it. It had been the front parlour in the days when the house had been a

Victorian cottage and was now used by Polly as the office to which she had become used when keeping an hotel. She opened the desk, sat down at it, and pulled a sheet of paper towards her.

My dear Jenny—the familiar sprawling hand spread over the page—*I am sending this to you instead of to A because you will know how it is best for her to spend it. Training for something, or on Savings Certificates. However, whatever is done, she must have a real say in it so it is made out to her, as you will see, I enclose a smaller one for you, dear, as a wedding present. See you both cash them at once and do not mention them to anyone, except your Bank Manager of course. As A. will tell you, and I expect you will see for yourself, this is goodbye. I cannot have either of you mixed up in anything not your business. I am sure you are a nice family and I wish I could have known you all, but there it is. I do not want any thanks for the cheques and no letters or messages of any kind to come to this house. If any newspaper should get on to you at any time—unlikely but you never know—simply say clearly that you have never seen me in your life and keep A. well out of the way.*

> *My love to you both,*
> *Polly Tassie*

P.S. Take care of A. She is almost too pretty just now, but it will wear off later, I expect. When I die there may be a little bit more for her, but not much, as I am about to incur some very heavy expenses. God bless you all.

She read the note through, took a cheque book out of her bag, and made out a draft to Annabelle for a thousand pounds and another to Jennifer for one hundred. She took time to scan them carefully and check the date with the calendar. Then she folded them into the letter and addressed the envelope to "Miss J. Tassie. By Hand."

She had put the envelope into her pocket and was rising to shut up the desk when she heard Annabelle pass the door and go upstairs, and at the same time her glance fell on the small steel box on the wall into which the telephone cable disappeared. It was a chance in a thousand that she should have noticed it because of an occasional chair standing just in front of it, but some faint change in the arrangement of the piece of furniture had caught her attention. She leant forward to touch the plaited flex with an exploring finger. The cable, which had been wrenched from the box and replaced loosely, came away in her hand. For an instant she looked at it stupidly and then, turning abruptly, sped out of the room and up the stairs with the agility of a woman half her age. As she reached the landing she heard Annabelle's laugh. It was shy but gay and innocently flattered.

The colour had gone from Mrs. Tassie's lips but there was no surprise in her expression by the time she had opened the door and come face to face with the man who had been waiting for her in the bright little room.

Gerry was standing on the hearthrug, staring at the girl, the expression of horrified incredulity which had made her laugh still showing in his face. He looked grey and excited. But the thing about him which startled the old woman was that he was without jacket or waistcoat, and the sleeves of his city shirt were rolled up.

As his glance turned slowly towards her, the sound of the front-door buzzer came floating up from the hall, two sharp and determined rings.

17

Hard Behind Him

Charlie Luke sat on the edge of the desk in a small private office off the main C.I.D. room in the new Tailor Street station, looking more like a black cat than ever as he listened to the telephone. His head was held on one side and his eyes were deeply pleased.

The voice at the other end of the wire belonged to his immediate superior, Chief Superintendent Yeo. It was blunt, as usual, but sounded content for a change and even conciliatory.

"A party from the lab is on its way down to Canal Road now and the preliminary report on the bus is positive, so I expect Mr. Oates to call a conference later in the night," he was saying, referring to the Assistant Commissioner Crime and conferring an accolade on the investigation at the same time. "For Pete's sake, keep in touch. Have you picked up your star witness again yet? Kinder needs his head examined for turning him loose."

"Waterfield? No, not yet. But I don't expect any trouble. We shall see him again any time now. Meanwhile Kinder did a very thorough job on him. His statement is full of good things."

"I know. I've got a copy here. By the way, Charlie."

"Yes?" Luke pricked up his ears. The use of the diminutive was a healthy sign.

"I've been taking a look at your chart of that pet district of yours." Yeo was apologising and was being short about it. "I'm inclined to change my mind. In fact, while I was looking at it I had a hunch myself."

"What was that?" Luke bent over backwards to avoid any unfortunate note of satisfaction.

"Well," the old man's grin was almost audible, "you remember the Kent car dealer?"

"Joseph Pound, found in a chalk pit, pocket case picked up by children in Garden Green."

"That's the man. As soon as I read Waterfield's statement something in it rang a bell and I turned up the widow's deposition." Yeo was proud of his memory, which was indeed remarkable. "Chad-Horner was the name of one of the holiday swells she and her husband were drinking with in Folkestone the night before the crime."

"Get away!" Luke's exclamation of delighted surprise was unquestionably genuine.

"Fact." Yeo was expanding. "Here it is on the desk before me. By sticking to your guns you've come up with something very interesting, my boy. I shall be happier when I hear you've got your man for questioning, but don't let anyone forget that if by chance you're right in including the Church Row case, you'll be dealing with a man who has shot his way out once and may do so again. Don't let anybody take risks. We're understaffed as it is."

"Quite," Luke said slowly. "I don't know if that particular guess is going to stick. Mr. Campion had an idea about it but . . ."

"Ah, Campion." Old Yeo had the grace to sound guilty. "I had a word with him this afternoon. He was coming up to see you. I don't know if he did."

"Oh yes, he's been with me ever since." Any note of reproach was gratifyingly absent. "He's sloped off now, I don't know where. He muttered something and next time I looked, there he wasn't."

"That's Albert." Yeo was amused. "He'll be back. He doesn't miss much. You'll find he's had an idea and trotted off to test it. Well, good luck to you. I still think you're asking too much if you try to link *all* those cases of yours. You haven't a ha'porth of solid evidence in one of them yet. Concentrate on the most promising and scrap the rest. Those people Lettice and Reginald Fisher, who may or may not have gone off to South Africa, for instance, I shouldn't waste any more time on them."

"Perhaps you're right, Guv'nor, but I've picked up one little thing that reminded me of them. Do you remember that in that enquiry the niece said that she had sent her aunt a white plastic handbag?"

"Was it a distinctive sort of a bag?"

"No, a chain-store product."

"Then I certainly shouldn't worry about it. You've got more than enough on your plate. I suppose Donne is concentrating on the Minton Terrace shooting? That's your best bet. Has he struck anything yet?"

"Nothing conclusive, but it's all very healthy. Donne has a girl friend of Chad-Horder's with him now. She's a woman called Edna Cater who runs the Midget Club."

"I know. Just round the back there. Well, she was handy to the crime. But all these cases without any real evidence are very tricky. I won't keep you any longer. Mention to Donne that what we most need are details of any further aliases. There's nothing on the files under Chad-Horder and nothing relevant under Hawker, but a chap like that could have half a dozen names, and there's always a chance that he's been shopped under one of them."

He hung up and Luke ducked his blue chin into his neck and grinned to himself as he heard the wire clear. Then, gathering up his folder, he went into the next office where Chief Inspector Donne, attended by a clerk and a sergeant, was interviewing Edna.

She was seated in the tub chair before the desk, her back straight and her suit and hairdo as crisp and formal as if she were in uniform. Luke shot a single glance at her and decided that he knew the type. It was not a bad one but in his experience seldom as hard as it assumed it was. She was trying hard, he thought. She looked scared but was determined to keep the party sweet.

Donne was putting her through it steadily, leaning towards her across the desk, his watchful eyes never leaving her face.

"About those oil drums which Chad-Horder described as making a wall to hide a racing car," he began abruptly as he heard Luke come in. "Do you remember if he gave you any picture of them? Did he say what colour they were?"

"I think he said they were black." She looked bewildered. "I doubt if they ever existed. I don't think that this boy Richard who was with him, and who made this long statement to you, understood Gerry at all. Gerry was romancing. He didn't even expect to be believed."

"I see. He's a liar, is he?"

"I'm not saying that," she said. "He embroiders things to make them more amusing, that's all." She was appealing to him to understand her, the suppliance in her eyes looking extraordinary amid the make-up. "You must know the sort of man I mean—charming, moneyed, good family..."

"Good family? Do you know his family?"

"No, I told you just now I don't know any of his people, although I've known him nearly five years. I don't even know if he has any. He keeps all the private side of his life very quiet. Some people do."

"Why say good family, then?"

"Because it's obvious. He's easy, assured, generous, attractive."

"*You* find him attractive?"

"Yes, I'm very fond of him."

Donne turned to Luke, who took the vacant chair beside him at the desk. The dark man with his powerful body and shrewd cockney eyes was very masculine and his approach was straight man to woman, with very little of the policeman.

"You still feel like that, even after the walkout on you this afternoon?" he enquired.

She shrugged her shoulders. "I can take it. I was just so pleased to see him. He hadn't been in for a couple of months."

"What do you think about him at this minute?"

"I think he's in a jam and I'm prepared to do anything I can for him."

"Do you know why we want him?"

"I can guess."

"Can you?" He was surprised. "Let's have it. We won't hold it over you."

"I don't care if you do." Her smile took the offence out of the retort. "I think that Warren Torrenden, the racing motorist, has made a charge against him. Something about a car or spare parts for one. I don't know what it is so I can't judge, but if I were you I'd make sure that I listened to the most reliable one of the two."

Luke did not speak but sat looking at her inquisitively, as if he could not make up his mind.

"Yes," he said at last, "yes, well, I hope we're not going to upset you, Miss Cater. Have you ever seen this before?"

He had taken up a brown-paper packet from the desk and now removed the wrappings to reveal the remains of the white handbag which he had brought from the Dump. She glanced at it idly and at first he thought that she was going to shake her head. But suddenly something about the ragged fold of plastic caught her attention and she put out her hand. She did not take the exhibit but turned it over on the desk and ran a strong white forefinger over a series of small flaws on the lower edge at the front.

"I'm not sure," she said at last, eyeing them cautiously as if she feared a trap. "Is it the one that was in the cottage at Bray that Mr. Chad-Horder rented? It was some time ago, you know, over two years."

"Is that the cottage that was mentioned in the conversation Waterfield overheard this afternoon?"

"It is." The colour was dark in her face. "A client of Mr. Chad-Horder's and his wife had been living there, waiting to go abroad. There were several of their things strewn about. I think this bag was one of them. Now I suppose they've come back years later complaining because everything they left behind wasn't sent on? It's extraordinary how people do make demands on comparative strangers."

Her voice had risen indignantly and Luke sat eyeing her.

"What makes you think it's the bag you saw at the cottage?"

"Those needle holes in the plastic." She nodded towards the white fold of material. "When I first saw it there were two gilt initials just there. Someone had tried to stitch them instead of sticking them on and they were hanging by a couple of threads. I thought they'd get lost so I cut them off and put them in the bag for safety. Gerry said he was going to send everything out to them."

"What were the initials?"

"One was an L and the other was an F, I think."

"How can you remember after all that time?"

Her slate-gray eyes with the darker edge round the irises met his own resentfully.

"Well . . . it was another woman who had stayed in the house."

Luke returned to the notes on the desk. "Fair enough," he said. "Did you ever hear her name?"

"No. Gerry wouldn't tell me. That's why I remembered the initials, I suppose."

Chief Inspector Donne cleared his throat.

"Was the bag in this condition when you saw it at the cottage?"

"No, the lining was in it then and it was ready for use. I didn't examine it, but there was a handkerchief in it and

a compact, I think, and—oh—one or two ordinary things."
The thick cream skin of her forehead had wrinkled and he
bent across the desk towards her.

"What are you remembering?"

She looked up and smiled in a startled way. "I was
remembering that I thought it rather—rather *poor*," she
said frankly.

"Not smart?"

"No, not that. Just poor. Poor for a client's wife."

There was a pause. Luke dropped his hand on Donne's
wrist and the other man nodded, and his pencil traced a
phrase on the blotter. *"Gal hasn't a clue."*

Edna took advantage of the pause to collect herself.

"Of course, it could only be carelessness on his part,"
she announced. "You do recognise that, I hope? Gerry
wouldn't steal a handbag. He's not that sort of person.
That's ridiculous. Wait until you meet him."

Luke did not look at her. "How does he make his
living?"

"I can't tell you exactly." She conveyed that she could
make a very good guess. "I told you he never discusses his
affairs. I should say he does a bit of car dealing, tunes up
racing cars for other people, and has a private income."
There was a faint primness, an old-maidish satisfaction on
the last word which stood out like a visible flaw on her
hard façade of sophistication.

The two policemen eyed her as if they could actually
see her feet leaving the ground.

"Is he sometimes much more flush with money than
at others?" Donne suggested.

"That's true of everybody but it's particularly so of
him. Sometimes he's—oh—quite absurdly over-generous
and extravagant."

"Are these intervals regular?"

"How? O, I see. No, I don't think it's when the
dividends come in. It's when the deals go through, I
fancy."

Luke sighed. He had a kindly disposition.

"At the time of the cottage at Bray, was that one of the
flush periods?"

"I'll say it was." She looked suddenly gay and
mischievous. "I hadn't seen him for ages, and then he

came in saying times had been fearful but that he'd got something cooking up. When I saw him again it had all gone through. The client had sailed earlier than expected and Gerry had got the cottage on his hands. That's one thing about him, he doesn't worry you with his worries. We had a wonderful time. There was money to burn for a bit."

Luke rose slowly to his feet and stood looking down at her. His face was sombre but not unkind.

"Did you ever wonder what kind of a deal it was?" he said slowly. "Money to burn. Did he get that from commission on a deal with a man whose wife had a cheap plastic handbag, with initials which she tried to stitch on herself?"

There was silence and the atmosphere of the little office was unpleasantly noticeable. The woman sat watching the Superintendent with that particular look on her face which indicates that a half-thought question has been dragged out into the open.

"What do you mean?" There was no bravado there, no defiance, only the simple query. "What are you saying?"

"How much did he get from them? If it was a lot, was it all they had?"

"But it couldn't have been. They were going away by sea and..."

"Did they go? The woman left her handbag."

They were unprepared for her sudden movement. She struggled up out of her chair and stood breathing heavily, as if she found it difficult.

"Do you mean... like Haigh?"

"What makes you say that?" Luke had crossed round from the desk and was holding her arm as if he feared she might fall. "Why did you say 'Haigh'?"

"I didn't. I... Oh, it couldn't be! Oh, my God."

Luke lowered her gently into the chair and put a cigarette in her mouth, which he lit.

"Now come on," he said, "be a good girl and clear your mind. We shan't involve you if we can help it but you must do all you can. Come on, what made you say 'Haigh'?"

She pushed her hand through her hair, ruffling the hard shell into untidiness.

"Haigh was the man who—who put—who got rid of—who bought . . . acid. . . ."

"Forget the acid." Luke was talking firmly and gently as if to a child. "Haigh was the soft-spoken friendly little crook who went the one stage further. Most crooks will take anything and everything from their victims, except the one final item. Haigh was the chap who thought that one final refinement was silly."

"Don't!" The word was a suppressed scream and she sat looking at him wildly. "That's what Gerry said. That was his word."

"Silly? About Haigh?"

She nodded, her eyes growing darker and her mouth pallid round the edges of the lipstick.

"We were discussing him one night and I said the man must have been mad, and Gerry said no, he was merely not silly, and that if he hadn't lost his nerve and confessed he'd be alive today still picking up a good living in a logical . . . Oh no, don't take any notice of me, I don't know anything."

"I should tell us anything you do." Donne made the recommendation sound friendly. "We shall get to know the whole story in the end and we're clumsy beggars. We make less mess if we're helped. Unless you still want to try to shield him, of course."

"Shield . . ." She spoke the word as if she had never heard it before. "Oh no, I couldn't. I couldn't. Not if it's that."

Her voice ceased abruptly and she sat staring ahead of her, all traces of charm and femininity in her face giving place to the stark practicalness of a human being confronted by the reality of self-preservation.

"You'd better look out if you take him," she said. "He was carrying a gun this afternoon. I felt it when he kissed me."

Donne glanced sharply at Luke and the thumb of his right hand turned upwards. When he returned to Edna he was very gentle.

"We shall want a statement, Miss Cater," he said, "but take your time. I should just sit here quietly and have a cup of tea if I were you. Then you can tell the sergeant the whole story and he'll read it over to you before you sign it." He smiled reassuringly at her stricken face.

"Don't worry too much. We shall be as discreet as we can. We don't go out of our way to make life difficult for anybody with a job to hold down."

Luke said nothing and indeed had no chance to do so, for at that moment a Detective Constable slipped quietly into the room and spoke with his back turned carefully towards the witness.

"Will you come outside, sir?" he murmured. "They've picked up the Lagonda."

18

It Occurred to Mr. Campion

Mr. Vick had installed his telephone in a small pantry at the back of the barber's shop, choosing it, no doubt, because his butterfly mind had noted that it was about the same size as a public booth. Since the cupboard was also used to store certain unguents and as a hide for the charwoman's equipment, it was not entirely satisfactory.

The uniformed Inspector making an interim report to his headquarters was forced to stand with one foot in a pail and his eyes on a level with rows of bottles of hair restorer, an expedient irritating to any man as bald as he.

"To return to the subject of the car. A Lagonda, details as previously stated," he was saying carefully. "It is drawn up outside the shop here, as given in my preliminary message. The boot is unlocked and is empty. There are, however, eight bricks... What?... Oh, they're red and they're old. Just ordinary bricks. Eight bricks which are arranged as wedges behind the tyres of the car. The road slopes. Have you got that?"

He listened while the paragraph was read back to him, and continued.

"There are a number of wooden boxes of varying size in the near vicinity. In this street it is the custom of shopkeepers to put their refuse out on the pavement at night and, amongst heaven knows how much other junk, there are several crates. The refuse is collected in the early morning... You'll send a couple of chaps?... Okay." He sighed. "The barber lives in a two-room flat above the shop," he went on. "I shall bring him in as soon as he's in a reasonable condition. At the moment he's upstairs, drunk as a lord, and my blokes are working on him. He has no idea how long he has been home, full stop."

There was an aggrieved query from the other end of the line and he relaxed.

"Sorry, Jack, but I'm clearing my own mind. I've got a story out of the man but it's no sort of statement. Either he's more than ordinarily plastered or he's a damned funny little man when sober. He says the car belongs to his dear old friend Major Chad-Horder, whose real name he doesn't know although he can take me to a man in a pub who does, and they've been to see Moggie Moorhen together and have been on the stage with him all the evening. Check that please. They appear to have returned home tight and I understand that the Major put his friend to bed and made up another for himself in the sitting room. After that point he seems to have vanished. There's a rug and pillows on the couch but they're not warm. There is no sign of him in the house and the front door is unlocked, so he must have gone out again, presumably on foot. Have you got that? Right, that's all for now. I'll report again. Goodbye."

He hung up and his message, when it was re-dressed in official language and flashed to Tailor Street, presented a single idea to Superintendent Luke's experienced ear.

"Hullo," he said, swinging round on Donne as they stood together in a corner of the C.I.D. room under the illuminated street map of the district, "did you hear that? The suspect is rigging up another alibi."

The Chief Inspector's eyes opened wide for an instant between their thick light lashes.

"Busy chap, isn't he?" he said absently as his mind fastened on the suggestion and weighed it. "He could be ditching the gun," he began.

"Why should he? He doesn't know he's coming unstuck, unless he's psychic." Luke spoke with savage satisfaction.

"Anyhow, wherever he's gone, it would appear that he intends to come back, so our chaps can just sit by the hole and watch like pussy. Tell them softly, softly. The Chief Superintendent is very anxious that we don't put any further temptation in his way. As he points out, the recruiting figures are down."

As Donne stepped aside to give the necessary orders, Luke remained alone looking at the map. The barber's shop in the side road off Edge Street had been ringed with a crimson marker and he could see at a glance just where it stood in relation to the Garden Green area, down in the adjoining division.

It was not in the same manor but it was on the way there and as he stood tracing the streets which crossed and re-crossed in little loops and squares without pattern or shape, he felt the thrill of catching wind of the enemy and he began to play with the coins in his pocket so that they made a music of mounting excitement.

When Donne returned he was still standing there, his neck looking very long and his head thrust forward. The Chief Inspector returned looking faintly embarrassed.

"That woman is coming out with the lot," he observed. "Goodness knows how much of it will be relevant but she's holding nothing back. I don't think she can know much of value because she had no idea what he was up to, but the shock has certainly loosened her tongue."

Luke turned to him. "Is she vindictive?"

"No. It's awful. She's dependent on him physically and suddenly finds..." He left the rest of the sentence in the air and Luke returned to the map.

"Little to depend upon," he said primly. "Poor wretched bitch. We're trying to comfort her with cups of tea, I suppose. Where the blazes has that chap *gone*, Henry? There's a whole section of his activities we haven't touched, you know. We've only got half the picture. Where's Campion?"

"There's no sign of him yet. He's a funny chap, isn't he? More like himself than one expects, somehow."

Luke made no comment. He was frowning.

"Campion wasn't altogether satisfied with the old lady and the pretty girl at the cockeyed museum," he said presently. "I was. I may be hiding my eyes but I just

cannot see either of them involved in anything of this sort.
We could go and rout them out of bed and ask them a lot
of damned silly questions which ought to wait at least until
the waiter has remembered where he saw the old couple
the first time." He hesitated. "No, I don't think so," he
said, answering his own question, "I don't."

"You took a fancy to them, did you?" said Donne,
unaware of trespassing. "Funny how one does sometimes.
Hullo, see who this is?"

Luke glanced up as a splendid figure strolled towards
them.

"Wot'cher, Cully," he said, "how's the Ambassador?"

Superintendent Cullingford was one of those stolidly
handsome men who appear to be the rule in Security. He
and Luke were old friends and each amused himself by
pretending that the other's was the glamorous job.

"Hullo, Charles, you're in the thick of it, I see."
Cullingford managed to sound wistful. "When I stepped
out of the lift on this floor I thought there was a fire, there
was so much excitement." He nodded to Donne and
stroked a magnificent yellow moustache. "Luke still finds
it absorbing even though he can't hang 'em any more."

His friend's dark face became a shade blacker.

"That's not a very popular line of talk, Cully," he was
beginning when Donne ventured to reply for himself.

"We'll hang the chap we're after now all right," he
said.

"Think so?" Luke sounded spiteful. "At the moment
I'm wondering if we've got enough evidence to bring him
to trial."

"It's murder, is it?" Cullingford made the enquiry as a
civility.

"It's about ten murders," Luke said, lowering at him.
"The bloke is lost in a snowdrift of suspicion, but snow has
a way of melting at the Old Bailey. If under the new
regulations we've got to see him sentenced twice before
he's eligible he may well escape topping. I can't see the
public standing for two trials for murder, first conviction
no hanging, the second it's laid on."

"You don't like the new legislation?"

Luke began to get angry. "I neither like it nor dislike
it," he said testily. "Once I've delivered the man to the

court, I reckon my business is done. I'm the dog. I bring in the bird. I don't expect to have to cook him."

"Oh, what a very interesting point of view." Cullingford had some of the manner of the eminent dignitaries whose safety was his care. "Should I be an impossible nuisance if I bothered you now with the little matter which has brought me up here looking for you? It won't take a moment. I telephoned your own office and they told me where you were. It concerns an old crime but I thought perhaps I should pass it on."

He was being long-winded deliberately and there was the ghost of a twinkle in the back of his eyes. Luke, who was aware he was being ragged, produced a packet of cigarettes.

"Try one of these, your Excellency," he suggested. "They won't hurt your throat. Just bung it up solid, I hope. Get on with it, you pompous old police officer, while we're still kicking our heels waiting for a witness."

"Very well. Have you ever heard"—Cullingford split the question to light his cigarette—"of the Church Row shooting? It happened some time ago I believe, and concerned a silk-stocking salesman who lost a glove." He paused and looked round to find both men staring at him with fixed expressionless interest. "I don't bore you, I hope?"

"Not yet. What do you know about that case?"

"Nothing at all. But about twenty minutes ago a very charming friend of mine—you must know her, the delightful old lady whose family runs the Grotto—told me over the telephone a very curious little story concerning the glove in that case. She thought nothing of it at the time but tonight something else happened which sent her into quite a panic. By the way, I've sworn to keep the family out of it."

"All right, if they're not involved already." Luke was not particularly gracious. "Get on with the something else that happened tonight."

"Well, that's another shooting. In Minton Terrace this time. A solicitor was killed, I'd rather assumed that you would know about it. Don't you?"

"Not quite as much as we'd like." Luke spoke cautiously. He was regarding Cullingford with a sort of superstitious awe. "Does this woman you know link those two cases?"

"Yes, she does. She has no proof, of course, but she was sufficiently frightened to get her son to telephone me tonight. As I understand it, she has an old friend who . . ."

Luke groaned aloud. "Oh, these old friends," he said wearily. "I thought for one blessed moment that you'd come staggering in with a genuine bone. The friend thinks she may have purchased the gloves, I suppose, and the friend never could make up her mind if the gloves which she gave as a present to someone or other (who afterwards turned out to be a disappointment) were the gloves in the murder mystery. And now when this new crime occurs the friend . . ."

"All right, Luke." Cullingford was frankly huffy. "You know much more about this sort of case than I do. It's hardly my province. I merely pass the story on because I thought it might be of use to you. But if it's a commonplace reaction . . ."

"Sorry, cock, I'm hungry. Takes me that way." Luke was contrite. "Sit down and I'll take the information in a decent copperlike fashion. Name and address of your friend, please."

"Mrs. Sybylle Dominique, the Grotto Restaurant, W. 1."

"Thank you, sir. And the name of her friend?"

Superintendent Cullingford was on the point of replying when he was interrupted by a clerk who came hurrying up to Luke.

"Mr. Albert Campion is on the telephone, sir. He'd like to speak to you direct if possible."

The dark man sprang off the desk and thrust his pencil at Donne.

"Henry, do this, will you? I've been waiting all night for Campion."

Donne did not reply. He was looking doubtfully at the Security man and Luke, after following his glance, took himself in hand abruptly.

"That's right," he said, "that's right, Henry. You take Campion's message. Now, Cully. Sorry for the interruption. What is the name of your friend's friend?"

Cullingford took his time. Presently he looked up from the neat pocket diary which he was studying.

"Her name is Mrs. Polly Tassie," he said slowly. "That is spelled T-a-s-s-i-e. The address is Number Seven, Garden Green. I don't know if you've ever heard of it. It's an obscure little district just off the Barrow Road."

Luke was still staring at him with his lips apart when Donne came back from the telephone in the adjacent cubicle. He stepped over to Luke and his discreet murmur was blurred by excitement.

"The old man is on to something. He says to tell you that he remembered that the bobby in the Barrow Road hospital spoke of seeing *two* people in Garden Green this morning. It occurred to him, he says, that if one of them had been Waterfield the inference might be interesting, so he slid off to the hospital and got a description. It tallies. He's now in Edge Street in a call box and he asks that someone should meet him there." He paused and his slow grin spread over his face. "I think his wish should be granted. He says Richard Waterfield has just walked up to the front door of a house you know of, Number Seven, Garden Green. Do you recognise the address? It means nothing to me."

19

Preparation for an Accident

In the upstairs sitting room of the house in Garden Green, whose gay colours seemed cold and unnaturally bright in the hard light, there was a period of complete silence after the front-door bell had ceased to ring. Polly, who was just inside the door, stood frozen, her chin up and her eyes fixed on the man on the rug.

Annabelle was still holding the tray and the flowered beakers upon it, the light burrowing into the depths of her hair, making the pale brown gold.

Gerry was listening. All the suppressed fire of the morning had gone out of him. His skin was grey and smudged and the hollows round his eyes and beside his temples were black-shadowed.

"Who's that, Polly?"

He spoke very quietly and the girl, aware that something was amiss but completely underestimating it, set down the tray with a rattle.

"I'll go."

"No." The others spoke together and the man kept his eyes on the old woman.

"Who is it? Have you any idea at all?"

The bell rang again, less aggressively this time, a single long-drawn buzz, and Polly's face cleared.

"Oh, it's Miss Rich," she said. "That's about it, Miss Rich, my old neighbour from down the road. She's come for her magazine. She must have seen my light in the office just now."

"Would she come as late as this?" His question was enquiry, not argument, and unconsciously her voice grew soothing as she reassured him.

"Later, I'm afraid, if she saw I was up. Old people are owls, you know. I get this paper on Wednesdays, you see, and by Thursday she expects me to have read it." Her relief was completely convincing and the other old woman became as real to them as if they could see her standing on the doorstep huddling a coat about her.

Polly was looking for the magazine and found it where she expected, under the sofa cushions. It was a thin but gay little folder with a dog and a baby on the cover, and she took it up and went back across the room with it.

"I remembered it this afternoon when I saw she'd left me a bit of water cress on the kitchen sill," she said, "but it slipped my mind again. Poor girl, she can't sleep."

"Don't let her in." He made it a warning and her eyes turned towards him again.

"No, of course not. I'll say I'm tired. If I shut this door and you keep quiet she won't know anyone's here. It's only if she thinks I have visitors and I'm going to be up anyhow that she insists on coming in for a chat. I'll just slip this out to her and come straight back."

She went out and as the door closed behind her, the

patent draught excluder upon it slid into its copper rim and shut the room away, secret and silent at the back of the house.

Polly moved quickly. She was very frightened and the single flight of stairs leading down to the front hall made her breathless, so that her voice sounded unsteady and alarmed as she tugged back the bolts.

"Don't ring again, Ellie. I've got it here, dear."

She swung the door open at last. "I was just off to bed.... Who is it?"

The final phrase was whispered as she caught sight of Richard's neat round head silhouetted against the street-lit arch of the porch.

"I'm sorry to disturb you, but could I possibly see Annabelle?" The demand came out in a shamefaced murmur. He had made the journey in the spirit of mingled anxiety and knight-errantry, but now, at the moment of arrival, he felt suddenly silly and embarrassed.

"Who are you?" She was still whispering and he noticed her glance nervously behind her.

"My name is Waterfield. I . . ."

"I remember." She opened the door a little wider to let the light from the hallway fall upon his hair, so that she might see its colour.

He blushed at the recognition and started again.

"I've known Annabelle all her life. I wouldn't have come round so late if the telephone hadn't suddenly got disconnected. I rang until . . ."

"Hush." Polly came out into the porch, pulling the door nearly closed behind her. "I've got no time," she said earnestly. "I don't want to explain but I can't let you in."

"I do want to see her," he said quickly.

"Yes." She was agreeing with him. "Yes, I was thinking. Could you put Annabelle on a train for me?"

"Tonight?"

"As soon as possible. I want her to be at home by the morning. If I got her out, could you do the rest?"

"Of course." She was aware of him staring at her suspiciously, but her hand was trembling on the latch and her ears were strained to catch the least sound from the sitting room. "The moment I can get her to go up to bed I'll send her down by the fire escape."

As a statement it was idiotic, but he caught the note of urgency.

"Where is that?" He was whispering too.

"Just here." She indicated the side of the house opposite to the museum. "You'll have to climb over or go right round to the other street. Wait at the foot of the stairs and I'll send her down the instant I can. I'm very grateful to you. God knows what I'd have done without you. I daren't wait now, dear. Hurry. Goodnight."

The door was closing behind her when she thrust it open again.

"You won't make a noise, will you? That's vital." She paused and he understood that she was struggling with a confidence. Suddenly out it came. "Tell them that whatever they do they're not to rush the house."

This time the door shut firmly behind her.

Richard came out of the porch thoroughly alarmed. Whatever he had expected of Annabelle's aunt it was not this. Obviously something was terribly wrong in the house and his suspicion that Gerry might have gone there had deepened into a certainty. However, his only real concern was Annabelle's safety and it was with relief that he had recognised a fellow feeling in Polly. He turned to the right across the front garden.

The rain was threatening again rather than coming down in earnest and a gusty, fidgety wind had sprung up, plucking the last of the leaves from the plane trees and ruffling the shrubs in front of the house. The street was deserted and the houses opposite dark.

He found the fire escape at once. It was a spiderweb of iron, festooning the blank side of the building nearest its left-hand neighbour. He could not reach it immediately because the entrance, which had evidently been there before the museum lot had been added to the property, was now bricked up, leaving him with a wall to circumnavigate. It was nine or ten feet high, hung with the evergreen variety of honeysuckle, slightly wet and abominably dirty, so he went out into the street and down to the museum door. As he feared, it was bolted and he had to come back to the wall.

As he swarmed up the creeper, it occurred to him that the return journey with Annabelle was not going to be easy, but he decided to meet that difficulty when he came to it, and presently swung his legs over into the narrow cul-de-sac to drop quietly to the gravel below.

Meanwhile Polly had her foot on the staircase before she recollected the magazine still in her hand. She hurried into the office with it, thrust it out of sight in a drawer in the desk, and was back in the hall just in time.

The door at the top of the stairs had opened abruptly and the angle of light appearing, gibbet-shaped and vivid in the gloom, made her jump.

"Is that you, Aunt Polly?" Her silhouetted form looking stiff in Jenny's tailored coat, Annabelle appeared, looking down at her. She was clutching her beaker of milk and hesitated uncertainly. "I thought I'd go to bed, if you don't mind. I'm rather tired."

She was frightened. Polly was as aware of it as if the child had stood there screaming her head off, and she came toiling up the stairs to her.

"A very good idea," she said as she arrived panting. "Wait a minute. Here's the note for your sister in case I forget it in the morning. Take great care of it and give it to her with my love." She noticed with relieved astonishment that her voice was quite normal. It sounded friendly and assured, and the breathlessness of course was due to the exertion. "I'll just see you up to your room."

"Oh no, please don't." The objection was frankly vigorous. "I know where it is. You showed me this afternoon."

"But I'd like to."

"Oh, cut it out, Polly." Gerry was exasperated. He was out of sight in the bright room, behind the angle of the door, but yet very close to them, only a few feet away. "Come and get me a drink and let the kid go to bed if she wants to."

"I'm coming, dear. I just want to scribble down an address on this note while I think of it. I shan't be a minute." As she was speaking she had taken the envelope for Jenny out of her coat pocket and now produced a stub of pencil from the handbag on her arm. She turned to the ledge which ran across the shallow recess at the foot of the second flight of stairs and began to write on it while the girl lingered unwillingly beside her.

> *Go out by fire escape. Landing window.*
> *Richard is down there. Keep quiet.*

"There," she said briskly, "can you read my writing?"

"Polly, for God's sake." There was an impatient movement in the room and the woman thrust the letter into the girl's hand and moved so that she was between her and the door. He did not come out, however, and Annabelle glanced at the message. Polly saw the expression change on her round face and caught her quick upward glance and nod of relieved comprehension; then she turned and went up the staircase like an arrow. Just before she disappeared into the greyness she remembered and looked back.

It was the last Polly saw of her, the pathetically grateful smile and nervous little wave of affection and goodbye.

"Goodnight," she called after her. "God bless." She turned away and went into the sitting room. "What was that about?" she demanded.

He wasted no time by pretending not to understand her.

"Stiff-necked little beast," he said. "I asked her what the hell she was doing here and she took offense. She says she's one of Freddy's brother's family, is that right?"

"Yes. Do you mind?" She was taking off her coat and he came over automatically and received it from her and threw it over a chair in the corner.

"No," he said mildly. "She took me by surprise, that was all."

The old woman's eyes followed her wrap. His own trench coat lay beneath it but there was no sign of his jacket and at the moment, so far as she could see, there was no place on him where a gun could hide.

"It was you I came to see," he went on. "You're very late. You went to the Grotto, she told me. How's the family?"

"Oh, all right, dear. Very well. Just as they always are."

They were neither of them aware of what was being said. Each was absorbed by tremendous and separate preoccupations.

Polly was listening for any betraying sound from upstairs,

and in that she was the more fortunate. Gerry had not the advantage of an interest outside himself. There was, so far as he knew, nothing between him and the project he had in mind. No danger. No need to hurry. The whole night was before him. The shadow on his face had deepened. He looked dirty with strain.

"I'll get us both a drink," he said suddenly and made a movement.

"No." Polly stepped between him and the door. "I'm going to have my milk. If you want anything I'll get it in a minute. How did you get into the house? I never gave you a key."

The sudden belligerence was unlike her and it astonished him. He took a step backwards and stood looking at her gravely.

"I've had one a long time," he said. "I thought you knew."

Polly went over to her chair and sat down heavily.

"When you had that set cut for me last year you bought another, I suppose?"

"I bought a second front-door key, yes. I thought it might be useful some time. And it was. I've been waiting for you for over an hour." He paused. "Wandering about the house, you know."

She nodded. It was a strange resigned gesture, which again was something he had not envisaged. She was leaning back against the chintz shell as high as her head and he saw her face as if he had never seen it before. It was such a harmless kindly old face. Not at all clever, but mild and peacefully beautiful in repose. He looked away hastily and there was silence between them until he forced his smile back and his eyes looked like a sorry ape's again. He was strangely loth to hurry and he began to coax her as he had done so often before.

"Sorry, old lady, it never occurred to me that you would mind. You don't really, do you? It was a damned silly thing to do but I knew you and Freddy so well that I suppose I thought I had some sort of right."

"Yes," she said, still in the same flat resigned sort of way which was making him uneasy, "we've been very close, we three. We loved you like a son, Gerry, and you loved us." She folded her hands with a gesture of finality.

"And we still do," she said, "and nothing can be done about that. Well, now then, run along and fetch yourself what you want from the dining room. Nothing for me. I shall drink that milk."

The man stood eyeing her. She had frightened him for a moment, but she seemed relaxed and unsuspicious and even, when she glanced at the little china clock among the figures on the chimney piece, relieved, as if some anxiety had been resolved.

He pushed the unformed question behind him and gave his attention to practical problems. The nightcap waiting already brewed was not in his programme.

"Very well," he said soothingly, "just as you like. I'll take this stuff down and bring you some fresh. It's gone cold and disgusting."

"Oh no!" She was horrified. "Don't you go and take my last pint. It's all I've got for the kid's breakfast in the morning."

"Then I'll reheat this," he insisted firmly. "Stay where you are and don't be so ruddy obstinate."

He went off with the tray, leaving the door swinging. Polly waited until she heard the familiar creak of the dining-room step and then rose quietly to her feet and crept across the room to the chair where the coats lay. Her hands were clumsy in her nervousness as she fumbled with the pockets, and when at last she found and drew out the heavy gun, it hung awkwardly from fingers which trembled. The problem of where to hide it seemed to overwhelm her. It was so much bigger than she had expected and infinitely more terrible to look at. She realised that it was most horribly unsafe and every line in her body conveyed her fear and distaste. With deep relief her glance fell on the big Meissen tureen, a mass of gilt and little coloured views, which stood in the china cabinet beside the window. Her own mother had always hidden things there and she remembered it from her childhood as secreting a long line of treasures.

It took her hardly a moment to unlatch the glass doors, lift the ornate lid, and slide the heavy thing out of sight. Then, shutting the cabinet, she was turning away when she saw that the window curtains were swaying. The discovery that the casement was open, and that therefore any sound the young people might have made by the fire escape just round the corner of the house could easily have been audible in the room, drew a net of nervous pain over her face.

She was bolting the window when Gerry came back and set the tray down on the table again. Besides the beaker there was a glass of scotch and soda upon it, but although he had removed the skin from the top of the milk she suspected he had not taken the time to heat it again, despite all his protestations. Something had happened to upset him. She could see it in his face.

"What are you doing?" he demanded. "Opening the window?"

"No. Shutting it. It's cold."

"Shall I light the fire for you?"

"If you do we mustn't close the door." She stood over him while he put a match to the gas. "Last time the gasman called he warned me it was dangerous. Those things I had put in here stop the draught completely and the fire can go out."

"I know. You told me." He did not look up and his tone was casual. "There," he said, "that's all right. Sit down in your chair and I'll bring you your drink. Polly, that boiler of yours in the kitchen, does it go out easily?"

"Not unless one tried to burn rubbish in it. It's no good for that." She had been in the act of resuming her seat in the shell-backed chair while he was still kneeling on the rug, so that she was looking down at him. Her face was close to his when the significance of her own words occurred to her. She drew slowly away, down, down, further back into the upholstery. *"You've been trying to burn your jacket. There was blood on it."*

The voice was not like her own at all. A hideous quality of panic had dried it into a whisper.

The man sat back on his heels, looking at her, and a strange dark blush spread over his face, more revealing than any change of expression could have been.

"What the hell are you talking about?"

It was bluster and she put up a hand to stop him.

"Don't, dear, don't. I tried to ring up Matt tonight. I know."

He remained where he was, kneeling before her

chair, and there was a moment of indecision, fleeting to him but to her as deliberate as a film in slow motion, while he chose the line to take. Finally he took her hand.

"You're making a silly mistake, old girl," he said. "You don't know what you're talking about and nor do I. I don't know Matt, do I?"

She sat forward and looked into his face to see if he was lying. It was a manoeuvre of the nursery and he met her stare with eyes which just then were like an animal's without the spark behind them.

"When you look like that, there's no one there," she said, "but that's not true always. Sometimes when I look into your face, Gerry, I can still see the lively boy that old Freddy and I were so fond of."

"That's right, Polly, while you love me I'm alive and kicking." He sat back on his heels once more. He was deeply relieved and was laughing, but the strange dark colour had not entirely faded from his face. "When you look in my eyes, darling," he said, "d'you know what you see? You see yourself. You're the life in me."

"No, I don't." She spoke with sudden vigour. "I see *you*, my boy. There's not much that's for ever in you, Gerry, but there's still a man there and not a snake, please God. I'm afraid, though, terribly afraid. Gerry, I know about the gloves. That glove we saw in the paper was your glove, one of the pair I gave you. You shot those people in Church Row."

It was his own turn to shrink away. The dull, orange blush returned, but this time he did not bother to make denials.

"If you knew, you connived, you approved," he said, and added, since even to his own ears the accusation sounded absurd, "you hid your eyes. You're like that. You deceive yourself very easily. You keep all that crashing junk of Freddy's because you think it must be wonderful, since he collected it, yet you know perfectly well that it's vulgar, tasteless, and a bore. Anything goes if it's done by someone you're fond of, that's your creed."

"That isn't true. You're changing the subject. You're trying to muddle me. Oh, Gerry, *they're going to catch you.*"

He cocked an eye at her. "They won't, you know."

Now that she was reacting as he had thought she might if ever she discovered him, he dropped his attack. He appeared completely confident. "I'm careful. I'm like a good racing driver. I never take a risk. I've got no ties and no rules. I'm so safe it's boring."

She sat listening to him, horrified and absorbed. It was as though, on looking at last at the Gorgon's head, it had indeed turned her to stone. She was dead to the gay room, to the fleeing children, to the blessed ordinary programme of sleeping and waking, lost in a single dreadful effort to comprehend.

"But it was Matt threatening to prosecute that scared you. And in Church Row you shot because you were frightened. All you did, you did in panic, Gerry." She was appealing to him in the teeth of her own intelligence to make the mitigating claim.

He sat on the rug frowning, as if he found the recollection shadowy.

"Church Row was the beginning," he said at last. "That was the start. That didn't count. The others were different."

"What others? Gerry . . . there hasn't been another besides poor Matt?"

"What? No, of course not. There hasn't been any, ever." He was laughing at her, treating her as he had done a thousand times before over less important issues. "You are inventing all this. This is in *your* mind." He was thrashing about, turning this way and that. "It's hysteria, old dear. Dreams." He paused suspiciously, warned by her expression. "What have you remembered, Polly?"

"Listen." She was struggling to control her breathing. "A Superintendent of police came here today."

"Oh. What did he want?" He spoke lightly and she found his assumed casualness terrifying.

"Nothing, as it happened. He was disappointed, I saw it. Some witness was confused about where he had seen two wax figures before and the local police thought he might have noticed them in our museum."

"Did you tell him I'd taken them?"

"No. He wasn't very interested in what had happened to them. All he wanted to know was if they had ever existed. If I know the police, they'll be sending the witness along to see if the place recalls anything to him."

Gerry sat looking at the fire, his eyes round and without expression, his lips parted slightly.

"A chance in eight million," he said softly. "Tenacious clots, aren't they? It won't help them. I may have to alter things down there a bit to stop argument, but even if I didn't, they couldn't prove a thing."

Polly did not speak at once. She was huddled in her chair, where she seemed to have shrunk as her suspicions became relentless certainty. Only her blue eyes were still very bright.

"That night when it rained you sent me the taxi," she said at last. "I knew that in my heart. And when I got the postcard telling me quite unnecessarily that you were somewhere else that night, I was even more certain. But I wouldn't, I couldn't believe it. That country bus with the old wax figures in it to stop questions, that was the sort of idea *you'd* have, Gerry. I thought that when I first read it, but I shut my eyes to it. I sat here and prayed to Jesus that I was getting a bit touched, living alone imagining nonsense."

He put a hand on her arm and shook it, not without kindness.

"You ruddy silly old thing," he said softly. "Why don't you shut up?"

She did not answer him and after a while he went on. He spoke very reasonably and in an intimate conversational way, as if he were making a business confidence.

"I'm in no danger at all, Polly. There's never any need to worry about me. You see, I'm careful and I'm thorough always, every moment of the time. I keep my feet on the ground and my eyes open and I never forget a possibility. I've never needed an alibi, yet I've always had one, you know. Besides, I have no sentiment to make me shrink from any move when the need arises. Even if a miracle happened and the police came to suspect me, they'd never prove anything. I clear up as I go."

Polly rubbed her hands over her face as if to brush away cobwebs.

"But to *kill*," she whispered. "To *murder*, Gerry."

He scowled and scrambled to his feet. He was red and irritable.

"That's a damned silly term. Murder is a word, a

shibboleth. People get killed every day and sometimes it's called murder and sometimes it isn't. Sometimes it's war and sometimes it's accident, sometimes it's... well, it's just the logical conclusion of a sequence of events. You're trying to make something metaphysical of it, setting it up as the one unforgivable crime. That's hocus-pocus. If you're prepared to strip everything else from a man, why not finish the job logically and take his life? You're going to sit there and tell me God wouldn't like it, I suppose. Is that it?"

Polly struggled to sit up in her chair and there was a flash of the old authority in her eyes when she faced him.

"I don't know about God," she said, "but I can tell you one thing. It's *men* who won't have murder. God's first commandment doesn't concern murder, but it's the first crime in man's law all right. If a man is a man with a spirit, and not a poor beast who hasn't one, he won't put up with murder even *if he's a murderer himself*. Men who murder turn against themselves and commit suicide by giving themselves away. They don't want to, but they can't help it. It's in the make-up, born there. You said you were finding it boring. That's the beginning."

"For God's sake, Polly, be quiet, and don't talk such cracking rot."

"I can't. *Murder will out*, Gerry. *That's what it means*." There was a moment of stillness after the words, like the silence after a thunderclap. The terrifying idea took the man by surprise and he escaped into anger. He swung away from her with an effort which contracted the muscles at the sides of his temples and drove the blood out of his face.

"It's time for these," he announced, turning to the drinks on the table. "I've also learnt to keep my temper, old girl. That's lesson A. No anger, no feeling, nothing to get in the way."

He handed her the beaker, which was on a saucer, and frowned as he saw that some of the milk had spilled over.

"Sorry about that," he said. "The old hand isn't as steady as it ought to be. Drink up. I put some whisky in it."

Polly took the beaker obediently, her glance resting

on his face. He looked older than she had ever seen him,
she thought, the lines deeper, the muscles more pronounced.
There was sweat standing out on his forehead and she was
relieved to see it, despite her sense of paralysed dismay.
She comforted herself; at least he was alive to it all, still
there.

She sipped the milk and made a face, but drank it
down as if it were medicine.

"You shouldn't have done that. It's filthy," she said
absently. "The kid must have put sugar in as well, or salt
or something, and the whisky makes it worse. Look,
Gerry, I've been thinking. Whether you like to believe it
or not, sooner or later we're going to need money for the
lawyers. They won't all be like poor old Matt. They'll have
to be paid. Well, I've got it, and when you need it both
Freddy and I would never hesitate..."

He made a gesture of blind exasperation, but she
persisted.

"Don't look like that, dear. We've got to face things.
I'm telling you this because I want you to know I'll see you
through, so don't do anything barmy like trying to run for
it, or... or... thinking you can do again what you did at
Church Row. You can't shoot your way out all the time."

She sat looking at him, the empty beaker on her
knee. She was mild and gentle and kindly, and her affection for him transfigured her face. He remained staring at
her, an extraordinary conflict growing in his eyes, part
apprehension, part eagerness, part passionate despair.

"You'd have given me away," he burst out at last,
dropping on the rug before her, putting his arms round
her, and peering into her face. "Admit it. You couldn't have
helped it. You and the kid between you, you're like glass.
You can't hide a thing. Can you? Can you?"

Polly closed her eyes tightly and opened them again.
An expression of childlike astonishment had appeared on
her face.

"I can't see you properly," she said. "It's funny. I
feel... Oh, Gerry! *The milk*. What have you done? What
is it? The chloral? It was still in the chest."

"Darling, it's all right, it's all right. Don't be frightened.
It's only a little. Only enough to put you out."

He was agonised, weeping even, suffocated by the

relentless compulsion. Polly looked very earnestly and stupidly into his face, so close to her own.

"I . . . am the last thing you love," she said thickly, struggling with the drug as its waves broke over her. "If . . . you . . . kill me, Gerry, you will lose contact with . . . your kind. There'll be nothing . . . to keep you alive. You'll wither like a leaf off a tree."

20

Betrayal

Annabelle came quickly down the fire escape in the rain, her cautious feet making no sound on the wet iron. Richard saw her white face in the darkness and heard her sigh as her hand touched his shoulder. She let herself drop gratefully into the arms he held up for her, and returned his squeeze with a wholeheartedness which warmed him with a glow to last a lifetime.

"What happened?" He was whispering but she made a warning movement and he seized her bag with one hand and, putting his other arm round her shoulders, led her round the back of the house under the single lighted window. In the few minutes he had been waiting he had explored the position and had discovered that, as he had feared, to return the way he had come was going to be impossible. However, the narrow path led through an archway into the adjoining plot where the museum stood, and he suspected that apart from the entrance to the collection there was a second way out through the gardens to the other road at the back of the houses.

By now it was raining hard in the city way, which to Annabelle's country ears was extraordinarily noisy, the water drumming on the roofs and gurgling in pipes and gullies. They could just see the path, white in the gloom, as it ran round beside the kitchen door just below the little passageway which led from the house to the collection. Then it followed the museum buildings, presumably right round to the entrance.

As they came round the arch and huddled under the wall, he bent closer to her.

"Was Gerry there?"

"Yes. Waiting for us when we got in. What do you know about him?"

"Not enough. What happened?"

"I don't know. He was just furious to see me. I thought he was going to kill me."

Richard grunted. "I don't think it's quite as sensational as that."

"I do." Annabelle's practical young voice quivered. "Aunt Polly was petrified about something. Richard, I think we ought to tell the police."

"No, we won't do that." His smile was wry. "I've had one little chat with the police about being on enclosed premises tonight. I don't think we'll risk another. No, you stand in this doorway and try and keep out of the wet, and I'll go and see if there's a back gate to this place."

He left her standing in the shallow porch of the side door to the museum, the one through which Gerry had come that morning to turn off the "Crossing the Barr" mechanism for her. As she leaned back against it, getting more and more wet, it occurred to her that she did not remember Polly locking this door when they had gone round fastening up together after Superintendent Luke and Mr. Campion had left.

She tried the handle cautiously and was rewarded by a waft of warm camphory air as the door slid open. She remained just inside, waiting for Richard.

He came at last and stepped in gratefully beside her. His face was glistening with water and there was a cape of damp on his shoulders.

"Thank goodness for this," he said softly. "We'll have to wait for a bit, I'm afraid. The whole blessed place appears to be surrounded by police. There's a carload just under the wall in front here and at least two bobbies are hanging about in a sort of alley which leads from this to the other back gardens."

He could not see her but he felt her shiver in the dark.

"Are they after that man?"

"I expect so. We'd better keep absolutely quiet in here until the hullabaloo is over, and then I promised I'd put you straight on a train."

"What will they do? Rush the place?"

He did not answer. Polly's final injunction had returned to him.

"What are you worrying about?" Annabelle was removing her coat. "I should take off yours, if I were you. If we're not to be caught and questioned, there's no reason why we should get cold. How just like Aunt Polly. She knew it was going to happen and wanted to keep me out of it, I suppose."

"That's the important thing." Richard seemed to have made up his mind. "We'll shut this door and lie low. They must know he's here, mustn't they?"

"Of course they do." Annabelle had seated herself on the edge of the centre dais. "Otherwise they wouldn't be here, would they? Come over and wait. Would you care to sit in an elephant or a giraffe?"

While the two were settling themselves, on the opposite side of the road, in a bed-sitting room in one of the unrestored houses a little lower down the street, Mr. Campion, Superintendent Luke, and Detective Sergeant Picot from the Barrow Road station, in whose division they were now operating, were listening to Miss Rich. This was Polly's old neighbour whom she had expected to find when she went down to the door to answer Richard's ring.

The bed-sitting room was on the ground floor directly beside the entrance and its large window was separated from the pavement by the deep chasm of the basement area. It had just emerged that Miss Rich was in the habit of deriving what light she needed during the night from the street lamp outside.

"I sit here in the dark looking out of the window and listening to the radio." The educated voice with the depreciating laugh in it came to them out of the shadows. "If you'd like to draw the curtains I'll turn on the light, but you'll see much better what I mean if you'll pick your way over here and stand behind me."

She had been a schoolmistress. The tone was unmistakable and they obeyed it, stumbling across the cluttered room to find her, a thin figure in a dark gown lying on a high couch which had been arranged very carefully beside the window.

"There, you see," she said with some pride. "I can see all the houses on that side of the road, the pillar box on the corner, and just a little tiny scrap of Edge Street itself. There is Number Seven, that's the wall by the dining-room window, and that's where I saw the man get over, as I told the constable."

"Yes, I see, ma'am." Luke was bending down behind the couch to share her angle of vision, and Mr. Campion, whose eyes were unusually good in the dark, was able to save a wavering column of books, boxes, and what he strongly suspected to be dirty plates as he stumbled against them.

"Put everything on the floor," said Miss Rich over her shoulder. "I have a woman once a week who cleans me right up. Then I start again. Now this young man, who was a stranger to me as I told you, walked up to the house soon after Mrs. Tassie and a girl, who I think is her niece, came in. He spent five minutes in the porch, where of course I couldn't see him, and then to my astonishment he came hurrying out and actually climbed over the wall. Had I had a telephone I should have used it. But I haven't. I know nobody I wish to ring up, so I spare myself that expense."

She paused reflectively.

"I might have shouted, I suppose. However, I didn't. No one in this house is very helpful. I knew Mrs. Tassie had a man over there to protect her, and a great schoolgirl who would probably have done something if necessary, so I waited a few moments when to my relief a constable came by. I rapped on the window and, as you already know, he stopped and I went out to the door and spoke to him. Well, I haven't seen your men go in yet, Superintendent."

"No, ma'am, you haven't." Luke could be as bland as she was. "It's the man who was waiting in the house as

Mrs. Tassie came in, he is the fellow we are interested in. Do you know what time he arrived?"

"Jeremy Hawker? You're interested in him, are you? Oh." Her face was in the shadow but each man could have sworn he saw thin lips folding tightly after the final word.

"Do you know him, ma'am?"

"I've met him." She considered and presently glanced to where Mr. Campion stood in the shadow. "I don't want to convey more than I mean," she began, indicating that while he probably knew what she was talking about, the police might not. "I have nothing against the man, and Mrs. Tassie is very fond of him, but if I had not known he was there then I think I should have put a coat over my dressing gown and gone across in the rain to warn her. I do go in sometimes at night in case she's lonely, but since he was there I didn't see why I should bother."

It was to Mr. Campion's credit that he did understand.

"Perhaps he takes up a great deal of your friend's time and thought?" he ventured.

"The woman thinks as much of him as if he were her own." The pleasant voice invited them to marvel. "And as far as I can see he's very seldom there and only gives her a lot of worry. I grant you he has a pleasant way with him and is a little more sophisticated than she thinks he is, silly idiot. . . . She's the salt of the earth. No one is too much trouble for her. No intellect, but a long-suffering heart . . ." Miss Rich broke off, leaving the sentence in the air. "Anyhow," she said suddenly, "she's the only person I've ever met who could put up with *me*! She's very fond of me. She buys and lends me the most horrible magazine every week. I pretend to read it to please her."

Luke cleared his throat. "At what time did Hawker arrive at Number Seven, ma'am? Did you happen to notice?"

"I did. I was listening to the symphony concert. It must have been about half past ten. He came up the road on foot, which is unusual. As a rule he has a large smelly car which he leaves about in front of other people's houses. He walked straight into the porch and did not come out again, so he has a key. I often suspected it. He was moving round the rooms after that until they came in."

"How . . . ? Oh, you saw the lights go on and off, I suppose."

"Of course. He went everywhere except the spare bedroom. He spent quite a time in the office. The telephone is in there. And he was also in the kitchen for a time. That's round the back. . . ."

Luke interrupted her. "Round the back," he echoed pointedly.

She laughed. She seemed delighted. "Bend down again and look," she said. "Can you see that lump like the back of a goose standing up against the sky? Over the studio where Polly Tassie keeps her husband's collection of monstrosities. You can? Well, when the kitchen light goes on in Number Seven it shines on that tree. It shows up far better in the summer than in the winter, but I can usually see it. I'm not often wrong. It was on for three or four minutes just before you came. Someone was heating a nightcap, perhaps. It's rather warm for a hot bottle. Is there anything else you want to know?"

"Er . . . no, ma'am." The Superintendent sounded both respectful and distant. "That'll do very nicely for the time being. Shall we find you in this room if we should need you again?"

"Oh yes, I shall be here, awake. I don't sleep very much." She sounded as if she were sorry for herself and found the emotion contemptuous. "Walk past the window and beckon and I'll come to the door. Don't ring. You'll wake the house and no one will thank you. I shall sit here and watch what you do. Goodnight to you," she continued, looking at Campion again. "If Mrs. Tassie should need anybody besides her niece, her as-good-as-adopted son, her burglar *and* the police force, perhaps you would let me know. I could go over, I suppose. Not that I should be of the slightest use."

"Now that's a type of woman I can't stand," said Luke as the three men walked away through the rain together towards the peeling stucco porch of an empty house about thirty yards down the street. "I can just see myself being comforted by her. 'Don't think of your trouble, think of *me*,' morning, noon and night."

"Just a nut," said Sergeant Picot, speaking for the first time during the incident. "They're not scarce. She produced what was wanted though, didn't she? There the suspect is, all ready to pack up and take home. Shall I walk up to the front door nice and fatherly? We couldn't lose 'im. We've got the whole place surrounded."

"Sorry, George. We're to take no risk. Those are orders." Luke shook himself to scatter the drops from his coat and perched on the parapet which spanned the sides of the square portico guarding the drop to the area beneath. "We wait and pick him up as he comes out in the decent and orderly manner best calculated to take the so-and-so by surprise."

Picot sniffed and nodded.

"Because he's suspected of being the man in the Church Row shooting, I suppose, sir? Is there any suggestion that he's up to mischief here now?"

Luke moved uneasily. "The idea is that he thinks he's safe here," he said. "While he keeps that conviction it's not very likely he's going to do any harm to the two women we know are with him."

Picot looked towards the silent house and back again.

"I thought it was said he had prepared an alibi for this trip," he muttered. "What does he want with an alibi if he's up to no harm? I don't feel comfortable about this. What's he doing in there?"

Luke leant back against the tall door column so that his face was in shadow.

"I think he's parking something he doesn't want to keep on him. The gun, even. It would be in line with his method. This is the place he regards as his bolt hole. He keeps the best side of his character here, perhaps."

"What about the old lady? Is she in it with him?"

"Course she is." Luke sounded weary. "I don't suppose she knows it yet. She's just fond of him. I've seen her sort so often I could tell you exactly what's coming to her. If you want to be certain that that chap's crimes are going to be paid for to the final farthing in terms of human agony, you can start celebrating now."

Picot said nothing for a minute and then he laughed briefly.

"It's funny how people do seem to pay up for one another," he remarked. "I wonder if one could compute it scientifically, if it would work out square. Those old women can never lie intelligently, can they? They fluff it and every word they speak puts the bloke in it deeper and deeper. That must add to the damage." His anxiety returned. "When you say parking evidence, you don't think he could be in there destroying it, do you, sir?"

Luke stretched himself. "I don't know," he said. "I don't think so. I hope not. We must not have any more killings tonight. My worry is that ruddy boy Waterfield. If he hadn't gone in, I'd be perfectly easy. He was in the porch five minutes according to Miss Rich. What was he doing there?"

Mr. Campion coughed. "To my eternal shame, I did not wait to see," he said frankly. "I'd just been to the hospital and picked up a description of him from the constable who had seen him with the girl in the morning. It was obviously Waterfield and I was drifting back to you with the information when suddenly I saw the fellow striding down Edge Street. I followed him and saw him turn into Number Seven. I had no way of telling that Hawker was there, of course, and I had no reason to suppose that Waterfield would stay very long. I had no authority myself, so I doubled back to the nearest phone box and called Tailor Street."

"Ah," said Luke, "did he knock and get no answer, or did someone come to the door and send him away? Miss Rich couldn't tell us. Yet something decided him to climb the wall."

"I don't see how anyone can tell what's happening without taking a dekko," said Picot. "I tell you what, sir. Let me nip round to the street behind this one and get into the garden. I can probably see something through the windows, if it's only where the lights are in the house."

"All right." Luke gave way unwillingly. "If you can find the boy in the grounds bring him out, if you can do it quietly. But frighten Hawker and we've had it."

"I won't frighten him!" Picot drew his narrow coat round his hips and turned up his collar. "I'd have to shout to make myself heard against this perishing rain."

He plunged out into the downpour and disappeared in the direction of Edge Street. Luke waited for a while. The road gave every appearance of being empty. All the houses were dark and the police discreetly out of sight.

Finally he sighed and grinned towards the shadow which was Mr. Campion.

"I hope you're comfortable, captain. This may take all night."

The thin man hunched his shoulders. "I was thinking how amazingly like any other big-game hunt it is, except that here one is spared any guilty feeling about being secretly on the side of the animal," he remarked. "There's something reptilian about this particular quarry of yours, Charles. Tortuous, dexterous, and very near the ground. Contrary to my usual reaction, I rather hope this chap will hang."

Luke grunted. "Hang! Everybody talks to me about hanging," he exploded. "How am I going to *charge* him? That's what's worrying me."

There was silence while Mr. Campion stared out at the drowned faces of the houses opposite.

"How very extraordinary," he said at last. "I hadn't noticed it. Nothing quite jells, does it?"

"Exactly." Luke made it a growl. "Every lead I pull out is as thin as a bit of cotton. There are hundreds of strings, but nothing that promises to plait up into a rope. The man is careful and he's tidy, just as I prophesied this morning."

"What will you do? Take him in and question him and hope for the best?"

"It's all I can do." The Superintendent kicked the stucco with his heel. "Anything may turn up at any moment. The lab boys may be lucky. The drinking-club girl may come across with some trinket which can be traced. The bullet in the lawyer may match those in the Church Row shooting. We may get positive identification of the wax-works in the bus from all five witnesses. But so far every clue relates to a different crime, and whereas we might try to prove method we might also come an unholy cropper doing it. He'll have a slap-up defence, remember."

"Who will see to that? The newspapers?"

"Or the old lady."

"Dear me." Mr. Campion was apt to use the term when shaken. "He could get clean away."

"Over my dead body." Luke spoke grimly. "We've had one little break and Donne has stayed at Tailor Street to investigate it. The commissionaire in the vestibule at the solicitor's office turns out to have been employed in his youth as a spotter at the Casino at Le Moulin. All gambling houses have these chaps, who are specially trained to remember a face whatever disguise its owner adopts, so that banned gamblers may be slung out without trouble. If by chance he took a good look at the delivery man he will be able to pick him out at an identity parade. That could be enough to convict, all other things being equal. But the old boy would have to be very sound in the box."

"Suppose you get the gun?"

"That would do it. That's why I'm sitting so quiet. If Hawker doesn't get wind we're after him he may keep it on him. If he smells a rat he'll ditch it first thing. There are a lot of ifs, too many."

Mr. Campion considered. "Very often this kind of criminal is betrayed," he ventured.

"I don't see who could do it." Luke indicated that the thought had been in his mind. "I am very much afraid that he's that rare bloke who is not dependent on anyone or fond of anyone. You can't be betrayed by someone you've never trusted."

"What about an enemy?"

Luke stood up. "There's just a chance, but only if it's someone he's never suspected, and I should say he's a character who suspects everyone. Hullo, see who this is?"

He took a step forward as Chief Inspector Donne stepped swiftly out of the rain into the porch. They could not see his face.

"Did he come across?" Luke's voice was husky.

"The commissionaire? Oh yes, he thinks he'd know the van man again." Donne sounded surprisingly casual. "He's very old and quaggly, though, poor chap. I don't think he'll live till the trial. This has been a terrific shock to him. I've sent him home with his daughter and told her to put him to bed. But don't worry, Super, we've got Hawker. He's in the bag once we get our hands on him."

"I'm glad to hear it." Luke was suspicious. "Something turned up?"

"Yes." Donne emitted a long breath. "The damnedest thing. I'd just finished with the old man and was feeling pretty doubtful about developments when a message came through from the sub-station in Siddon Street. The proprietor of a small restaurant just across the road from the Royal Albert Music Hall had brought in the dead solicitor's wallet, which had been left on a table in his shop by a customer who just got up and walked away after taking all the money and a couple of letters out of it. The rest was intact."

"Phillipson's wallet? I don't believe it."

"I don't blame you. It's not credible." Donne had forgotten all his affectations and was a plain policeman, very nearly incoherent with excitement. "But his name and address were all over it. That's how we got it so soon."

"Can anyone there remember the customer?"

"Oh, it's Hawker all right. The waitress and her mother who minds the urns say they could swear to him. They noticed him particularly because he put on some sort of act. They say he was frightened by a letter he read. After he went out two young working chaps, who were facing him in the eatery, spoke about him. They are regular customers. They'd know him too. He gave himself away completely and utterly. He must have had a brain storm."

Luke began to laugh softly in the moist darkness.

"There you are, Campion," he said. "Who betrayed him? Friend or enemy?"

"The only man he didn't suspect, at any rate," said Mr. Campion.

21
Tether's End

Up in the gay room which looked so homely with the old woman sleeping heavily in her chair, Gerry went on with his preparations. He was in a state of mind which was new to him. The suppressed excitement of the morning had left him quiet and intelligent at first but now a fresh change had taken place and he had become clumsy, his body feeling heavy and unwilling to obey, as in a nightmare.

Although convinced that he had all the time in the world, he was trying to hurry but was finding it very difficult. The black shadows under his skin had intensified. His clothes hung upon his stiffening muscles and there was a sweat on his forehead like a mould. He kept his eyes away from Polly now, turning his head like a sulking child whenever he passed her.

Yet so far all had gone fairly well. With both door and window sealed, the little chamber was already growing airless and the fire was burning blue and very low. In an hour, perhaps less, he would let the flame die and then the gas, insidious and lethal, could pour out into the room.

He looked down at the stove for a moment and then crossed to the door and turned to survey the scene. The little adjustments he had made to the original scheme to meet the new circumstances were satisfactory enough. The chair drawn up on the opposite side of the hearth to Polly's own looked as if it had always been there, and he had put an occasional table beside it to hold the second beaker. He felt sure he had nothing to fear. With reasonable luck the tragedy must appear the most natural of accidents. An old woman and her unsuspecting visitor chatting over the fire, unaware that the door had swung shut behind them. Any coroner's jury, after hearing of the gas official's warning, would bring in misadventure, adding the usual rider drawing public attention to the danger of imperfect ventilation, and another accident in the home would make a half day's wonder in the press.

Gerry opened the door and stood listening at the foot of the stairs leading to the upper floor. The house was quite quiet in its cage of hissing rain. He hesitated and his thought was quite apparent as he glanced over his shoulder towards the room where the soft cushion he had chosen lay ready on the table. Upstairs the girl was doubtless in her first deep sleep.

He made a movement, paused, glanced down at his hands, and appeared to change his mind. It was clear that he found the improvised plan, which had been made necessary by the accident of Annabelle's visit, difficult or perhaps even distasteful, and he was reluctant to implement it until the last moment.

At length he went back to the room, set his own empty glass and Polly's beaker on the tray, ready to take down, resumed his raincoat and strapped the belt tightly round his ribs as he liked to wear it.

Just before he took up the tray he felt in his pockets and missed the gun. Incredulous astonishment appeared in his eyes, but cleared at once as he glanced over at Polly and smiled with the same half-amused exasperation with which he had watched her on that other rainy night when she had stood in his path and he had sent a taxi to take her out of his way.

He found the weapon at once. He knew exactly where it would be. He opened the glass cupboard, lifted the lid of the tureen, and took it out, together with the handful of assorted documents under it. Polly was a creature of habit and this was the place where she always hid the things she did not want to lose but was yet a little ashamed of keeping. He had seen her slip trifles there a hundred times.

The yield on this occasion was much as he had thought it might be and included a wad of raffle tickets for a workingmen's club draw, bought at the door, a treatise on vitamins to restore energy from the packaging of a patent medicine, and a current driving licence renewed every year although she did not own a car and had not driven since she came south.

He put them back, his mouth twisting suddenly out of control. He remembered her so vividly. Then, thrusting the gun back in his pocket, he took up the tray and went swiftly down to the kitchen.

The room welcomed him with its warmth and faint smells of food and ironing, and he took his time washing the glass, polishing it, and when he set it back in the cupboard he held it with the cloth. He rinsed the beaker very thoroughly indeed and made it dirty again immediately with some dregs of milk which he found in the saucepan on the draining board. And that, too, he held and wiped with the cloth when he replaced it on the tray to take up stairs again.

His next problem was the boiler. This square coke-burning box of cream enamel matched the stove beside it, and they were both crowded into the original square hearth where the Victorian range had once stood. Gerry opened the door at the bottom and found that, as he had feared, the fire was dead. The ragged jacket which he had crammed into the top whilst he was waiting for Polly to come home had stopped the draught completely.

He got up, cursing, and went over to the cupboard beneath the sink, where he found a half-used packet of the old-fashioned fire lighters which she always used. They were pale brown slabs of greasy wax which looked like fudge and smelled like turpentine and were used broken up into small pieces and lit directly beneath the solid fuel.

He prised the jacket out of the top of the boiler, filled the cavity with coke which he found waiting in a tall thin galvanized hod or scoop by the stove, and spent the next few minutes and a third of the lighters getting it to burn again. Once he was sure of it, he got up, dusted his hands, and gave his attention to the jacket which lay, a smouldering mass, upon the shining black top of the closed stove.

He could not be sure if it was actually burning or if it had merely retained some of the smoke from the original fire, and he prodded it dubiously. It was warm but by no means hot and the padding on the shoulders looked indestructible.

He was turning the garment over in an attempt to find out if any part of it was alight when his hand touched something bulky in the inside breast pocket. A sudden stab of apprehension touched his heart and, with colour flooding savagely into his face, he put in his hand and drew out a roll of notes and Polly's letters to Matt Phillipson, both of which he had taken from the dead man's wallet while he was sitting in the café. He remembered he had put them in his coat as soon as the waitress had warned him about displaying the money, and he had not thought of either of them since. From that instant they had vanished from his mind as completely as if a sponge had wiped them off a plate.

He stood holding his breath, realisation breaking over him in a wave.

The wallet. Where was it?

To him the most terrifying thing was that he knew, he knew quite well. He had known all the time. He knew he had walked directly out of the café, leaving the leather folder behind him on the table, and he had done it almost but not quite deliberately. Only the finest veil of unawareness had hung between him and that suicidal act.

He shied away from the certainty in trembling fury and searched through every other pocket, both in the jacket and in the clothes he wore, and finally opened the boiler plate again and, with a gesture which he knew was futile, thrust his bare hand into the coke.

At last he became very quiet. His shoulders were hunched and all his movements became a little smaller as if he was shrinking into himself as the old seem to do. He took up the jacket and the fire lighters and pushed them together into the empty coke hod, and turned from the stove. His glance travelled slowly across the room to come to rest on the dark window sprinkled with raindrops, and in that instant his eyes met another pair of eyes looking in.

Sergeant Picot, who had been watching from the yard ever since the light had appeared in the kitchen, stepped back at once and would have taken his oath on it that he had not been seen.

Gerry gave no sign of alarm but he slid the paper money and the letters into the hod which he was carrying and walked on smoothly to the door with it, where he turned up the switch. Then he drew his gun, and with that in his right hand and the scoop containing the smouldering jacket in his left, he crept back to the window.

There is always a certain amount of light from a city sky, but while he could just make his way about the house by the faint glow from the window, the garden, lying low between high walls, was in complete darkness, and out there he could see nothing.

He came away at last and moved very softly into the small square lobby outside the kitchen door. A short flight of stairs directly in front of him led up to the front hall, and as he stood at the foot of them his eyes were almost on a level with the floor, so that he could see a narrow ribbon of grey light from the street, where the front door did not quite fit its worn step.

As he stood watching, an unmistakable shadow passed across this line and back again, so that he knew that a man stood waiting in the porch.

He crept up into the hall and turned into the little office, where he stood flattened against the wall beside the window, peering over his shoulder into the street. There was no one actually loitering outside the gate but a heavy figure hurrying up the pavement on the opposite side of the road had something about him which was unmistakable.

Gerry moved away. Stepping very quietly, he regained the hall and turned down the passage to the museum. The door to the corridor which linked the house to the studio was kept fastened at night, but, as he knew, the key was always left in the lock. He got the latch undone without noise and felt his way through the yard or so of wooden tunnel carpeted with matting and smelling of varnish, to push open the swing door to the collection.

As he stepped into the airless, aromatic atmosphere he saw the square skylight, a patch of yellowish grey in the dark roof. Below it there was a cluster of grotesque shapes just discernible against the deeper shadow.

For a second he hesitated, his hand tightening round his gun. He thought he had heard a movement somewhere amid the shadows. It had been a rustle or a sigh, as if someone had caught his breath. He listened but it did not come again, and after a time he went on, advancing slowly down the side aisle past the dais.

He was so stunned by the discovery of his self-betrayal that his behaviour was largely automatic. Just as a hunted animal will continue to run for some time after a bullet has killed it, so he pressed on with the plan he had made.

He was making for the old iron stove which heated the room in very cold weather and was almost certainly not empty. When he had carried Polly's milk down to be reheated and had discovered that the boiler was out, he had decided that this stove in the museum was the one place where the cremation of the jacket could be accomplished successfully. He had been anxious to destroy the ragged garment because he realised that it had been the outstanding item of his costume when he had carried the wooden box into the house in Minton Terrace, and he knew that over ninety per cent of the people who had noticed him at all there would in fact only have noticed the coat.

It was very dark in the side aisle and although he knew the place so well he found that he was brushing against the crowded exhibits as he passed. To get away from them he swerved across the parquet towards the dais.

The shadows sitting there, crouching so still not three feet away from him, seemed to materialise while he stared at it. He stopped, gripping his gun, his hairs prickling on his scalp. The shape changed in contour and a blurred white face peered up at him.

"Oh," said Annabelle, her voice shrill in the darkness. "Oh, you've got a revolver!"

In the instant of paralysis while his slowed mind registered the astonishing fact that the girl he intended to silence was here, and not where he expected her to be, upstairs asleep in her room, a second shadow streaked out of the blackness and a blow under his wrist sent the weapon spinning out of his grasp. Immediately afterwards a fist crashed into his face, catching him under the cheekbone.

The scoop dropped out of his hand and rolled away into the dry darkness and he struck out savagely, to meet a whirlwind. Richard plunged into the fight, as some small men do, with a reckless belligerence which offsets almost any disadvantage. He was used to giving away enormous amounts of weight and his reach was inadequate, but he was hardheaded and very fit, and on this occasion he had the advantage of surprise.

All day he had been growing more and more angry. He did not understand the world which had threatened to absorb his newly found and beautiful Annabelle, but everything he had so far discovered about it had struck him as inexpressibly second-class and tawdry. And now her statement, coming to him out of the tingling dark, touched off an explosion.

For the first time in his life he experienced outrage. He hurled himself at Gerry without doubting it was he, and after a minute or two of hard milling had the extreme satisfaction of feeling him go down with a crash before his right. He flung himself upon him without pause, fought for his throat, and twisting his tie round his wrist achieved a strangle hold.

"You pulled a gun on her," he muttered, drumming his knees into the narrow ribs as if he was riding a recalcitrant horse. "A *gun*! You had the blasted impudence to draw a gun."

On top of the attack, which was utterly unexpected, Gerry recognised the voice and the last flimsy shreds of illusion dropped from his eyes.

"You . . . followed me from the Tenniel?" The words were breathy in the airless dark.

"I followed you from here to the barber's this morning." Richard could not resist telling him. "I brought Annabelle here, and as she's only a kid, I wanted to know what sort of life she was going to find. Now I know. I've been to Rolf's Dump and so have the police. They're round this house now waiting for you to come out. I don't care if they catch you or if they don't, but I won't have Annabelle mixed up in any mucky little scandal. Do you understand that or don't you?"

Gerry did not move. The discovery that Richard regarded him as some sort of small-time crook flourishing a gun to frighten a woman had an extraordinary effect upon him. It arrived like a brief mercy, a little screen to hide for a moment his naked horror, which had become terrifying even to himself.

He let his body go limp. "All right." He sounded merely sulky.

Richard released his hold and got up. As he stepped back his heel knocked something heavy and he stooped and picked it up. It was the gun and he stood holding it.

"Buck up, Gerry, and clear out of this building," he said. "I don't care if you go back into the house or not, but I don't want you found in here with us."

The young voice was strong and authoritative, and a little way down the room Annabelle, responding to it, opened the door into the garden, to let in a great swirling gust of midnight air.

Immediately, from somewhere just behind them, there

came the sound of a strange sucking breath, followed at once by a small blunt noise like a toy balloon bursting, and a sheet of orange flame shot up from the edge of the dais and began to spread.

As Gerry reeled to his feet the whole of the far end of the museum appeared to catch fire at once. It happened in a moment and without warning, like the descent of a fire bomb.

The explanation was simple. At the beginning of the fight, when Gerry had dropped the coke scoop, it had rolled over and over and the jacket had fallen half out of it with the fire lighters amid its folds. The heat had melted the wax and the sudden draught from the garden door had fanned the cloth into flame. The museum was ripe for burning, like a bonfire saved for a celebration. Even the stuffed beasts, impregnated for many years with a naphtha spray against moth, were dry and tinder-like with age and dust.

The ostrich lamp with its silken shade blazed like a sacrificial torch, flinging sparks up into the roof, and as they fell they started other fires, so that the whole building was as good as lost in the first three minutes.

"Aunt Polly. We must get Aunt Polly!" Annabelle's choking cry from the doorway reached Richard through the sighing rustle of the flames and he swung towards her.

"Get out before you're suffocated!" he gasped and pushed her into the garden. "Mrs. Tassie is all right. She's not in the same building. She can get out through the house, can't she?"

He threw the final question at the man who had reeled out behind them.

"Get the door shut. The air's making it worse in there."

Out in the rain the darkness was newly alive. On the other side of the wall at the end of the garden someone was shouting and from the path to the back road the sound of running feet came thudding towards them. Already the glare from the museum was lighting the dark branches of the trees, so that the watchers in the street in front had been alarmed.

Richard's arm was round Annabelle's shoulders.

"It's no use us assing about any longer. We'll have to

see the police," he said to her. "Come on, pretty. We'll go and meet them."

He glanced back at the shadow beside him. "You'd better go in through the kitchen, Gerry, and warn the old lady, hadn't you? Or are you going to make a dash for it while the going's good?"

His dislike and contempt, which were both so essentially youthful, had not lessened, and the face of the silent figure beside him made no impression upon him. He did not even see it. The notion that something a little less than a man might be trembling there, struggling feebly to wrap itself in the shreds of a false and shameful identity which had been casually created for it by Richard himself, was something quite outside his imagination. It was an aspect of hell, which, mercifully, was not in his comprehension.

"Anyway," he said fiercely, "don't stay here. We don't want to see anything of you again, and I don't want to have to explain this either, so take it with you, please."

The clatter of the wooden gate less than forty feet away from them lent emphasis to the words. Gerry felt a cold weight thrust into his hand. He turned back blindly into the fire, his fingers closing round the gun.

The museum of oddities, the collection of nonsense, the jokes in bad taste, and all the other naïve banalities, were about to burn to the ground, but so far most of the actual blaze was confined to the dais and the further end of the building, so that the creeping figure holding the weapon was able to cross the few feet of parquet to the swing door in the passage. He burst through the second door and closed it behind him, and came safely into the cool hall of the little house where all was dark and quiet, as he had left it.

He went down the short flight of steps towards the kitchen and turned back to see the grey streak showing under the front door. For a minute he watched it fixedly and dropped slowly down until he was lying on the stairs, his eyes level with the top step. But the grey line remained unbroken. The watcher had been distracted by the fire. The shadow had gone.

The house was silent as the end of the world. The noises from outside, the shouts and the hollow alarums of the firebells, the police whistles and the stamp of feet, were far away from him, as if already they belonged to a place in which he had no claim, and as he lay there in the little dark hole, with the gun in his hand, he heard them without interest.

He was nothing, and there was nothing for him.

After a time he put the muzzle of the weapon into his mouth, but although his finger curled round the trigger he did not press it.

The time crept by. The corner was very cool, very dark.

In the end he stirred painfully. The gun slid out of his hand, dropping into the carpeted well below him, and then, very slowly and as if he had no strength in his body, he began to climb hand over hand up the steps, across the hallway, and finally, as if it were a mountain he was essaying, up the main staircase.

It was an hour after dawn when Sergeant Picot placed a cup of nice black tea on the desk where Luke sat writing in the office which had once been his own in the Barrow Road station.

"It's like the good old days, Chief," he remarked, demoting his hero in a fit of pure nostalgia. "Well, that's that, and very satisfactory." He jerked his square head in appreciation of good work done. "He's a cool one. I hope he gets what's coming to him. That was only done for show, you know, him bringing the woman out. Do you know what he said to me?"

Luke had heard, for it was all over the station, but he was a kind man even in the early morning. He made an interested noise and took up the tea, for which he was very grateful.

Picot leaned across the desk, his solid face shocked as a child's.

"I said to 'im as I put on the bracelets, I said, 'What made you go back for the old girl?' 'Pon my Sam he looked me square in the face and spoke as straight as if he was saying his prayers. 'Because I need her,' he said. It was as crude as that. Serve 'im right if she turns on him when she comes out of hospital and sees what's happened to her property and hears what he's been up to."

"She won't." The Superintendent spoke with utter certainty.

"Then she's a fool," said Picot, "because that chap really is the cold-blooded monster that the papers are going to call him. D'you honestly think she'll stick by him when it all comes out?"

Luke sighed and went back to his report. His vivid face was furrowed with weariness.

"I know it," he said. "She'll forgive him without question, whatever he's done to her and however high we hang him. *And he knows it*. It's no use you blaming her. She can't help herself. She's only a vehicle. That's Disinterested Love, chum, a force, like nuclear energy. It's an absolute."

Picot shrugged his shoulders. He was disgusted.

"Well, he left the wallet on the café table and his gun on the stairs, so he made pretty certain of hanging," he observed with some satisfaction. "He couldn't stand himself any longer, that's what it amounts to."

"I doubt it." Luke put another sheet in the typewriter. "In my experience that kind of blackout always indicates an explosion. Either some unexpected idea or demand set off an emotional spark which he didn't know he had in him, or some force from outside suddenly succeeded in penetrating his hide and startled him out of his senses for a minute. We shall never know quite what it was. It's not the sort of evidence which comes out at a trial."

Picot said nothing but sat down at the other desk and put on his spectacles. There was a great deal of work to be done.

ABOUT THE AUTHOR

MARGERY ALLINGHAM, who was born in London in 1904, came from a long line of writers. "I was brought up from babyhood in an atmosphere of ink and paper," she claimed. One ancestor wrote early nineteenth century melodramas, another wrote popular boys' school stories, and her grandfather was the proprietor of a religious newspaper. But it was her father, the author of serials for the popular weeklies, who gave her her earliest training as a writer. She began studying the craft at the age of seven and had published her first novel by the age of sixteen while still at boarding school. In 1927 she married Philip Youngman Carter, and the following year she produced the first of her Albert Campion detective stories, *The Crime at Black Dudley*. She and her husband lived a life "typical of the English countryside" she reported, with "horses, dogs, our garden and village activities" taking up leisure time. One wonders how much leisure time Margery Allingham, the author of more than thirty-three mystery novels in addition to short stories, serials and book reviews, managed to have.

BANTAM MYSTERY COLLECTION

Kinsey Millhone is...

"The best new private eye."   *—The Detroit News*

"A tough-cookie with a soft center."   *—Newsweek*

"A stand-out specimen of the new female operatives."
        —Philadelphia Inquirer

Sue Grafton is...

The Shamus and Anthony Award winning creator of
Kinsey Millhone and quite simply one of the hottest
new mystery writers around.

Bantam is...

The proud publisher of Sue Grafton's Kinsey Millhone
mysteries:

☐	27991	"A" IS FOR ALIBI	$3.95
☐	28034	"B" IS FOR BURGLAR	$3.95
☐	28036	"C" IS FOR CORPSE	$3.95
☐	27163	"D" IS FOR DEADBEAT	$3.95
☐	27955	"E" IS FOR EVIDENCE	$3.95